*By Judith Rossner*

To the Precipice

Nine Months in the Life of an Old Maid

Any Minute I Can Split

Looking for Mr. Goodbar

Attachments

Emmeline

August

His Little Women

Olivia

Perfidia

# Perfidia

*A Novel*

# JUDITH
# ROSSNER

Island
BOOKS

ISLAND BOOKS
Published by
Dell Publishing
a division of
Bantam Doubleday Dell Publishing Group, Inc.
1540 Broadway
New York, New York 10036

PERFIDIA by Alberto Dominguez.

ISBN 0-440-22613-9

Reprinted by arrangement with Doubleday

Printed in the United States of America

Published simultaneously in Canada

October 1998

10  9  8  7  6  5  4  3  2  1

OPM

*For Stanley Leff
and Alexandra and Gabriela*

# Chapter 1

I was five in 1976, when my mother packed me and her other possessions into our station wagon, said goodbye to my father and drove me away from our home in the cool, lush little town of Hanover, New Hampshire. We rode around and across the country for months before we came to rest in Santa Fe, where we met Wilkie at the first restaurant we went to. She must have gotten pregnant with my brother about two hours later. I think she and Wilkie broke sexually early on, but they never stopped being involved, one way and another.

My father was—is, I imagine—a professor of American history at Dartmouth. A true academic. I was an

excellent student. A model girl, when I was in school.
My mother said later she'd thought I wouldn't know
the difference if she took me away from my father, he
cared so little about me. We don't always remember
things the same way. Didn't always. In fact, she remembered things differently from one time to the
next. Some of her stories had a sad version and a funny
version, with such a difference between the two that
you had no idea of what had actually happened.

She was raised on a farm west of Montreal, ran
away from home when she was sixteen. In 1965. She
packed her knapsack with some clothes and necessi-
ties, plus she stole her favorite two of her father's 78's
that the two of them listened to together on the
phonograph in the kitchen. "Perfidia" and "Remember." Her mother had no use for music and they'd
never bought a more modern system. She stayed with
the first man who gave her a hitch until she lied about
her age and got a job as a waitress. She'd changed her
name a few times, but I think that she'd settled on
Anita by then. She always insisted that she wasn't
pretty, though I thought she was beautiful, and she
was terribly sexy, with a big bosom, great legs, and a
lively, teasing manner with men. She had no trouble
connecting with them in those days when even the
middle class had begun to think that sex was free and
easy. After a couple of years in Montreal, she hitched
to Toronto, which she'd say she eventually left because
it was too clean. She had stories about the café and

restaurant owners she worked for and slept with. She called them Pierre One, Pierre Two and so on, though they mostly weren't French. (My given name was Madeleine. She claimed it was one of the few things my father ever insisted upon. She didn't like it because it was French.) When she told the umpteenth Pierre that she was leaving Toronto, and he said she had to stay until he found another waitress, she suggested he bring in the cow who was his wife, it wouldn't hurt for *her* to know what it was like to work for a living.

My mother told stories like that more readily than she told ones in which she did something nice. Nor did she ever make any effort to conceal her sexual adventures from me, though she was occasionally surprised or amused that I knew as much as I did.

After three years she hitched down to the States with a Dartmouth student, worked in a luncheonette in Hanover where, one day, she waited on my father. She asked him whether the snow was lightening up, said she didn't have snow tires on her car and she was afraid she wouldn't be able to get home. (She was boarding in a room in someone's house. She didn't have a car.) My father asked if perhaps she'd like to have dinner at his place. It was only a few blocks away and he'd made a good stew.

She said, "A man who can cook? I'll go anyplace with you."

Or so she said she said.

Rupert Stern was a thirty-seven-year-old bachelor

who owned more books than she'd ever seen in one place, including her school's library. She liked the way they looked. She didn't care about the way he looked, one way or another. He was a little taller than she, a bit chubby. His brown hair had more kinks than she'd seen in the whole city of Montreal; she always said, Thank God I had inherited her hair. His study was the only room where he smoked his pipe, although there was no woman around telling him he couldn't do it elsewhere. He'd furnished the house on his own, mostly at auctions. There were a lot of old sepia photos on the walls, none of his family or anyone else he knew. For her birthday, he gave her a working Victrola and a carton of 78's that he'd found at an auction.

By May she was pregnant with me. He told her he knew a woman who'd had a very easy abortion by a doctor in town. She said she'd do anything he wanted her to, including leave town, but she couldn't take a human life. He went for it. He married her and she stayed with him, *we* stayed with him, until 1976, the five years I remember as the good ones in my life. I'm still not sure why it had to end. She said he didn't love me or anybody, but I don't think I could tell when I was little. For a long time I thought of him sweetly. By the time my mother and I settled in Santa Fe, his study was the only part of the house I remembered. Book-lined walls, huge desk with orderly stacks of paper, maroon-background Oriental rug. When she was busy, I would stay in there with him, drawing, looking at picture books, being read to, taking my nap. (I could read by the time I was four but I still wanted him to read to me.) Someone gave me a wooden puzzle map of the United States. Each state was one piece. I think my mother learned where the different states were from doing that puzzle with me. I don't know how much more she knew about any of them when she picked me up and left.

In the months that we were on the road, I would dream that I was in my father's study, but it was all right when I awakened because my mother was next to me in bed. Once we got to Santa Fe, my mother was in bed with Wilkie, and when I awakened, nobody was there.

❍

*M*y mother would have been twenty-seven, Wilkie about ten years older, this huge, soft-voiced teddy bear with wavy brown hair and bushy brows, his eyes set so deep under them that they looked trapped. He got by because he'd had an inheritance of maybe forty thousand dollars and, bumming around the West, he'd landed in Santa Fe several years before the real-estate boom. His then artist-girlfriend persuaded him to buy a crumbling adobe house on a large lot on Canyon Road. Outright. She left before long, but there were always other artists *(artist* mostly in quotes) ready to move in with him. The males and maybe some of the females paid rent. He had good offers for the whole piece of real estate but he turned them down. He couldn't imagine where he'd go afterward. Wilkie was one of the few people I've ever known who didn't need to *do* anything, even when he was sober. He could sit at home or in the coffee shop for hours without even looking at the newspaper, waiting for people to come by and talk. Or not talk. Just drink coffee at his regular table. Sober, my mother could do that for five or ten minutes. Even drunk, she didn't stay still for long. Anyway, I wasn't so much aware of the difference between drunk and sober, in those days. And she wasn't drunk so much of the time.

They struck up a conversation in the Pink Adobe, called by regulars the Pink. His girlfriend had just left. A couple of hours later, we moved into his room. No mystery about how my mother got pregnant; the marvel is that it didn't happen more often. She loved babies. She loved anything that didn't talk back.

She did not love Wilkie's two remaining woman-artist tenants. She kicked them out and persuaded Wilkie to get financing to develop the place into the Sky Galleries, later usually shortened to the Sky. She dealt not only with the bankers, but with the architects, contractors and tenants. All this while she was pregnant. My mother was too angry and restless to sit in a classroom and absorb information, but she built the Sky into a major tourist trap because Wilkie let her use her brain.

The new building was shaped like half a hexagon that went right to the outer edges of the property. In the center was a lovely courtyard with plants and flowers at the edges, benches in the middle. The stump of one huge tree they'd cut down had become a bench; part of its great trunk was now a table inside for the cash register. Some of the stores changed over the years but the art gallery was at the center and dominated. On its left, facing you as you entered the courtyard, was a store called Farolito, which carried pottery and a lot of Santa Fe souvenirs—chili-pepper key chains, Santa Fe T-shirts, postcards. My mother had a mug made up, sky blue with a big white cloud and *Sky Gallery,* in Santa Fe turquoise and fuchsia, printed on the cloud. They sold a fantastic number of those mugs over the years in both the gallery and Farolito. (At one point my mother had the mugs taken out of the gallery because she felt people who might have bought a painting were copping out and just buying the mug. Nothing much happened and after a few months, she brought the mugs back in.) Then there was a small jewelry store with a lot of good Navajo jewelry and other silver. To the right were Wilkie's Coffee Shop (my mother's idea, from his nickname; his given name was Philip Wilkerson) and the tiny place first occupied by Rahji Cohen, Photographer.

When the buzz about the Sky began, artists looking

for a gallery started to come by. She was very pregnant, by this time, but she must have tuned in to the
social possibilities of running a gallery in a town full of
artists who wanted their work shown. She told Wilkie
she was going to manage the gallery and set out to
learn what she needed to know. It wasn't much, beyond the size and shape of the artists she liked. The
gallery had plenty of space. It was about fifteen feet
deep and more than forty feet wide, with the space
interrupted only by a couple of windows in the front
and an entrance to the storage room at one end of the
back.

She'd hoped we could live in different parts of the
building while it was being reconstructed and ex-
panded, but at some early point in the renovation, she
decided this wouldn't be minimally comfortable. I
liked living there and I didn't want to move but my
mother patiently explained to me, holding me on her
lap, hugging and kissing me as we tooled around the
mountains in Wilkie's jeep, that we needed more
space so we could have real bedrooms again.

I didn't know the meaning of the word *patient* in
those days. It was just the way my mother was with me
all the time. She never got mad at me before my
brother was born, though she yelled at other people
once in a while.

◗

*L*eaning hard on everyone, my mother had managed to save enough from Wilkie's mortgage money for him to buy the shack on Cerro Gordo. It was on a tiny piece of land and the adjacent plot's owner hadn't had enough money, after putting up his new house, to pay the high price the owner was asking. We moved there a week before she gave birth to my brother. Cerro Gordo went up a mountain, and they talked about the beautiful view, but as far as I was concerned, there were no beautiful views in Santa Fe. Everything was brown. No grass, just some weeds. Hardly any trees. Our "home" looked like a big version of some clubhouse nailed up by kids. One reasonable-sized room with rusty kitchen equipment in a corner; two cells the broker called bedrooms; a closet with a sink and a toilet. No heat or hot water, but it had electricity, unlike some of them. Later we had hot water, too. It had once been one of several shacks on Cerro Gordo, but by this time there were real homes, mostly down where the road was paved. There was a playground about halfway up, but I never went there; I was always more interested in what was happening at home. She put a couple of canvas butterfly chairs and some big pillows in the "living room," along with a table and three chairs. There was a real bed that barely fit into their bedroom, a cot and my old car bed, the kind they don't make anymore because they're not safe enough (now they just make a car seat you strap the poor baby into; it's sort of like an electric chair without wires). My mother said someday there'd be a baby in the car bed, but I wasn't terribly curious about it, although I did ask what "someday" meant. I knew I was to begin school someday in September, and that someday was taking forever.

In my mind, the teacher sometimes looked like Wilkie, other times more like my father.

◑

*S*he went into labor in the middle of the night and seems to have forgotten, or ceased instantly to care, that I existed, that I was six years old, and that I was asleep in the next room. I don't think they even checked to see if I was awake. Wilkie drove her to the hospital, left her there and headed back toward the house, probably stopping on the way to smoke some weed, have a couple of beers, take a long nap.

Maybe it was the noise of his car engine starting that had awakened me. I'd been dreaming that I missed the beginning of school. Awake, I thought maybe I really had. It was dark. I went to their bedroom, which was empty. Nobody was anywhere in this house I was just getting used to! I thought one of them must be outside. I called, but no one answered. I pushed open the door and went out. Nobody was there. She'd put a butterfly chair out there, too, on what would later be a terrace. It was just dirt, then, at the top of our little hill, with a few cacti and the usual scrubby chamisae. One of Wilkie's hilarious jokes was that other men's girlfriends fell off the roof once a month, but his was going to fall off a mountain. I'd taken it literally, and this was the first time I left the house without my mother. After some hesitation, I climbed into the chair. Once settled there, I realized I needed a blanket, and maybe some books to hold until it was light enough to see the pages. I craved both, but I didn't feel like struggling out of the chair. I wanted my mother to see what she'd done. How cold she'd let me be. I wanted her to be *sorry*.

It was utterly quiet, the birds hadn't even begun to sing. My breath still catches when I hear that silence. I think I only began to breathe normally when the first chirping began, just before the sky lightened, but I never fell asleep. I don't know what else I was think-ing. I'm sure there was no baby on my mind. When we were traveling cross-country, if my mother cried out in her sleep in the middle of the night, it was always about a fire. Maybe this was about a fire. But then, why would she have left me here?

The sun was way up when I finally heard Wilkie's jeep on the mountain, then watched it pull onto our hill. It stopped. I didn't get out of the chair. I assumed my mother was with him and I needed her to know that I was angry with her for leaving me alone like that.

"Hey, Maddy," Wilkie said. "You have a brother."

I was confused. Not just because she wasn't there. A

brother made it sound as though there would be another person.

Wilkie laughed. "You look like you been smoking
what I been smoking."

I remained silent. I would have hated him if he
weren't the only person in the world, just then.

He said, "Come on. Let's go in the house."

I tried to move, but my limbs had been asleep too
long, and they had pins and needles, and I ached all
over.

I said, "My legs don't want to move."

With a groan, he picked me up out of the chair and
carried me into the house. But when he tried to put
me down, I held on to his T-shirt and began to cry.

"Where's my mother? I want my mother!"

"She'll be home in four, five days," he said. "I hope
you're not gonna cry the whole time."

He might as well have said I'd never see her again. I
don't think she'd left me for more than a couple of
hours before that night. As he tried to free himself, I
clung to his T-shirt. Wilkie was such an ass, but even
if I'd seen him that way then, he was all I had. What
he finally did to get me out of his arms was, he
brought me to my bed, sat on its edge and struggled
out of the T-shirt without taking it away from me.
Then he slowly let me and the T-shirt down to the
pillow, where I cried myself to sleep in a much worse
world than the one where I'd awakened.

〇

*T*he next day he drove me to school. He didn't comb my silky brown hair, or kiss it and tell me how beautiful it was, he wished he had curly hair like mine, or help me choose what to wear, or do the other things I was accustomed to my mother's doing; he just gave me cereal and milk, then dumped me in school. Santa Fe was still a small town, though its chichi-ing had begun. Wilkie explained to the principal, whom he knew, about my mother, and promised to pick me up at three. He hadn't thought to pack me a lunch, but the teacher, Miss Munroe, shared her sandwich with me, and one of the kids gave me a cookie I wasn't hungry. It all seemed like a dream, and I was never hungry in my dreams. Wilkie didn't come back until almost four but Miss Munroe sat with me outside the school and read stories to me, until she left out a sentence and I corrected her, so she realized I could read, and then she made a big fuss over me and let me read to her. I was crazy about Miss Munroe. I don't know that I'd have gotten through that year without her.

Wilkie had promised I could go to the hospital with him after school on Thursday to get my mother, but he tricked me. Picked her up after he left me at the school-bus stop on Palace Avenue, at the foot of Cerro Gordo, in the morning. He didn't even come for me, just called the school and told them to put me on the

bus. It changed everything from the start. I was preparing myself to be a hostess, but it never occurred to
the other mothers that nobody was picking me up and
I had to walk all the way up Cerro Gordo. My mother
was settled in when I finally reached home, exhausted
and angry.

I marched into her bedroom, prepared to bawl her
out for all the terrible things that had happened in the
last few days, so she'd take me into her arms and
comfort me; she'd always comforted me when Wilkie
did dumb things. But she was sitting up in bed, holding something I must have known was a nursing baby,
although I don't appear to have taken that into account when I scrambled up on the bed and tried to
throw myself into her arms.

"Whoa!" she said, pushing me back so I wouldn't
land on top of the baby. "Ow!" she said, because as
she pushed me back, the baby's mouth, which had
been around her nipple, came off it. "Watch it,
Maddy, this is a person I'm holding!"

At the edge of the bed, I stopped. A person? It
looked more like the pink octopus in one of my picture books. I stared at its ugly face and waving limbs;
it wasn't a nice pale pink, like the octopus, it was
practically red. My mother said I could touch its
hands, but I didn't want to. I just wanted it to go away
so there'd be room for me in her arms.

I said, "Put it over there," pointing to the empty
place on the other side of the bed.

My mother laughed. The baby was back at her breast, held close, the way she'd once held me.

"How about, *you* go over there, and when I'm finished feeding Billy, then you and I can . . ."

She didn't even finish the awful sentence before she was looking down again. Furthermore, she'd given it a name without asking me. It was my baby, too, if it was going to live with us, and she shouldn't have done that. It was a stupid name, anyway.

"You left me alone!" I howled, and burst into tears.

The baby began to cry, too.

"Wilkerson, where are you?" my mother moaned. She got out of bed. She was angry but she didn't let go of the damned baby, she just began walking around the house with it. She was angry at everything else, not the baby, though the baby, the baby octopus, was what had caused the trouble. My mother began to cry, too. I stopped crying and told her if she would put away the baby, I could make her feel better, but she didn't smile or stop crying, she *ignored* me. She'd never ignored me before. I began to cry again.

I want to write that it was weeks and months before I stopped. It isn't true, but it might as well have been. I could have been crying for the remainder of my childhood, for all I remember of home pleasures in those years, for all the concern my mother showed for me. (The exception being when I was ill. I had awful cases of both measles and chicken pox and she took wonderful care of me, then. She told me stories she didn't usually have the patience for about the time when we'd been on the road, and cooked food the way she had in Hanover instead of just bringing it in.) None of the explanations I've heard since then of why she stopped being halfway decent to me—postpartum depression, and so on—seems to explain what happened. Sometimes I thought it was because Billy had a penis that she liked him more than she liked me. She'd play with it and tickle him when she changed him. (If I tried to do the same thing, she stopped me.) Other times, I thought it must be some different person who'd come home from the hospital in her body. Occasionally, I thought it might be worthwhile to make friends with this new person. I gave her a name, Maxine; I'd heard it someplace and thought it sounded like someone who wasn't nice. The old person was Mommy. I'd say something like, "You look very nice today, Maxine," trying to turn Maxine around, but she didn't like that or anything else I did. Even the good things.

I think at some point I stopped being able to do what she wanted me to do; it made me feel craven to obey someone who couldn't stand to have me around.

School was another matter. I could do no wrong there and didn't try. I was the smartest kid in the first grade, but I wasn't a show-off. I never had fights, got along with everybody. I was invited to all the birthday parties, and to play at kids' houses. I had a friend halfway down Cerro Gordo, Laya Candelaria. Often

I'd go home from school with her and sleep over because my mother was too busy or too tired to pick me up. Laya didn't come to my house, nor did the other girls. My mother told Miss Munroe she'd be pleased if my friends visited, but I think Miss Munroe could tell that my mother didn't really want anybody there except herself and the baby. I realized when I was much older that the mothers knew there was a lot of dope around our house. Wilkie and my mother both kept their supplies there, but even Wilkie felt extra around my mother and the baby. He found himself a new girlfriend and stayed at her house most of the time.

At first I didn't have anything to do with Billy, except once in a while I'd flick the bottom of his feet with my fingers when my mother wasn't in the room. Or make scary faces at him. After a while, though, he began to seem almost human. He stopped being red and his eyes got a little bigger, they no longer looked like slits in a piggy bank where you could drop in some coins. They began focusing on me. That was it. I'd felt unreal because nobody looked at me when I was home, as though I didn't exist. Wilkie had never noticed me much, and my mother had stopped seeing me the day she brought Billy home from the hospital, and I felt as though I existed again when Billy looked at me. I began to talk to him, make nicer funny faces. I could make him laugh better than anyone. I didn't call him Billy, which was my mother's name for him. I called him Belly, because he had such a big round one.

This irritated my mother, so I couldn't have given it up if I wanted to. Sometimes I think I'm giving most people false names in this book for legal reasons; other times I think I'm just trying to get a rise out of her.

She was still nursing Belly when he was two. He'd turned into an adorable little boy I loved as much as I hated. When my mother went to work or on a buying trip, she took Belly with her. She only took me if she needed me to keep an eye on him. Otherwise, I stayed with Wilkie and his girlfriend, or just Wilkie, when a girl left him. Sometimes Mrs. Candelaria invited me to stay there. By this time I was used to being treated like some animal my own mother put in a kennel when she needed to go someplace. I was always well behaved when I stayed at one of the kennels, but that wasn't where I wanted to be. When she met her next boyfriend, she started neglecting even Belly, except she kept nursing him because it turned on the boyfriend. Belly had me to mother him when he wasn't being nursed and barely noticed that my mother had gone AWOL. She was never mean to him.

I'll call her new boyfriend Rex. Or the Lion King. No. This was 1979, long before the movie, but it's also wrong to evoke the king of anything, just because my mother treated him like one. Lion Dung might do. Or just Beast. He was huge and really ugly, if you looked at his tiny eyes and big nose, but women, not just my mother, went wild for him, because he had a mane of gorgeous golden hair that nearly covered his back to the waist when he didn't tie it into a ponytail, and a beard and mustache just a little darker, and his body was all covered with golden fuzz, just like the men in the romances my friend Anthea read later that we teased her about. *The sunlight danced on the golden hair of his powerful arms.* Lion Dung had golden hair everyplace except on his penis, his backside and his feet. I knew, because he walked around the house naked when it was halfway warm. He said he hated clothes but he was mostly just showing himself off. He teased my mother because she wouldn't do the same, she'd show off her breasts, but not the rest of her. They'd come together, so to speak, over her breasts, on a winter Saturday when the Sky's salesgirl had called our house early because it was snowing and she was afraid to drive to work. My mother brought me to the gallery so I could look after Billy when she was occupied. Lion the Liver-Hearted, Cowardly Lion had come north from Texas to ski. The woman he'd been with in Texas had given him a jeep to get around her ranch, and he'd skipped town in it. He'd only been in Santa Fe for a couple of hours and he hadn't found a woman to live off, yet. He met my mother over coffee in Wilkie's. He asked if she knew where to rent some skis, and she told him where the shop was, said she didn't know how to ski, though she was dying to learn. (Some of what I tell you about when I wasn't there might not be exactly right, but it's never far wrong. When my mother told me things in a friendly

way, it wasn't mother-daughter friendly, but pal
friendly. She didn't keep grown-up girlfriends for
more than a couple of weeks at a time.)

She probably told him she had to go nurse her
"baby." He came back with her to the gallery, where I
was sitting in the rocking chair, reading. There were
no customers. Belly, who was two, was in the little
play space she'd made for him—a piece of blue carpeting, a little table and chair, a bookshelf with toys—
doing one of his puzzles. From an early age, my
brother could look at puzzles and see where the pieces
went without having any idea of the picture. He was
perfectly content, but my mother ran to him as
though he were crying, said something stupid like,
"You poor baby, you must be starved," then scooped
him up and brought him over to the rocking chair,
which I'd vacated before she could tell me to. She sat
down, pulled up her shirt and began suckling him.
Lion, looking at her breasts, asked the baby's name.
My mother said his name was Billy, but his sister
called him Belly; it was the first time she'd thought the
name was cute. Lion began to sing, "Belly Hi, may call
you," etc., as in "Bali Ha'i," from *South Pacific*. Lion
mostly listened to rock, but he knew the songs my
mother loved (she hated all music that didn't have
words). Most important, he knew "Perfidia"—in
Spanish. She loved it. She began learning Spanish from
that song, and she taught him the words in English.
*Perfidia, my heart goes out to you, Perfidia. For I found*

*you, the love of my life, in somebody else's arms.* He owned her from that day. This was important, because he needed to own someone who worked. Actually, she owned him, too, she and drugs, the latter having the controlling share.

They gave each other skis the next Christmas. She paid for both pairs. He reigned in our household like some hereditary monarch who had to do nothing to support his claim. Just walk around naked and fuck my mother. I think he was faithful to her during that year or two they were together. Why not? She gave him everything he needed. Lion never met a drug he didn't like. They smoked weed as though it were Lucky Strikes, dropped acid as though it were the sixties (she only did it when he needed the company), sniffed coke when she could find it. And at some point, when he'd talked my mother into procuring it for him, Lion began shooting heroin, as well. His father had disinherited him over drugs and he'd left home. She wasn't going to take a chance on his leaving her.

Unlike me, Billy seems *genuinely* to have taken all this in his stride. Maybe younger siblings have a gene for stride. I did what I had to do, but I *felt* what was happening all the time. I took care of the two of us when my mother and Lion weren't around. Lion was the last man she cooked for. She made steak or chops every night because he liked the texture, didn't notice the taste. I washed the dishes. I also did whatever housecleaning was done. My mother never cleaned, and she didn't want anyone else "snooping around the house." Since Lion, she'd stopped even pretending my friends were welcome, though she had volunteered him to meet the school bus on Palace Avenue. The other mothers said, No, thanks. My mother didn't act friendly enough to them for me to be confused by their standoffishness. I had been trained not to talk to anyone about anything that went on in our house. I don't know if she ever had to train Billy; it wouldn't have occurred to him to discuss anything but sports with his friends. I don't know when I understood that stoned wasn't the same as sleepy.

On a hot autumn day (I remember that I was wearing a T-shirt and shorts) in 1981, when I was ten, the school bus let me off, along with Laya Candelaria and a few other kids. Laya wanted me to come to her house, but I thought I'd better go home to see if I was needed for Billy.

Lion's radio was on full blast, playing rock, and my mother was sitting on top of him, he must have been in her, on the serape in front of the fireplace. She was leaning over him so her breasts were hanging over his face, and he was holding one of them, sucking at it like a baby. Except she was groaning, which of course she didn't do when Belly was at her. Belly wasn't around. They didn't hear me come in. I doubt they would've stopped if they had. Lion Dung, even more than my mother, failed to grasp the idea that there were things you didn't do in front of anybody else, especially if they were children. Actually, there are all different ways not to give a shit what happens to children, and Lion Dung's and my mother's were quite different. He really and truly—it would've been deeply if he had any depth, but he was about as deep as the stream of dirty water that ran from the house pipes after the dishes were done—Lion Dung really and truly didn't care what happened to us. He never distinguished between Belly and me in that way, though he was generally nicer to my brother because Belly allowed him to be. Belly was a more amiable child than the one I acted like at home. He didn't look for arguments the way I did. My mother no longer brought Belly to the gallery. He just hung around the house with Lion, playing by himself or with some of the other hippies' kids. There were still some who came to the playground on Cerro Gordo. My mother didn't mind if Belly was happy, she just couldn't be bothered to do anything about it while the Beast was around.

Actually, there was a brief time when my mother was doing more acid and she got nice, even to me. If Lion Dung passed out first, as he usually did, and Belly was in bed already, she'd hold me as if I were her little girl again, kiss me, smooch me, notice that my hair was a mess and brush it, tell me what a pretty little girl I was. I heard this occasionally from other people, but not normally from her. She bought me clothes like the other kids' but she never took me to the store; she just brought them home and usually they were okay. After someone like Mrs. Candelaria told me I was pretty, I would look in the mirror to see what she meant. I had straight brown hair, like my mother. Brown eyes. A face. I didn't know what was pretty about that. When I asked my mother, she laughed and said it just meant that I didn't look like her. That made the whole thing senseless to me, since I thought her beautiful. She also told me stories about when I was little. Some of them couldn't ever have happened, and others I remembered had happened to my brother. Or maybe to her. Some of them happened on a farm, and I'd never been on a farm, but it didn't matter.

From that day on, I went to Laya's after school unless I'd been told I would be needed at home. The Candelarias were very straight. Spanish. (People in Santa Fe still identify themselves by one of the three groups—Spanish, Indian or Anglo—that they or their parents or grandparents or great-greats, or whoever, were when they settled here.) Laya's father worked as a security guard at Los Alamos. Her parents were both very nice to me. They were nice to *her*. She had no brothers or sisters, there were just the three of them. And two cats. It was Laya's job, which she hated, to keep the cats' box clean. I remember that I was always surprised when Laya got upset about that—or anything—because I thought that if I lived in a house with my mother and father, nothing would ever bother me much.

❁

*O*ne day later on my mother said I should come home after school because she was going to Taos and she wasn't sure whether she'd take Billy. She was interested in a gallery there that was for sale. (Lion liked Taos more than Santa Fe, which he said was getting too gentrified. *Gentrified* was the only long word he ever used.)

When I got to my house, Lion was lying on his back on the serape, staring at the ceiling, arms splayed out from his side. I drank some orange juice and called the gallery and was told by Ruth, the girl who worked there, that my mother had taken Billy to Taos. I did my homework, but when I finished, it was getting dark and Lion hadn't moved yet. I was too uneasy to just sit and read. I turned on every light in the house, but he still didn't move. I called Laya. Of course I didn't mention Lion, or drugs. I asked if I could come to her house, maybe sleep there. Mrs. Candelaria said it was okay, but to make sure I left a note for my mother. I wrote the note, put it on the dining table under the tequila bottle, gathered what I needed in my canvas bag, and left. I'd never walked down the trail in the dark. There were only a few houses, and I didn't know the people in them, so I walked very fast and tried not to think about snakes or coyotes. When I got to the door, I was freezing. Santa Fe always gets cold at night, and I hadn't thought to put on warmer clothes. Laya's mother greeted me.

"You poor child," she said. "I didn't realize until a minute ago that you must be walking."

I began to cry. Mrs. Candelaria put a hand on my shoulder and I moved up against her, but I couldn't stop crying. Mr. Candelaria looked up from his paper and Mrs. Candelaria explained that I was upset because my mother hadn't come home. She asked if something else was upsetting me, but I was afraid to say anything about Lion, and then Laya came out of her room and gave me a hug and I stopped crying and apologized for being a baby. Mrs. Candelaria told Laya to give me a sweater.

Their house wasn't much larger than ours but it was a real home, with plaster walls like our house in Hanover, a regular cloth-covered sofa in the living room, and six chairs at a nice, round dining table. Oh, yes, and a TV. I had to go there to watch television. I went to the bathroom to wash my face and hands, something my mother never made us do at home but I'd seen other kids do it. We had sausages and the beans and the tortillas I'd once hated but had come to enjoy at my friends'. I was really hungry, by this time, and I ate every bit of food on my plate, tried not to show that I wanted more. After dinner, I helped Laya with the dishes and then we went to her room, but I couldn't concentrate on schoolwork or anything else, I just grew more and more uneasy. Finally, I asked Mrs. Candelaria if she'd mind if I called my house.

The phone rang a few times and then it was picked up. I remember that I was relieved at the moment the ringing stopped, and I almost hung up, but then a man's voice that wasn't Lion's said hello.

I said, "Hello. Who'm I speaking to?"

The man's voice said, "Who's calling, please?"

I must have been staring at the phone, not answering, not knowing, except I understood right away that something was wrong. I could see Lion on the floor, and the sight was more ominous than it had been earlier. I must have dropped the receiver, or let it go slack in my hand, because Laya's mother took it from me and, identifying herself, said that Madeleine seemed to be upset about something and couldn't talk.

After a long time, she said, "I see. I see." Very quiet. Her arm was around me by this time. She said that Madeleine had been expecting to sleep at their house, and that if it was all right with her mother, they'd just keep me for the night. Then, suddenly, she recoiled. My mother had grabbed the phone. I could hear her shrieking. Mrs. Candelaria tried to be nice. This woman, after all, had had a shock. After a while, Mrs. Candelaria said, "I'll see if I can find her," and covered the mouthpiece, and said to me, "Your mother wants to talk to you, Dear, but she's very upset. I guess they told you, her friend died. I don't know . . ."

I took the phone from her. She remained next to me.

My voice holding just enough, I said, "Hello?"

"What did you do?" My mother screamed it, so that I had to move the earpiece away from my ear. I'd been prepared for something bad, but not this. "Why didn't you call Ruth?" she was screaming as Laya's mother took back the phone.

I just stood there, feeling guilty without knowing, yet, what I had or hadn't done. I was beginning to understand why Lion had looked peculiar, but I was afraid to admit that to my mother. I didn't know what it would mean. I was afraid to tell her I *had* called Ruth. The rule of my life had been not to tell anybody anything.

Mrs. Candelaria took the phone from me. After a while, she said she was really sorry, she could understand why my mother wanted me home, but they had a flat tire on the car and they couldn't do anything about it until morning. Yes, it was true that it wasn't such a long walk, but might it not be just as well if Madeleine stayed, why should the child have to deal with, see . . . You know. And then Laya's mother recoiled because my mother had smashed down the phone. Mrs. Candelaria hung up, shaking her head.

I thanked her for helping me, but said that maybe I'd better go home. My mother was going to need my help with my brother, if nothing else. Mrs. Candelaria said she would take me, but she wanted me to know I was welcome at their house at any time of the day or night. She thought I was wonderful.

In the world away from my home, most people thought me a bright, pleasant girl who would never give anyone a bad time if she weren't provoked. At home, I was seen by my mother as a time bomb that was waiting to go off—or that already had, and must be trying to conceal the damage. What I couldn't have predicted was the extent to which her view would remain with me. Happy moments. Rotten ones. Her songs, too. My head still runs on her old 78's. *Perfidia, my heart goes out to you, Perfidia. Remember.* The part where she says her lover promised he wouldn't forget her but he forgot to remember. It's as though her mind has come to nest in my own brain, entered into an eternal dialogue with it. If her voice had often followed me beyond the house, I'd once been able to wrestle it into a cage where I didn't have to think about it.

Not on a night like that one, of course. When I talk about Mrs. Candelaria bringing me home that night, even if I manage to describe only how *I* was feeling, I am wondering what my mother would say if she could read it. I want her to read it. I want her to read every word I write. Her intensity, happy or unhappy, spoiled me for other humans. Have I told you that she was a terrific ballplayer? It was the only thing she did in a team. She didn't keep friends for as long as the baseball season, but she kept teammates. She became a good skier, though whatever she'd told Lion that first day, he had to convince her to learn. She was afraid of going downhill, out of control. (She didn't ski after he died.) More important than sports was the way she was at home. She was never still. The men who lived with us weren't adept at plumbing or carpentry, but she could fix anything that went wrong in the house. I don't think she cared, half the time, whether it was fixed or not; she just needed something to *do.*

Long before my brother was born, my mother had spoiled me for everybody else. When she left me, withdrew from me, whatever you want to call it, it was as though I'd been dropped in a place with no sun. No moon, either, for that matter. I could only look through a telescope and see her rays shining elsewhere, too far away to matter to me. There were no rays for anyone, after Lion died.

Mrs. Candelaria said she would take me home to check things out. Laya came out of her room and asked, "What's going on, Maddy?"

I was in a knot because I needed to tell her but I thought I shouldn't.

Finally, I said, "Lion died. I don't think I can talk about it."

She said, "You don't have to if you don't want to."

I sorely wanted to, but I was afraid. Finally, I said, "My mother needs me." Then I hugged her and said I'd see her in the morning.

Once we were in the car, Mrs. Candelaria asked me

if I was going to be all right; my mother was terribly upset.

"Thank you," I said. "My brother must be home, too. I think I can help with him."

"Oh, of course," Mrs. Candelaria said. "How old is your brother now?"

I said he was four. Mrs. Candelaria didn't talk for a bit. Finally she asked, very slowly and carefully, whether I'd like her to wait for me for a while . . . just in case . . . my mother or I . . . needed help. Needed some help with my brother.

"No, ma'am," I said. "I appreciate it, but I really don't think you have to do that. If we need help, she can ask one of her friends."

Maybe Mrs. Candelaria didn't know my mother had no friends.

◗

We could see the swiveling rays of the police car's top light even before we rounded the bend. The car was parked on the road below our house. The policeman was standing at our door. Mrs. Candelaria told me to wait until she'd talked to him, but I was up the hill before she'd even gotten out of the car. Then I stopped. I wanted to go to my mother, but I didn't want to look at Lion, now that I knew he was dead.

I ran back to Mrs. Candelaria, buried my face in her bosom, began to cry. She understood and asked the policeman if she could go inside with me. They began speaking in Spanish. The cops were mostly Spanish; second-, third-, umpteenth-generation New Mexico, and nice, unless they thought you were one of the people bringing dope into their beautiful town.

Mrs. Candelaria said, "Maddy, this is my friend, Johnny. He'll bring you inside and take care of you."

I hugged her more tightly.

"What is it, Honey? Tell me."

I made her lean over and whispered in her ear, "Who's on the rug?"

It wasn't what I'd meant to ask, but I couldn't figure out how to ask it properly.

"On the rug?" she asked.

The policeman heard her and said, "The body, Betty. The body's on the rug."

I'd stopped crying but now I began again, full force, my own body shaking, my arms around her, my face against her chest. I thought they wouldn't hear me, that way. Mrs. Candelaria held on to me, stroked my hair.

"It's covered, Honey," the policeman said. "You're not gonna see him when you walk in. And soon the ambulance'll be here, take him away."

Slowly, I was able to calm down. Reluctantly, I moved back from Mrs. Candelaria's bosom.

"Atta girl," Johnny said. "What's your name? Madeleine? How old are you, Madeleine?"

"Ten." Usually if someone asked I said what I was

almost, and I was almost eleven, but now I didn't want to be a day older than I was. "Where's my brother?"

"He's inside with your mom, Madeleine. Now, let's see if you can be grown-up, and we'll go in together, and you can see them, and Officer Perez will take care of you."

As we walked to the door, the policeman holding my hand, Mrs. Candelaria called to me that she would wait awhile, in case I wanted to go back with her. I didn't answer. I was trying to imagine what the room would look like, where my mother would be, but I couldn't picture anybody except Lion, on his back with his eyes open, like a dead man on television. If Johnny hadn't been holding my hand, I would have run back to Mrs. Candelaria. As it was, I squeezed as hard as I could and let him open the door to the house.

But he'd lied to me. He'd promised I wouldn't see Lion, and Lion was all I could see. At first, I didn't even notice my mother, rocking and weeping in the chair near him. Or Belly, asleep on one of the big cushions on the floor on the other side of her chair. There was just Lion, covered by a sheet but his contours clear—his forehead, nose and chin, his big chest, and—oh, God! His bare toes were sticking out of the bottom of the sheet.

I tried to scream but nothing came out. I shook my hand free of Johnny's, and ran to my mother, who let me sit on her lap. I snuggled against her breasts and she held me as though she were still my mother.

"This is the child who left the note?" the second policeman asked.

She was nodding.

"Your name is Madeleine?" he asked me.

I nodded.

"I just need to ask you a couple of questions, Madeleine."

My mother clutched me more tightly.

"You found Mr. Lion on the floor?"

I nodded.

"How did he look when you found him?"

"Same as usual," I managed. My mother's grip on my left arm was beginning to hurt. I sat up, but she didn't let go.

"What do you mean by that?" he asked.

"I need to blow my nose," I said. My mother handed me a wet tissue, but even after I blew, it was hard to breathe. "He was sleeping," I said. "He always sleeps on the floor. We don't have a sofa."

"Does he sleep a lot in the daytime?"

I nodded. I was beginning to feel glad that my mother was hurting my arm because it helped me remember to be very careful.

"Why do you think that is?"

"Because he doesn't work."

"You think everyone who doesn't work sleeps on the floor all day?"

I didn't know how to answer that, so I just looked at him. The feeling of not being able to breathe had moved down to my chest.

"Why did you go to your friend's house?" he asked.

"I was hungry," I said. "My mother was in Taos."

"Is that a usual place for her to go?"

"I don't know."

I heard a car drive up and stop. For a second I thought it must be Lion, but then I remembered.

"Even if he was still alive when you got here," my mother moaned, her voice shaking, "he'd be dead by now."

"But he wasn't alive when we got here, ma'am," the policeman said.

"I don't mean you," my mother sobbed. "I mean her." (That was one of the lines that got around, from Johnny to Mrs. Candelaria to God only knows who else, and made them even more sympathetic to me than they would have been.)

The ambulance people came in, then, and I broke from my mother and ran into my room. I didn't want to see if he moved when they picked him up. I got into bed, pulled the blanket up over me. I was hoping that when Lion was gone, my mother would come in to me. I didn't want to close my eyes because I was afraid if I did, I'd see him. I don't know how long it was before I fell asleep in spite of myself. When I awakened, it was because my mother was putting Belly

into his bed. Briefly, I thought it was Lion she was
leaning over.

"Mama?"

She turned as though she hadn't known I was there.
She was drunk. I don't know if I recognized it then,
but I can see it clearly, now. She'd always liked to
drink—too much, I suppose—but she began, that
night, to put away an incredible amount of booze,
plain José Cuervo tequila, or real margaritas. She
called them margaritas or Josés. *Where's José?* and so
on. She kept a saucer of salt out on the counter and
salted the rim even when it was just a José.

She reached for the light.

I said, "Please leave it on, Mama."

She said, "I'm not your mother."

I bolted up to a sitting position, frightened and
confused.

"Why aren't you my mother?"

"Why didn't you call me?"

"When?" I was frantic to understand. "When you
were in Taos?"

"You could've called the hospital. A doctor. The
operator. The *police!*"

I was dumbfounded. I'd been trained not to even
say hello to the police, whom she'd always called cops,
and the subject of doctors had never even come up.
We didn't have doctors, we had vitamin C. If there
was a hospital in Santa Fe, I didn't know about it. I

started to tell her I'd tried her at the gallery, but she interrupted.

"Do you know what an emergency is?" Her voice was getting louder.

"I didn't know it was an emergency," I said, my voice barely holding, perhaps because I knew what was about to happen.

"You're lying!" she screamed.

My brother woke up and began to cry.

She didn't notice, yet.

"You left him here to die, you wanted him to die!" She broke into howling sobs that sounded more like a coyote in the hills than like a human. She sat down on the edge of Belly's bed and reached for him, but he was frightened, and he edged back into the corner of his bed.

I just stared at her. Could it be true? I hadn't liked having Lion around, but I hadn't thought he needed to be dead to be gone. My mother was saying he hadn't been dead when I came home, and it could be true. It certainly hadn't occurred to me that he was dead. Maybe I should have known. Maybe I could have saved him. I should have, if I could; it wouldn't have been any worse than this.

She went to the living room for the tequila. I followed her. She stopped sobbing for long enough to take a big gulp from the bottle, then she began keening again. I wanted to comfort her, to make up for what I'd done. I wanted her to stop making those awful noises. But when I approached her, she began calling Lion's name, begging for him to be there in my place. When I stayed there, she put "Perfidia" on the record player—so loud that it hurt my ears. Finally I went back to the bedroom, where Belly was hiding under his blanket. He didn't want to talk to me or to anyone. I only understood much later that Belly must have believed what my mother said about me. At least, he must have believed it some of the time.

◊

*T*he autopsy showed Lion to have died of a combination of heroin, acid and marijuana. The funeral was held in Taos so it would be okay when nobody showed.

◊

*M*y mother's milk dried up overnight and she became a different person. Her once-pink cheeks were white and puckered, as though the flesh behind the skin had been drained out. Or she'd been pickled. It was partly that she got very skinny, but that wasn't all of it. Her face was entirely different. The first time I saw her on the street near the gallery without knowing she was there, it took a moment to realize that the old woman walking slowly toward me was my mother. (She was thirty-two.) She still liked my brother and not me, but there was no energy to either feeling. No grabbing Billy and telling him she loved him to pieces. No screaming about the day I let Lion die. When we were home, I took care of Billy. He was just four, but he was very independent. He didn't like being inside the house. During the day he walked down to the playground on his own, played with the little kids and their mothers if there was nobody his age.

I started cooking simple things like hamburgers and ravioli from a can, so we'd have something to eat when my mother didn't come home. At night, if he couldn't fall asleep because it was cold and I was sitting up in bed, reading or doing homework, he'd come over to the bottom of my bed and pull up the quilt and curl up under it, his feet touching mine for warmth.

There was a photo of my mother with Lion and Billy that she'd had enlarged, then hung up in the living room. It had been taken by Rahji Cohen during the time when he had a studio in the Sky. (He hadn't been able to survive on the tourists, who mostly brought their own cameras.) In the picture, Billy stood in front of Lion; one of Lion's arms was around my mother, the other rested on Billy's shoulder. Mr. and Mrs. America and their adorable little boy. That was the whole family. It was harder for me to do what she wanted me to do if I was in sight of the picture. Once, so drunk she could barely stand up and look at it, my mother said that if she'd known Lion then, he would have been Belly's father instead of Wilkie. She smacked me when she heard me tell Belly that Wilkie, not Lion, was his father. Belly didn't seem to think twice about how peculiar her whole line of reasoning was. Partly that was about his being younger and a boy, but, in general, he didn't get absorbed in her craziness the way I did. He stayed under her radar.

Other signs of Lion had remained around the house but were less bothersome. His sheepskin coat was still on its hook. (Belly called it "Wilkie's coat.") The guitar Lion'd supposedly been able to play, though I'd never heard him do more than strum a couple of chords, stood in a corner in my mother's bedroom. Sometimes she held it on her lap, one hand resting on the strings, the other holding her drink.

After a couple of months she began to spend time with Wilkie and his girlfriend. But soon his girlfriend had had enough. At that point, my mother picked up a hippie kid on the street and brought him home. The problem with him was, she wouldn't allow dope in the house. She'd stand there, half out of her mind on tequila, lecturing this kid about the dangers of drugs. He couldn't understand what the big deal was. When he tried to give me money to buy some weed for him from a dealer near my school, I told him I wouldn't because it was illegal. He thought that was funny, for a kid my age to be worried about what was legal. I told him I was glad I'd said something he thought was funny, even if he wasn't that much older than I was. A week later he was gone. My mother said I kept getting

rid of her boyfriends, wanted to know what I'd said to
him, but she wasn't intense about it. I think he'd
stolen money from her. He didn't have his own car
but he'd begun to stay out at night, anyway.

Laya and her mother were wonderful to me, although DRUG DEATH had been in the paper, and some
of the kids with straight Spanish parents (the Indian
kids went to their own school and they'd never mixed
as much) weren't allowed to have me in their homes
anymore. Occasionally I slept at Laya's house, but not
as often as I could have. It wasn't just because of Billy.
I wanted to be in my own house when my mother
became herself. When she did, I had to be prepared.
I'd need to know what was going on in her life. If
she'd just met a man, home would be safe because
she'd be happy. If she'd just had a breakup, home
would be safe because she'd be low. In between, I
never knew.

◐

*I*t was a long time after Lion's death before my
mother began to inhabit her own body, stopped playing her old records all the time, dancing around the
room as though someone were with her. And singing
"Remember." Or "Perfidia." *Forget the love, all promise
of love, or sharing another's charms.* She stopped being
drunk all the time and started paying attention to the
gallery, which had deteriorated. She found some new

artists, a couple of women, as well as men. She'd been on the lookout for artists since the Sky opened, would consider any picture or sculpture that didn't have Jesus or saints in it, but now she began to learn a little more about the Santa Fe painters and sculptors, which ones might be wanting to switch galleries, which ones she might lure from others, and so on. They ranged from the George O'Keeffers to the Billy el Kids; most of the stuff was ghastly and/or imitative, and she knew it after they broke up if not before, but in the meantime, they had a gallery and she was getting laid.

Before Billy was five, she persuaded Wilkie to get mortgage money to turn our shack into a house. We lived there and slept there, or in a tent outside, most of the time while the work was being done. Perhaps I should say, Billy and I slept there. During that time, my mother would as often as not stay in town or go back after supper. Sometimes she didn't return until the morning, after I'd given Billy breakfast and brought him to the playground or, once he began school, to meet the school bus. The shack was a nightmare of splinters and sawdust, plaster dust and rusty nails. At different times, both Billy and I had to get tetanus shots. But when the work was finished, we had a real house with a living room and three small bedrooms, wooden floors throughout, a bathroom with a shower and a tub, a kiva (the standard Santa Fe corner fireplace) in the living room, an adobe exterior and a tiny terrace, as well as a paved driveway that ran up the small, steep incline to the front door. She furnished the living room with a sofa, some tables and three chairs, all with classic Santa Fe carved-wood frames, and Navajo rugs. She set Indian pottery on the various shelves and in the *nichos,* the little wall recesses where traditional people put saints and other religious pieces. And we had a decent kitchen, although it was still part of the living room.

She was justly proud of the job she'd done and became more likely to bring home her casual lays. She needed people to admire the house, but not that many townspeople spoke to her. She had friends from Tiny's, a hangout for locals across the street from the school for the deaf, but they didn't go to one another's houses. I was thirteen before she had a house boyfriend again and she stopped moaning over the way I'd let Lion die as soon as she had a few ounces of tequila in her.

◐

She met El Shrinko at Tiny's, not long after he hit town. (I'll call him Ellery when I begin to like him. Ellery Queens. Queens was where he'd been born and raised; I'd never heard that place name before and thought it was funny.) I think it was '83. There'd been an article in *Esquire* magazine, Santa Fe as Shangri-la, and a lot of people had come to visit. Some had stayed. El Shrinko had fallen in love with the town when he and his wife visited their son, Keith, who was living in Taos. When Keith threatened never to speak to them again if they moved to Taos, his mother returned to New York but El Shrinko rented a room in a bed-and-breakfast in Santa Fe. Keith continued to speak to him, maybe because his sister back East barely did. My mother helped him make up his mind to settle there and get a divorce. He planned to buy a house and start a practice, once the divorce was settled and he knew how much money he had. He was much older than my mother, somewhere in his fifties. He had a round face, wore glasses, he was bald on top, and he drank coffee all day, couldn't keep his eyes open without it. In Taos, Keith had persuaded him to smoke weed for the first time and he'd become a fan. My mother told him about the love of her life, who'd died of drugs, so that she'd never again get involved with someone who, etc. El Shrinko persuaded her that a man who'd never smoked a joint through the sixties or seventies was unlikely to become an addict in the eighties. But he was probably impressed by the strength of her convictions. With all the commotion about weed, he might not have noticed at first that she was a drunk. She drank less for a while, anyway. And maybe he didn't want to notice. He was having a good time, the way you're supposed to when you move to a beautiful place like Santa Fe.

She was happier than she'd been since Lion's death, and she treated El Shrinko well. When he had back problems, she bought a firmer mattress. When he found the Navajo rugs dangerously slippery, she put rubber mats under them. El Shrinko thought adults should be dressed when they walked around the house, so my mother bought a couple of cotton muumuus and stopped going around without her top. She also tried to convince him that she was a cook. His mouth wouldn't buy that one. He acquired a fancy coffeemaker, and he'd eat breakfast at our house when he could buy the Indian bread they made on the pueblos, the only kind in Santa Fe he considered worth eating, but that was it, until he started cooking, himself. Then he bought spices and pots and a set of knives. He had a lot of time for cooking. Sexually, there was no way he was hot stuff. He was very calm. Unexcitable. There weren't the shrieks and moans there'd been with Lion, though it's hard to say for sure because we had better walls between us. My mother didn't complain about El Shrinko, but once in a while she sighed and said there would never be another Lion.

That was just as well, of course, though I wasn't crazy about El Shrinko at the beginning and Billy couldn't bear him. Not only did he have no interest in sports, but he approved of my mother's stand on TV. My mother hated television far beyond the rational hatred many parents have. She was suspicious of electrical equipment in general, had never wanted a more modern music system than our little radio and her old phonograph, talked about TV as though it were the electric chair, this monster that could fry your brains in a minute if you just switched it on. When we had a school assignment that required seeing a show, I had to watch it at somebody else's house. El Shrinko thought his son's brains had been ravaged by too much television.

Maybe it was because my brother could hardly stand to be in a room with him that I began to see his good points. Or maybe it was because he paid for a housecleaner, and I didn't have to do it anymore. In general, he treated me like a person, not just the bulky baggage of my mother's life. When he started cooking, he'd occasionally ask if there was something one of us would enjoy. (Billy's response was to stop eating real food at home and concentrate on things like peanut-butter and marshmallow-fluff sandwiches. When El Shrinko told him he should have some greens, Billy tore off a piece of lettuce about two inches square and put it on his sandwich.) He'd inquire about my life. My mother never asked me about school or anything else. She signed my report cards without reading them, although El Shrinko was certain she was proud of me. I began high school the year he came to live with us. He remembered Keith's New York high school curriculum and was interested in comparing it with mine.

Another reason it was good to have him around was that my mother was more likely to answer questions I asked instead of just smacking me, even if she was in a bad mood.

○

*I* acquired a boyfriend, Arnold Taylor. His family had moved down from Utah the year before. His father was an accountant who had a job in the Santa Fe government and his mother also worked, at a gallery. Arnold was sixteen, two years older than I. A lot of the kids thought he was too square to talk to, but he was another top student, we both read a lot, and we talked about school and books.

El Shrinko's divorce settlement was reached during that year. It was less favorable than he'd hoped, and buying a house became problematic. My mother wanted him to stay in ours and rent an office in town, but he thought it was important to own some real estate. He got a little tight about money. He wanted to eat at home most nights and resisted going out just to drink. That worked out well for me, but a hint of tightness made my mother start to ask for things she didn't even want and they began to have little quarrels.

On one late-autumn night, the two of them had driven to Taos so he could introduce her to Keith, who blamed her for the divorce and had resisted meeting her until now. They were going to the restaurant where Keith, a painter, waited on tables.

Billy had gone to bed. I'd spent the time doing

homework and talking to a couple of my girlfriends on
the phone. I couldn't settle down. I was thinking
about walking to Laya's when I heard the car pull up
in the driveway.

It took a long time for them to reach the door.
When I went to open it, I wasn't being nosy. There'd
been a couple of robberies and we'd all begun to lock
our doors at night. El Shrinko was helping—practically dragging—my mother up the path. He was a
slighter person than Lion or Wilkie, so it would have
been difficult even if she hadn't been stinking-laugh-
ing-hostile drunk. She'd been that way plenty of
times, but not in the year since El Shrinko had come
to live with us. She was singing *Remember*. As they
entered the house, her arm was around El Shrinko and
she was singing "Remember," that same old part
about how her lover forgot to remember.

El Shrinko tried to propel her into the bedroom,
but she wasn't having it. I think she was upset because
she was singing to him and he wasn't noticing. She
broke away from him and lurched toward the sofa,
almost making it before she fell to the floor on her
knees, her elbows on the sofa-seat pillows. She was
laughing in a hostile way as he came to help her up,
then let her swivel back onto the sofa. She didn't open
her eyes.

He said, "I'm going to bed."

She said, "Ellery's going to bed."

I didn't look at him; we were both embarrassed.

She said, "Madeleine, would you make me a José?" She grinned. "I told the bartender that at home I didn't bother with the triple sec and the lime juice, we just made Josés, and he said we should call them Anitas, but I told him we didn't change names all that easily." She winked as though we had a secret.

I made her a José, dipping the glass (we only had eight-ounce glasses in the house; she found small ones offensive) in the bowl of coarse salt, then pouring some tequila. She was awake, by now, and not un-friendly, at least not to me.

"How was your dinner?" I was curious about Keith.

"Oh," she said, "the food's fine, even if some Very Fussy People don't think so."

I waited.

"Or are you asking about Little Tight Ass, son of Big Tight Ass."

I was shocked. She'd never said anything remotely nasty about Ellery.

She laughed. "You didn't know having a tight ass was in the genes? Sure it is. Practically everything's in the genes."

I'd noticed she was beginning to talk about genes, maybe because Ellery sometimes referred to the *reasons* people did things.

I said, "I guess that's what I meant. Who I meant."

She shrugged. "Not much to say. Just another dopey kid who's got his father by the balls. I should've known better than to go. His mother's a perfect hu-

man being, and he can't understand . . . He doesn't
know or care that his father never had a sex life. A life.
He doesn't know a fucking thing except that his father
belongs with his mother in New York. Not with me,
having a good time." She struggled to her feet and
toward the tequila.

I said I was going to bed.

She said, "I wasn't nice to Ellery."

I turned, not knowing whether to agree with her or
keep quiet.

As though he'd been listening, Ellery came out in
his pajamas.

My mother, in a way that could have been inter-
preted as either mocking or childlike, said, "I was upset, Ellery."

Ellery smiled benignly. "I understand."

"You do? Really and truly?"

But she'd slipped over some border and I grew uneasy.

"Of course I do," Ellery said. "Why don't we all go
to bed, now."

Eager, if still sloppy, my mother struggled to her
feet, staggered toward the bottle to refill her glass.

Ellery said, "Maybe you should leave José out
here."

My mother said, "Maybe I should leave *you* out
here." Then she went ahead of him into the room,
holding the half-empty glass.

Ellery looked like a little raw egg someone had

smashed and thrown into the sink for its insides to drain out. He shuffled into the room after her.

I took a very long shower, washed my hair and brushed my teeth. When I came out, I could hear murmurs and giggles from behind their door. She'd made up to him, and he was letting her do it. I felt disgusted, nearly nauseated. I went to Belly's room and looked at him, sleeping quietly in his bed, and then I went back to my own dark room and empty bed. It could just as well have been a coffin; there was no way I was going to lie down in it. I put on my jeans and a sweater without having any definite idea of where I might go after midnight on a weekday. Finally I decided I'd walk past the Candelarias' and see if a light was on. If not, maybe I would keep going down the hill and hitch a ride to Tesuque, where Arnold lived. He'd told me he read and listened to music until all hours. If I could find the house, locating his room should be easy.

My hair was wet. I didn't care. I got my parka, packed my knapsack with what I needed for school the next day, and took off.

Laya's house was as dark as I'd expected it to be. I was sorry, but I was also glad, in a way. After Lion's death, my other friends had tried to find out more about what happened than Laya would tell them. I'm not sure how much her mother even told *her*. I liked them all, but there was no reason for them to know any of it. If I saw Laya right now, I might find myself talking about my mother and Ellery. The distance between Arnold and me, not the physical distance, of course, but the mental space, made it easier to not talk about things I wanted to keep private.

I continued down the road to Palace Avenue, and then to the highway, where I got a lift to Tesuque with a truck driver who lectured me on the dangers of a pretty young girl hitching rides from strangers. I never had a lift from a man who didn't lecture me about the dangers of other men. This one would have left the road to drop me off in front of Arnold's, but I told him it wasn't far to my girlfriend's house and I didn't want to wake up her parents. He made me promise that I'd never again hitch a ride. By the time I stepped down from his truck, I was glad to be on the road again. I wasn't scared. I was seldom scared of the things normal people are scared of.

I'd never been at Arnold's house but the name was on the mailbox. From a distance, it all seemed to be dark, but when I walked around the brand-new one-story adobe to the back, I saw light around the shades of one room. Symphonic music was playing, but low. I wasn't worried about how Arnold would react to a surprise visit. I was just concerned that his parents would hear me. The window was open at the room with the music. I called his name softly, waited, called again, but either he was asleep or he didn't hear me because of the music. Finally, I set my face in the space between the window and the sill, and said, with my full voice, "Arnold? Are you there? It's Madeleine."

He said, nearly shouted, "Huh?" and I thought I heard him leap out of bed.

I said, "I'm at the window."

After a moment, he pulled up the shade, peered at me through the glass.

I said, "I'm sorry. I was desperate for someplace to go."

He remained motionless.

I said, "I had a fight with my mother and she kicked me out of the house."

He pushed up the window farther and asked how I'd gotten so far.

"I hitched a ride."

"You're kidding."

"You were the only one I thought might be awake."

He nodded, but he didn't move to let me in.

I was beginning to feel very cold. My hair was still damp.

"D'you think I could come in for a little while?"

"Here?"

I didn't respond, and after a while, he pushed open the window as far as it would go and said I should climb up. I handed him my knapsack, stepped on the ridge at the bottom of the adobe, and let him help me hoist myself over the sill. Then, facing the window, I slid to the floor. I couldn't bring myself to turn and face him. We hadn't gone beyond a few hugs and kisses. I had assumed it was for lack of opportunity, and of course it had crossed my mind that being hidden in his room late at night would provide an excellent one. I knew I was ready to do whatever he wanted to do, but I couldn't make myself turn around. He asked me what had happened, and I began to cry. He placed a sympathetic hand on my shoulder, squeezed it. That small gesture encouraged me to turn, very slowly. He hugged me and then sympathy turned sexual, as everything but algebra does when you're a teenager, and we kissed for a long time. When he moved back from me, we were breathing quickly.

He said, "I'd better shut the window."

I watched him. He was wearing baggy pajamas. When my mother wanted to be nasty about my father, she'd imitate him shuffling around in baggy pajamas.

I asked if it was okay to take off my jacket.

He shrugged. "I guess."

Piqued, I said, "Maybe I should keep holding it in case I have to make a fast getaway."

He said, "You won't have to. They're all at the other end of the house." But he moved to lock the door.

I said, "Oh. That's nice."

He turned back to me, scratched his head. I found him terribly handsome, even in his funny pajamas. He was tall and skinny and sort of craggy, for someone of that age, and most of the girls preferred smooth looks, but I thought his more manly.

I got more and more nervous as he remained where he was, and finally, I said, "Checkmate."

Arnold was a chess player, and it turned him on. He came back to me, a distance of about two feet because it was a small room. He smiled for the first time, told me checkmate was what you said at the end of the game, not the beginning. I said I was terrible at all games. He took me in his arms, and he kissed me, at first lightly, but growing passionate, pressing his body against mine. The first time I'd seen Lion walking around with an erect penis, I'd run into my room, terrified by the sight of this huge, stiff thing that I'd been told went into my mother to do something that made babies, except I'd been certain there was some mistake in what I'd learned. Nothing that went into her could look like that. All I'd wanted was to get out of its way whenever I saw it. But I wasn't a child, now, I was fourteen, and excitement lent Arnold's organ a different cast as it pressed up against me. His hand cupped my breast. With some difficulty, I reached behind me and opened my brassiere. Carefully, the hand reached under the loose cloth to find my flesh. I felt him breathing fast, heard myself moan softly as he played with my nipple; I'd never been told how good it all felt; sex was just something you did because you were old enough. And Arnold was even more excited than I, this shy, inward boy who some of the kids laughed at because you couldn't imagine his having a dirty thought, much less . . . I pulled up my sweater and bra, but could barely get my head and arms out of them before he'd pushed me back onto his bed and he was on top of me, playing with my breasts and sucking at my nipples and breathing so hard you'd have thought he'd come up from underwater. I wanted to get undressed and under the covers, but he seemed to be content just to lie on top of me, press against me.

After what seemed a long time, I whispered, "I'm all tangled up in my clothes."

He stopped, looked down in a puzzled way.

I said, "Do you want me to take them off?"

He backed off me, sat back up on his heels. "Here?"

"Not if you don't want me to."

He said, "I do, but I . . . I never . . ."

"Me, neither," I said. "I . . . They just feel too warm, now."

He nodded slowly. But he didn't move.

I said, addressing an unidentifiable issue, "We could get under the covers."

He remained on his knees for an interminable period, as though he'd been offered a choice of his life or twenty years in the Gulag. Then, finally, he decided. He slapped his thighs, got out of bed, lowered the shade and turned off the bedside light. I took off my sweater and bra, got under the covers before removing my pants. Then I waited for him to decide to come back to the bed.

It was that way the whole time, excitment driving

him on against his will, so that when he came under the covers and pressed his body against mine, and his penis stuck itself between my legs, he froze for a moment, then came at me more passionately than before. Eventually, as he rubbed, I moved backward, and he pushed into me, then stopped, briefly softened enough so that he wasn't hurting me the little he had, then after a moment grew stronger than ever. When he finally came, I actually came along with him. True. Together, we shuddered to stillness.

He seemed to have fallen asleep on top of me. I remained quiet for as long as I could, but then his body grew too heavy, and I began trying to extricate myself. He startled awake, shook out his head, as though for cobwebs, looked down at me. He didn't know what I was doing there.

I smiled. "I need to move."

Abruptly, he pulled out of me and rolled off, leaving a wet trail across my thighs. Then he lay on his back. He seemed to be looking at the ceiling.

I moved from the moist spot under me on the bottom sheet, used the top sheet to wipe off my legs. I was beginning to feel as though something was wrong.

He said, "How do you know you're not pregnant?"

"You don't get pregnant that easily." I was certain *I* didn't.

He was silent. Our bodies were barely touching, though it was a narrow bed.

I asked, "Do you want me to stay here?"

He said, "My mother wakes me up in the morning."

I said, "Well, maybe I could sleep under the bed. I don't see how I can get home, now."

He asked, "How'd you get here in the first place?"

I said, "I hitched. Remember?"

He didn't respond.

I said, mildly sarcastic, "Maybe you'd like me to hitch back. It's only two o'clock in the morning." And was surprised, in spite of myself, when he didn't say no.

I was going to have to get out of that bed. Sleep under it. Do *something*. I scrambled over him to the floor, turned on the light and found my clothes. I got dressed with my back to him.

"Can you please just tell me," I asked, sitting at the edge of the bed to get on my sneakers and socks, "why you're acting mad at me?"

He took a long time. Then he said, his eyes still on the ceiling, "You seduced me."

"Oh? That was a crime?"

He looked down toward me for the first time. Suddenly I could see why the other girls thought he was bad looking; he might have had fangs instead of teeth, for all the attractiveness I saw now.

"I didn't want to be seduced."

For a moment, I just stared at him. Then I got on my parka, grabbed my knapsack, unlocked his door and found my way through the living room to the front of the house, where I unlocked the big door and allowed it to slam behind me.

He could tell his parents it was a raccoon.

◑

*I* walked down the dirt road and onto the highway without seeing a car. I didn't mind. I was too agitated to be tired. It was only a few miles to Cerro Gordo and at first I thought I'd just as leave walk home.

My great concern was that I not miss school. That Arnold Taylor not be allowed to ruin school. If he wanted to dodge me, fine. If he didn't want to sit next to me in Spanish anymore, fine. Let him do anything he wanted to do, including stay home. But I wasn't going to act as though I'd been humiliated. I wasn't going to let him ruin the most carefree part of my life.

At first, I stayed a few yards off the side of the road, thinking of the nice driver I'd promised I wouldn't hitch. But eventually I grew tired and achy. My knapsack felt heavier and heavier. I began to worry that I wouldn't have time to shower and sleep if I didn't get home pretty soon. Finally, I came out onto the highway. A few cars passed me, but then I got a lift to Cerro Gordo with the man who delivered the *New Mexican* to the stores in town. It was half past four when I reached my house, exhausted, aching all over, and still determined to get to school.

The house was quiet, but a light was on in the

living room, both bedroom doors were open, and as I was struggling out of my backpack, Ellery came into the living room in his maroon bathrobe.

He said, "Hi, Maddy. I was worried about you. I went to get some juice and I saw that you weren't in your room."

I tried to smile but I was too tired. I was also too tired to cry. I sank into the sofa, just looked at him. I'd been despising him when I left the house but now he just looked very kind, not at all foolish.

I said, my voice quivering like a little kid's, "It's very important for me to get to school today."

He nodded. "Will there be a problem with that?"

I said, "I haven't had any sleep. And I have to shower."

"Hm." He treated it with the seriousness I felt it deserved, further endearing himself to me. First, he asked if I'd mind if he smoked a cigar. I said, Of course not. He lit up, paced the room, finally said that "we" could get a little extra time if he drove me to school instead of my having to meet the bus. Perhaps he could wake me up at eight, instead of my usual seven, and then I could shower, have some breakfast, and he would bring me to school.

I said, "Oh, Ellery, that would be wonderful. Thank you so much."

He sat down in the chair nearest me. He looked terribly benign, yet he wasn't even smiling.

I said, "I'm so tired, I don't know why my eyes are open."

He said, "I think it's because you're upset."

I began to cry. As though he'd pushed a button. I said I was sorry to be a crybaby and he told me not to be silly; crying was what people did when they were upset . . . if they were lucky.

I smiled, though I was still crying. "Or play baseball."

He nodded, but he remained serious, which allowed me to cry for a little longer.

"Do you feel like talking?" Ellery asked when I stopped.

I shrugged. "Dunno." Then, after a long time, I said, "I went to bed with Arnold." I waited, and when Ellery didn't seem shocked, I said, "I needed to get away from here, and it was too late to go anyplace else. I know he stays up late." I felt like an idiot because I thought Ellery must know everything before I told him.

After a long time, he asked, "Was it not a pleasant experience?"

"It was okay," I said. "But afterward, he was horrible." And then I really began crying, much harder than before, so loud that I was afraid of waking up my mother.

When I'd calmed down again, Ellery said, "There's this idea, now, that just because it's easier to keep from **getting pregnant, or just because dope makes it easy to** be casual about sex, that it's fine for young people to be doing it . . . having it. That it's easy. But it's not so easy. It stirs up all kinds of feelings. And if someone's not ready for them, they can be bad feelings."

I looked at him as though he'd opened the gates to the Emerald City of Oz. I said, "Arnold definitely wasn't ready for it."

Ellery nodded.

"He said that I seduced him and he hadn't wanted to be seduced."

Ellery smiled. "Well, he had and he hadn't. If he simply hadn't wanted to, it wouldn't have happened, would it."

It wasn't a question. I smiled back. For the first time, my eyes were willing to close.

I said, "I like the smell of cigar smoke."

Ellery said, "I'll tell you something funny, Maddy. I never smoked cigarettes, and I don't think I'd ever have picked up a cigar, if I hadn't read when I was in graduate school that Freud smoked cigars."

I was half-asleep. I smiled, said, "My father smoked cigars."

Ellery said, "Ah, yes. It's interesting, isn't it. So many people doing the same thing, for so many different reasons."

# Chapter 2

I didn't have much to do with boys from that night until the end of my junior year, even ones I liked. I was on the student council, hung out with Laya and the other straight kids, talked a lot with Ellery when I was home. There was an unspoken rule that we didn't speak directly about my mother or my brother. If she was being awful or if Billy was being maniacal about, say, not being able to play ball because of the weather, we might talk about the responsibility of being a single mother and having a job, or the necessity for a young boy to become a little independent of the females in the house. Then we'd discuss my friends and teachers more specifically, and human nature in general, always in a way that wasn't demeaning.

He was renting a room from a doctor in town, working just a couple of hours a day. When my mother was around, he didn't talk about setting up a practice in his own home. She still wanted him to stay with us and he still hadn't found a house he could afford, and he'd begun to think he might rent office space, after all. I don't think he'd made up his mind that he couldn't live with my mother. I think that happened on her birthday.

We played a lot of gin rummy, and a little chess. He wanted to teach Billy chess, but Billy wouldn't let him. And my mother had no patience for cards or chess or any other games. If we were occupied, she might put on a record, dance around the room, sometimes looking at a fashion magazine or one of her trade journals at the same time. She'd still stop in front of the photograph of herself and Billy and Lion, and dance in place for a while.

*My dreams have faded like a broken melody*
*While the gods of love look down and laugh*
*At what romantic fools we mortals be.*

She wasn't going into town by herself at night.

◖

*E*llery bought her a music system for her birthday, not a big-deal one, but much better than the record player and small radio we'd always had. When he had told me his plan, I'd reminded him how she was about equipment, but he was convinced she would love tapes and discs because they were so simple—and it was just one not-so-large unit containing everything. After buying it, he told me he'd hesitated over the one with the disc player, then decided my mother would want it because it wasn't at all complicated.

The four of us were to go out for dinner. The music system was wrapped in foil because it was too big for gift wrap. It sat on the coffee table, along with the gifts from Belly and me. When she opened the door, we all shouted, "Happy birthday!"

She took off her jacket, came to the kitchen, where I handed her a real margarita. Ellery had one as well, raised his glass to her. Billy and I had Cokes. Ellery was all excited about his gift, finished his drink before my mother did hers. A first. She circled the sofa and coffee table, pretending to ignore the monster package but glancing at it when she thought he wouldn't notice. Trying to figure out what it was. She didn't actually like surprises. Also, she might have suspected it was in the category she called "equipment."

Finally, he asked, "Would you like to open your presents before we go to dinner?"

She deliberated at length, handed me her glass for a refill, picked up the smallest package. A pair of silver earrings, selected by Billy with my help, and a home-made card from Billy. She thought they were the most beautiful earrings she'd ever seen, took off the ones she'd been wearing and put them on, insisted upon kissing Billy, though he'd become squeamish about being kissed.

Ellery beamed.

She opened the next package, a necklace that matched the earrings, thanked me but didn't kiss me or put it on. Ellery glanced at me to see if I'd noticed. I wanted to laugh, but I just winked at him. Once in a while he still tried to persuade me that my mother really loved me, but I was sure it was garbage.

"Mmm," she said. "Now, what's this big lump?" She pushed at it. It didn't budge. "Not an Indian basket. Too heavy. Not a dinosaur turd. They're hard to get, this year." This sent Billy into a paroxysm, as did any joke about shit, piss or vomit. She began to peel off the foil, looked more and more puzzled. Finally, drink in her left hand, she pulled down a whole strip of foil with her right, and could read what it said: Pioneer Component System.

She continued to seem baffled. Ellery still looked pleased. But gradually, as she stared at the carton without making a move to open it, he grew uneasy. He really hadn't had any feeling for the possibilities. Billy and his radar went to the bathroom.

After an incredibly long time, my mother said in a

hostile voice, "What's a component system? Components of what?"

Ellery, momentarily relieved because he thought she really didn't know, began to explain. He peeled back another side with a picture of the piece. But by that time, my mother had finished her drink. She stood, yawned and asked where we were going for dinner.

Ellery's mouth went slack.

I felt so terrible for him, I didn't know what to do.

Billy came out of the bathroom, asked my mother if he could unpack the system.

"Later, Love," my mother said. "We're going out to dinner, now. I'm famished!"

She was never famished.

Ellery was just standing there. His mouth was closed, but nothing else had moved. When my mother went to the bathroom to fix herself up, I gave him a hug around the middle, and he put an arm around me, squeezed me back. He let go but I held on.

Billy was in that state males enter when a new piece of machinery is around, couldn't wait to see what it looked like, get a feel. It was the first thing Ellery had ever done that he approved of, but watching him, you wouldn't have known the system had anything to do with Ellery. Billy probably would have passed up dinner, if it hadn't been my mother's birthday. As it was, she came out of the bathroom when he'd just gotten the top of the carton open. She clapped her hands loudly.

"Ready! Let's go!" She glanced at us. I was still holding on to Ellery. "If I'm not interrupting anything." He pushed me away gently; he had a better idea of her filthy mind than I did.

He was so crushed that he let my mother drive. He sat beside her, not talking when she went too fast or moved to the wrong side of the highway to pass someone. No one talked. Such a pall was over us that its creator had to announce, as she pulled into the only parking space on San Francisco Street, that from now on, everyone should have a good time.

It didn't happen that way, though I had a glass of wine with dinner, Ellery kept drinking along with my mother, and she, giggling, let Billy sip at her margaritas. Ellery didn't appear to notice that or anything else; it was the only time I ever saw him get stinking drunk.

Having plunged all of us—at least, Ellery and me—into gloom, she announced that she didn't know why everyone was in such a foul mood for her birthday, but it was time to lighten up. She began singing some song or another, stopped suddenly.

"D'y'know," she said, "when I left home—Montreal, I mean—I took two of my father's 78's with me. The only thing I took. That's how *your* father knew about the 78's, Maddy. He got the Victrola and the first carton at one of his auctions. And then, whenever he saw records, he'd check through them for me. He knew what I liked."

I nodded. I'd never heard about that or anything else nice he did for her.

She said, "I like the way things sound on 78's."

Ellery was just looking at her, not giving a loose crap for her reasons, not understanding that this was as close as she could come to an apology. Her mouth couldn't form the words, *I'm sorry.* Billy was reading the dessert menu. I was woozy on my one drink, not feeling what she was doing to Ellery as much as I might have, except I was nervous, kept eating when I wasn't hungry anymore. Billy and I finished every roll in the basket. Ellery could barely keep his head up, by now.

"Somebody," my mother said, "should be able to not like a present without ruining a whole birthday."

He managed to look up at that one.

"Mmworryaboutit," he said. All one word. "Icanreturnid."

"No!" That got Billy's head out of the dessert menu. "I want it, Ma. It's a good system."

Ellery looked at Billy, the hint of a smile on his face, maybe because Billy still hadn't said a word to him.

My mother shrugged. "Fine. You got it."

Ellery struggled to his feet and staggered out of the restaurant.

"Son of a bitch," my mother said, signaling the

waiter to bring another margarita. "Leaving me to pay
for my own birthday  dinner."

◑

*T*hey didn't recover from that night. They might
have been having sex for a while, but they weren't
having conversations. She started going into town at
night after dinner. Often she wasn't back by the time I
went to sleep. She was drinking all the time when she
was home and the drunken-looser she got, the tighter
Ellery became. He and I were very careful not to do
anything she could imagine was ganging up on her,
but there were moments when she'd stumble in so late
that the three of us had finished dinner and were sitting around, at least Ellery and I were, reading or
talking quietly, and she'd walk in and make some
comment about the Gang of Two, or the Conspiracy,
or how she was so sorry this was the only home she
had to come home to, when the two of us were having
such a good time without her. It wasn't wrong, of
course. It was just different from how she made it
sound. We never did anything vaguely improper. I
couldn't have. He wasn't the least bit attractive to me,
even aside from his age.

The first time he went into town by himself it was
because she came home, drunk halfway out of her
mind, when we were talking about colleges. Ellery had
been explaining to me why he thought I should try to

get into a really good college, perhaps in the East. He didn't say a word about putting distance between myself and my mother. He said that his own parents were very smart but uneducated, and Yale had broadened his sense of the possibilities, showed him that there were more choices than being a medical doctor or a lawyer. My mother came in while he was saying this and somehow got the idea he was talking about her. He couldn't convince her otherwise and, finally, he gave up and walked out of the house.

That might have been the night he met Cona the Barbarian, the Fat Bleached-Blond Real Estate Barbarian. It doesn't really matter whether it was then or later. He began drinking with her at the Dragon. He only went to places my mother didn't frequent. There weren't many heavy boozers at the Dragon, so my mother didn't like it.

Cona and my mother had crossed swords three seconds after Cona hit town. With some of the proceeds from the big house on Long Island she got when her husband left her, she'd bought a tiny old house close to the plaza, in what would later be the central historic district. Cona decided, without talking to anybody, that the little sign in her window wasn't big enough to be noticed by passersby. She put up a neon monstrosity that wasn't large but was still absurd in terms of its location. She argued that it was inside her window, and she tried every way she could to get the town to let her keep it. When that failed, she delayed for weeks while the new sign was supposedly being painted. My mother was one of the people she tried to enlist on her side. My mother had often tried to push the envelope for Sky tenants, but she couldn't stand Cona and there was no way she was going to help.

Ellery also began going up to Taos more frequently to see Keith, who'd never become used to my mother even to the point of sitting down to a meal with her. It had angered my mother, before larger angers took over, that Ellery was willing to "cave in to the little bastard," and visit Keith alone. But it was part of Ellery's goodness, in those days, to accept his son's feelings.

He introduced Cona to Keith a few weeks after they met, and Keith claimed to like her.

◑

*I*n my junior year, I started working after school at a jewelry store several blocks from the Sky that called itself Sheila's Studio. (Nothing in Santa Fe is a *store;* it's a *gallery* or a *studio.* My mother told me she'd said at a town meeting that we needed a convenience studio in town, and nobody even laughed.) Sheila was one of the few "Indians" then calling herself a Native American. That was because she was actually an Irish-WASP princess from Texas. She had a generous soul, and she was always nice to me, but she was too selective in her niceness, too moody to be trusted. She had

some kind of deep stake in every sale, and a decision
not to purchase by some customer, especially a female,
on whom she'd expended time and effort upset her as
much as though someone had told her she was stupid
or ugly. If there were other customers around, she'd go
into the stockroom and circle the shelves, talking to
herself. Then, when the shop emptied except for us,
she'd begin with something like, "D'y'all hear that
one?" and proceed to a ferocious and/or funny imitation of "that one" who hadn't bought anything. I
once teased her about that, thinking she'd deny it. But
all she said was, "Damned right, dahlin'. They're the
ones who're a pain in the ass."

Sheila and my mother had been on some town
planning committees together and couldn't stand each
other. (If I've given you the impression that my
mother didn't get along with any women, then I've
given you the correct impression.) I wouldn't say a
word against one to the other, and Sheila trusted me
more because of it. Everyone trusted me, except my
mother. And Arnold Taylor.

**❍**

*I*n the second half of my junior year, there began to
be excitement about college. My whole crowd was going to the University of New Mexico at Albuquerque,
which is less than fifty miles from Santa Fe. Ellery kept
saying I owed it to myself to go to a better school. He

thought that with my record, and coming from where I did, I had a chance of getting into Harvard or Yale. We talked briefly about Dartmouth because, with my father teaching there, I might be eligible for free tuition, but then we dropped the idea because I was afraid of how my mother would react if I so much as mentioned the possibility. My practice College Boards came out very high and Ellery went to my school to speak with the college adviser. He came home to say she felt there was no reason for me not to try for the best colleges. I told Ellery that the hardest thing for me to imagine about going away was being far from him because he'd become like a father to me. He said he was certainly a good friend and adviser, but it was important for me not to grow too dependent on him, either. I couldn't understand why he would worry about that. Ever since my mother's birthday, he'd spent more evenings away from the house, but that seemed natural. I hadn't thought about it a great deal.

My brother, who had no interest in anything taught in school, had let me teach him chess and we played a lot. He was already a better player than I.

Then, Ellery met me after school one day and said he'd like us to have a private conversation. Why didn't we get in his car and drive someplace where we wouldn't be interrupted. I was curious but not unduly; sometimes he came just to tell me it would be a good idea to sleep at Laya's that night because my mother was very "upset." Now, he drove to the far end of Acequia Madre, where prices hadn't zoomed to the level they had on Canyon Road, and parked in front of a corner house with a beautiful border in front of its adobe wall—daffodils and hollyhocks and various tropical flowers whose names I didn't know, in those days.

He smiled. "I haven't asked you about school in a while."

I said, "You haven't been around as much as usual."

"Mmm. That's true."

I was beginning to feel a heaviness in the air between us.

"Well," he said, "the reason for that is, I've been spending some time with a woman."

I smiled. "Good." I wanted him to know that I was glad he was having some fun. It wasn't just my mother who had the right to stay in town when she felt like it.

"I think you know," he said, "I'll always be there when you need me. But you also know life with your mother . . . in the past year or so . . . has become much more difficult for me."

I nodded. He meant for both of us.

"I'd hoped to be able to remain with you until you graduated. Went off to college. Made a good life, as I expect you will."

Uh-oh. Something bad was happening. *I'd hoped to be able to remain with you.* That meant he wasn't remaining. My first conference with the school adviser on the matter of applications was coming up, and it crossed my mind that I might put Dartmouth back on my list.

"I was looking at houses in a leisurely way, thinking I wouldn't actually move out before next year. After you graduated."

*Move out.* There it was. *Next year.* At the moment, I couldn't remember where we were in *this* year.

"Then . . ." He smiled, and his voice got nearly hushed, "I fell in love with a woman and a house at the same time."

*No. Wait a minute.*

"A house?" My lips were dry, and my head hurt. It was the first of what they call my migraines, which to me are simply what happens when life squeezes my head very hard.

*Why couldn't someone let me be the one to leave, just once?*

He nodded toward the house with the beautiful flowers in front of the wall. They didn't conceal the fact that it was a wall.

"Cona was the broker who showed it to me. She became a broker when she moved out here. Needed to earn her own living, for the first time. She has one of those tiny houses near the plaza. Maybe you've seen the little sign over the door. She lives there and works there. Anyway, we've bought this one together. We're going to be married in it."

I hadn't exactly absorbed the words. I didn't want to. But I must have looked stricken, and he must have taken this to mean that I grasped what he was saying. He smiled. He would have preferred me to be happy for him, but he knew. He might not have known, yet, that Cona was a reptile; that would take eleven or twelve minutes after they were married. But he knew how I was likely to feel about what she was doing to my life. If everyone in the world knows how a daughter, real or pretend, is likely to feel about her "father's" new woman, no matter who it is, then Ellery knew how I'd react to Cona.

"When?" It was all I could think of. My head hurt so badly I could barely see.

He told me the date, close to the end of June. I still couldn't remember which month we were in, but I knew his birthday was in June. I was making him a beaded belt in my crafts class.

"The wedding, that is. I might have to move out a little sooner. We'll talk about that. There's a lot to be done with this place."

Darkness fell. My mouth screamed; I don't remember if any sound came out of my throat. I just remember that there was worse pressure than before on the top of my head, and I couldn't see. He grabbed my arm, held it tight, said my name, kept telling me that he was there, or there for me, I don't remember whether it was a simple truth or a dumb cliché, but in either case, it didn't help. I began to sob, though my eyes stayed dry. I wasn't even thinking about Ellery anymore, only about whether I'd be blind with an aching head for the rest of my life. I couldn't live forever that way, but how would I be able to kill myself if I was blind?

A woman's voice outside the car said, "What's going on, Sweetheart?"

She sounded as if she was really from New York. Awful. Not at all like Ellery. Cona the Barbarian. I stopped breathing.

Ellery's voice said, "I thought you were at the office, Dear."

Cona said, "Well, I was, but then I had to check something at the house, and I thought you'd be finished, by now."

Silence. Ellery got out of the car, then came back. She seemed to have gone away.

Ellery's hand was on my arm. His voice said, "We had to buy the house right away, make the down payment, or someone else would've gotten it. It's a real gem, Maddy. You're going to love it. And, of course, you'll be welcome here whenever . . ."

*Whenever.* Whenever I wasn't unwelcome.

"When the gate's open, you can see a little path."

I nodded. I didn't want him to know I couldn't see.

"The path continues around the house, there's a back entrance to a nice room that'll be perfect for my practice. Maddy? I can't tell if you're listening."

I was squinting, trying to get some vision back under the weight on my head, but I could hear him perfectly. I told him I just needed to be left alone in the car for a few minutes.

"You're sure that's what you want?"

"Yes."

"Okay. But if you don't come in soon, I'll be out again."

After a while, he took the keys out of the ignition and left the car.

I waited until I was certain he was in the house. Then I opened the door, felt for the curb with my foot, stepped out and quietly closed the car door behind me. I didn't hear people on the street. Or cars. I remembered the wall. I walked cautiously toward where I thought it was, stopped when a prickly bush against my leg made me realize I'd gone too far. I backed away from the bush. I was close to the corner. If I walked back down Acequia Madre, I could make my way over to Canyon and the Sky. To my mother. My mother was nice to me when I hurt myself or I was sick. Besides, when she heard about Cona, she'd stop worrying about Ellery and me. I moved slowly, feeling along the sidewalk before I took each step, as though I might fall off the world. I was absorbed in trying to remember how many blocks it would be to the Sky, telling myself there'd be someone around to help me if I couldn't find it, when I stepped down from the curb, out into the street, and was hit by a car and hurled back to the sidewalk.

I'm not sure I even screamed. I think that although

I definitely hadn't done it on purpose, I was glad of it, even at that instant. My vision cleared when the car struck me, and my headache faded so rapidly that by the time the driver ran over to me, it was gone. My right leg and foot had been broken and the pain was extreme, but I welcomed the exchange.

She was older than my mother. Gray hair. I could see her. I smiled. I was half on the sidewalk, half in the street. My leg was in a funny position, which, it occurred to me, was related to the pain.

"Oh, my God, oh my God," the woman said. "Are you awake? Can you hear me?"

"I'm really okay," I assured her. "It's just my leg."

"I'll be right back." She ran toward the closest house, then dashed back to me. She said they were calling the ambulance. She asked if she could do anything to make me more comfortable. Without waiting for an answer, she took off her suit jacket, folded it and set it under my head. She remained half-kneeling in the road next to me, wailing, saying it had never occurred to her that I was going to keep walking.

I said, "It wasn't your fault. I wasn't looking. Or listening."

She stared at me.

"You're amazing. What's your name?"

I said, "Madeleine Stern." And smiled at her. I was enjoying the role of Plucky Heroine. My brain still wasn't minding the terrible pain in my leg. A couple of people had come out of their homes, by now, and were watching us.

She asked where my mother was. I said at the Sky Gallery, and told her the phone number. She relayed it to one of the other people, and my mother arrived about two minutes later, flew out of her car, ran over to me, kneeled at my side, booze on her breath.

"Maddy! Maddy! Are you all right?"

I began to cry. It was that simple, you see. My mother was there, so I could cry.

"My leg!" I bawled.

She stared at it and I really looked for the first time. It went out at the knee in a way that it couldn't have if it weren't cracked.

"Oh, Jesus!" Her voice was cracked, too. "You poor baby! Where's the goddamned ambulance?" As she asked it, I could hear the sirens. "Where's the son of a bitch—"

The woman looked terrified.

"It wasn't her fault, Mom," I said, but I couldn't stop crying. "I ran in front of the car."

My mother didn't want to hear it. "Has somebody got her license number?" she called to the five or six people who were there by this time.

The ambulance pulled up. I get the rest confused with all the hospital stuff I've seen on television since. The police, the medic, or someone, asking me questions. Then they had to do things to my leg so they could get me into the ambulance. I was still crying, but my mother held my hand. She was crying, too; I remembered that later, whenever she said she didn't give a shit what happened to me. The woman who'd hit me handed my mother a business card and a piece of paper with the insurance information on it, asked for our names and addresses. My mother, tight-lipped, told the woman she shouldn't worry, we weren't going to disappear from her life. I smiled at the woman, trying to show her that I wasn't angry, trying to balance out my mother, but it was difficult while I was crying.

That night, when my mother finally left me in the hospital and went home, she wouldn't tell Ellery why I wasn't there. She refused to speak to him at all. He didn't know what had happened until the next day, when the accident was in the news. He came to the hospital to see me, smacked the side of his head at the sight of me in this monster cast held up by pulleys. I assured him that our conversation had had nothing to do with the accident, and said I hadn't even told my mother why I was on that street.

"So," he said after thanking me, "there isn't even a reason she's not speaking to me."

I said, "Maybe she knows something, anyway. About . . ." I couldn't say the name. "She could've heard it, you know. Someplace."

He said, "I'm sorry you were so upset, Madeleine."

I said, "I wasn't all that upset. Honest. I was thinking about something else, and the car was very quiet."

He watched me for a while. A look I knew from when he was trying to decide whether to bother arguing with my mother. I asked if he and my mother were speaking now. He said he didn't believe in not speaking to people, but my mother appeared to be angry with him. He'd assumed it was about the accident.

I smiled.

He asked why I was smiling.

I said, "I'm thinking, my mother's taking very good care of me, and you're dying to move out . . . There's really no reason to wait."

The truth was, by this time, I was eager to be rid of him. He was going, anyway. It would just be tense if he were there when I came home.

He said, "It seems to me I can be helpful to you, to your mother, during the time when you can't move around."

I assured him we'd have all the help we needed. I'd been promised people would be coming from school with the homework, and my mother would stay with me as much as she could. Furthermore, his moving out didn't mean he couldn't drive up and visit. If I was lonely. During the day.

I really just wanted him to be gone. And by the time I came home from the hospital, huge, gruesome cast and all, he'd moved out.

◯

*I*t was a peculiarly blissful time. My leg was broken in several places, my foot was in two pieces. I was in the cast for the next six weeks, until close to the end of my junior-year school term, and comfort—my mother's attending to me, caring for me, neglecting work if I needed her at home or to take me to the doctor, whatever—lasted a little longer, while I was on crutches, and then used a cane. She'd always been tender when I needed her for some physical reason. The problem was, I hardly ever got sick. It was a temptation to be hurting myself all the time, but I never did it on purpose, including that accident. I don't really mind pain, once I have it and know what it is. But I'm scared when I know it's coming and can't tell how bad it will be.

If I hadn't been afraid of being hurt before I was dead, I might have let her smash the bottle into my face later, when she came at me.

My mother said she was delighted not to have Ellery around; he'd really begun to get on her nerves. She wasn't aware that he was visiting me some afternoons, after he'd checked to make sure she'd gone to the gallery. But he began to get on my nerves, as well. He seemed ill at ease, just being in the house. He looked at his watch after he'd been there a short time. If he knew I'd noticed, he would explain about some painter, contractor, whatever, who could only meet him and Cona at such and such a time. I didn't need him there, anyway. From then on, when he called, I told him my mother was home. After a few times, he got the idea.

Billy was ten that year, a real athlete who needed to be moving all the time. While I was in the cast, he was worse than usual about hanging around. It made him uncomfortable to look at me. It. He'd always joined every team or club he could, and now, unlike most of the boys, he'd do sleep-overs, even at the house of some kid I knew he didn't like. When he didn't have a school activity, he hung out in the playground down the hill. Boy heaven. They'd had all kinds of lectures about letting the girls play there, but mostly it hadn't worked, and once the girls were old enough to care whether they were welcome, most stayed away. My friends visited after school, brought me the home-work, the gossip, and so on. Their mothers made them come two or more at a time, like nuns, to make sure Vile Sex and Dope wouldn't take them unawares. Laya brought me the bead belt I'd been making for Ellery's birthday and the beads to finish it. She thought it was a good thing for me to do while I was in bed. I put the plastic bag they were in under my mattress and forgot about them.

My mother just went to the Sky for a couple of hours a day. She didn't go out at night, hardly left my room. She brought in the tequila bottle and the salt saucer so she wouldn't have to keep hopping up for them. Then she'd sit at the foot of my bed and talk to me. That was when I learned a lot of what I know about her lovers, as well as a great deal I'd never heard about her parents and her life before I was born. She'd always refused to speak of her family, even on the rare occasion when I asked questions about them. On the day she brought Lion back to the Sky, he'd asked where she hailed from and she'd told him, Hanover, New Hampshire. But when that didn't appear to ring a bell in his tiny brain, she said her parents were actually French Canadians, from Montreal, which was what I'd grown up thinking. Now she told me they were both Irish, from County Fermanagh, and had immigrated to Detroit, where they had relatives. Her father had worked at the Ford plant, but her mother had decided, at some point, that Detroit was not a good place to raise their three sons. They'd migrated to Canada, found jobs at a big, fancy hotel called the Manoir Richelieu, in the Murray Bay Colony of Quebec. My mother had been born there, the fourth of seven children, the first of two girls. Her father tended the grounds, her mother was a housekeeper. Meaning, my mother said, she washed out other people's toilets. The face my mother made when she said this was as full of disgust as though she'd just finished cleaning up a pile of shit. Her own mother had lived for the day when they would get away from the hotel, but they never did. For one thing, her father had never forgiven her mother for pushing him to leave Detroit, and he refused to move ever again. He said they were lucky to be there, though my mother didn't think he believed it. She said her own mother was always tight and angry, if not at her father, then at her. They were devoted Catholics, her mother especially, and my mother had been forced to put in a staggering number of hours in church, which she hated.

As far back as she could remember, her father's great pleasure in life lay in listening to his records, mostly from the big-band era, though there were a couple of musicals. She'd listened with him and she knew all the songs by heart. She'd left home when her father beat her because he found her smoking. He'd never lifted a hand to her before that, though he had whipped her brothers.

She'd said more than once that she had to marry my father because of me, but now she told me she had been glad to do it, not only so I'd have a father (she hated everything about the Catholic Church except its stand on abortion) but because he was accustomed to taking care of himself. Not just cooking, but cleaning up afterward. He had grown up with a working mother but not enough money for a housekeeper, and he really preferred doing it to letting a "stranger" into the house. Of course, at some point that changed, as everything good did when you were married, and he started wanting her to do the cooking and cleaning, become a "proper wife." He wasn't a bad man, really, but he wasn't a good enough husband or lover to get her to do that. He didn't have much in the way of feeling. She'd fallen in love with his home, not with him. She described all its beautiful rooms to me, sounding as though she'd been there last week. In her first days there, she had wandered around as though she'd been let loose in Windsor Castle. I couldn't remember the whole house, only his study, but she sounded so reasonable when she talked about my father that I began to think I might be able to apply to Dartmouth. On the other hand, it was difficult during this period, when she curled up at the foot of my bed and told me I was the sister she'd never had, to contemplate ever going so far from Santa Fe.

The closest thing we had to an argument was when we had to make out the insurance forms and she said I couldn't tell them I'd run in front of the car. I told her I'd already apologized to the woman for doing it. She asked if I was bucking for sainthood. I didn't argue more because I was afraid she'd want to know why I'd been at the end of Acequia Madre. None of the insurance forms had asked that.

❍

Sheila came to see me, brought me a batiste nightgown my mother thought was beautiful until I told her who it came from. Sheila said neither of the girls who'd worked for her since my accident was good, and I could have my job back whenever I was ready. My guidance counselor visited, brought me a stack of college catalogs to look over. Ellery had tried so hard to open me up to the idea of exploring new academic worlds, but I'd never been able to get interested in any of those worlds, except maybe psychology, which didn't interest me anymore. I read course outlines as though they were historical romances, wasn't drawn to one more than the others. It was the descriptions of the buildings and locales that I pored over, trying to imagine what the real thing was like from each short paragraph and photo—like my brother with his first copy of *Playboy*. My mind had frozen when Ellery talked about Yale and Columbia because I pictured monstrous buildings without grass around them. No amount of assurance about a park that was a couple of blocks from the school assuaged my anxiety about being stuck in a place with no grass or trees. In grade school I'd had to write about a place I liked, and I'd written that I liked all of Hanover because it was green, didn't like Santa Fe because it was mostly brown. The teacher had told me about Georgia O'Keeffe, New Mexico's Great and Famous Painter, who'd said there was nothing to paint in upstate New York because everything was green. There, in a nutshell, was what I couldn't stand about Georgia O'Keeffe. (I'd just nodded as though my mind had been changed; I was able to do that in school, with my teachers, but not at home, with my mother, where something larger always seemed to be at stake.) I also wanted to be able to walk places, as we had in Hanover. In Santa Fe, we needed a car to buy a roll of toilet paper.

The Sky began to deteriorate because my mother was spending too much time with me. Then her old Ford station wagon got so decrepit that the mechanic advised her to buy a new one. One night, while she was roaming around the house, complaining that she couldn't bear to go into hock for a piece of machinery, she saw my college catalogs and got very upset. At first, I wasn't certain what the upset was about, but finally, with a slightly hysterical edge, she told me that she couldn't buy a new car and pay tuition at a fancy college at the same time. When I said the guidance counselor thought I could get a scholarship, she wasn't reassured, asked if I knew what these places could cost in the way of transportation and "real" clothes. She knew all along that a big check was coming from my accident, but she wouldn't talk about it, dismissed the sum as inconsequential when I asked.

A few days before my cast came off, a newly hired salesgirl failed to show up for work so that my mother had to be at the Sky all day, and Wilkie called to say that he and his new girlfriend, Courtney, would like to visit. It must have been three or four years since he'd been there, though we'd seen him in town.

Occasionally, when he met that year's love of his life, Wilkie got high. On this day, he was high and lively, astonished at how terrific "the old place" looked. Courtney had been born the same year I was,

Wilkie informed me, as though it were a huge joke. It was also a laugh riot that Courtney was his first girl-friend who was like him about the cold. They were wearing T-shirts, shorts and rubber thongs. This was Wilkie's outfit, almost no matter what the weather, though in the bitter cold he put on sneakers (no socks). His brain was like his feet—sprawling, no walls —but there was nothing inside that might jump over a wall, anyway. Aside from a few gray hairs in his beard and some lines in his forehead, he looked, he *was,* exactly the same as he'd been on the day my mother and I arrived in Santa Fe. You've heard of Growth and Change? Forget them. The only thing that changed was his girlfriends and how much they liked him and, accordingly, his mood. He hadn't overseen the renova-tions of our house, hadn't done anything but make out checks. Now, though, he puffed with pride as Courtney oohed and aahed over the place, told her what a shack it had been when he bought it, showed her what "we got the guys to do." Neither seemed to notice my cast or my crutches. At one point, when they were in my mother's bedroom, they lowered their voices as though they had a secret, but I didn't think about it.

When my mother and Billy came home, she was in a foul mood because the second mechanic had given her the same prognosis as the first.

I said, "Guess who we had a visit from."

Billy, grinning, said, "Santa Claus!" Then he took

some cookies and went down the road to play stickball.

"So?" my mother asked. "Who's the mystery guest?"

I grinned. "Mr. Wilkerson and his new teenager."

She said, "Uh-oh," and rose rapidly from the sofa. "He brought her? What did he do? What did he say?"

I didn't ask why she was in such a panic. Questions or attempts to get her to explain something before she was ready just confused her. I tried to re-create the visit, the conversation. She interrupted me at a couple of points to question some nuance. When my little narrative was finished, she made herself a José and began looking through the kitchen cabinets. She found a bag of Fritos, took a couple but didn't eat them, opened the front door, stood in the entryway for a while. When she came back, I was on the sofa, crutches nearby. She sat down in a chair, threw the Fritos on the table, took a sip of her drink.

"I think," she said, her voice quivering, "there's trouble in River City."

I didn't get the allusion to the song from *The Music Man.*

She said, "Wilkie's giving me a hard time. I think he might be looking for an excuse to fire me and let his little chipmunk run the place."

I couldn't believe it. The Sky was much more hers than his. Except, of course, that he owned it.

"No way," I promised my mother. "She couldn't

run a stocking. Anyway, why would he bring her here?"

My mother smiled, but she looked about to cry. She licked all the salt off her glass rim, sipped at her drink.

"Just showing off. She doesn't have to do it right. She just has to be there, draw a salary. He can get someone else to do the work."

"Not the way you do."

She shrugged. "He might not know the difference. Or he might not care. He might have enough money to coast for a while. He had some last year. I don't know about now. If he needs money . . . the Sky can't support two managers."

She was known for what she'd done with the Sky, but she was also known for her fights with other owners and managers—over "stealing" painters, potters, jewelers. Her big fight with Sheila had been when she persuaded a weaver named Alma to move from one end of Sheila's store to the space Rahji had vacated. She had a lifelong quarrel, not just a competition, with the owner of the little mall closest to us, who'd won out in a competition with her for a guy who imported dhurries and kilims. Then there were the quarrels over city-development issues. Over planning for events. If there was a fight to be had over an issue, she'd had it. She appeared to believe whichever side of the argument she was on at the moment, even when it was opposed to the side she'd been on weeks or months earlier. Still, she'd turned the Sky into such a bonanza, it was hard to believe someone wouldn't want to grab her.

I suppose it was a measure of our attachment to the house that we didn't think realistically about why Wilkie would have brought Courtney to see it.

"Anyway," I said, "there're plenty of other people who'd love to have you."

She didn't cry, but I began to.

She was touched. She set the brochures on the coffee table, came over to hug me, reassure me.

"Listen, kid, I'll have quite a résumé. Just telling the story of the Sky. People in Taos know about it, already. We'll go to Taos, if we have to. I mean, *I'll* go to Taos, if I have to."

I smiled, stopped crying. "Or Boston. Or wherever I go to school." Now *I* was reassuring *her.*

"Hey, now." It had worked. "There's a thought." She finished her drink. "Boston. Why not? You get a scholarship to Harvard, and I'll follow you there."

I laughed. "I don't know about Harvard, but there're all kinds of possibilities." This wasn't the time to bring up Dartmouth. "Billy'd be better off someplace with decent public schools, anyway."

"Mmm. Right. He's never even been East, for God's sake. It's time." She made another drink. She was getting excited. But then, suddenly, she lost it.

"Oh, shit. I don't know what I'm talking about. I could never . . . I could never match what I have here anyplace in the East. Even if I got a job, I couldn't make the kind of money I'd need for rent. I can't imagine what you'd need to get a place like this in Boston. In the East. There *are* no places like this in the East."

She started pricing cars. She said she had to be able to move around the country if she was job hunting. She was about to go into hock for a new Honda when Wilkie informed her that Courtney had fallen in love with "his" house and they wanted to live in it.

She left the gallery early, so thrown off balance that she forgot it was one of Billy's after-school club days and she was supposed to pick him up at six. She stormed into the house calling, "Maddy, where are you?" although I was sitting right there on the sofa. My cast had been taken off and I was moving around with one crutch but I was uneasy putting the slightest pressure on that foot. I tended to sit for long periods in the same places as I'd sat when the cast was on, though the doctor had said a little exercise would be good for me. I was trying to read something or other, having trouble concentrating. I was scooping up peanut butter with Fritos, although I didn't eat peanut butter if anything else was around. When she burst in, the Frito I was scooping with broke off in the jar. My memory of that is as clear and strong as my memory of the moment when the edge of the bottle cut her neck. I don't know why. It had to do with the Frito's breaking.

She sat down next to me. "You're not going to believe this. We're being evicted."

I thought she was talking about the gallery, but Wilkie couldn't be evicted from his own building.

"Evicted?"

She nodded. "Wilkie and his little corn pone. They want to be up in the hills, away from the world. Isn't that darling?"

I thought of Ellery. "All of a sudden, everyone's getting married."

"Everyone doesn't own the house we live in."

"Oh, my God." Finally, it was sinking in. "This house? I didn't— We can't be evicted, it's ours. I mean, I know we don't own it, but . . . but . . ."

"But nothing. Mr. Wilkerson owns it, and Mr. Wilkerson wants us out."

I couldn't imagine it. Even my dreams of going far away to school had always involved coming back here, maybe with some nice boy I was in love with. Or, at other times, with some not-so-nice boy whose presence would keep my mother in check in a different way.

The phone rang. It was a friend of Billy's, which reminded my mother about picking him up. She'd have to drive back down. I said I'd keep her company, if she'd wait for me to hobble to the door.

" 'Course I will," she said. "That way we can finish . . . We shouldn't talk about all this in front of Billy," she said, as I stood, picked up my crutches and began the arduous walk to the door. "There's no sense worrying him until we know . . ."

At the car, she opened my door and helped me to my seat. We agreed I would leave my crutches in the driveway. I wouldn't need to walk anyplace.

As we approached the school yard, we could see Billy, sitting against the fence, reading a magazine. The car pulled to a stop and he climbed into the backseat. She asked him why he hadn't found a phone and called the house. Billy said he'd figured she'd remember, sooner or later. My mother laughed.

Later that night, she cited this as an example of the way "the male mind" worked. I was much more like her than my brother was; that was why he hardly ever quarreled with her. It made me uneasy because it reminded me of the days when she'd only wanted to know why I couldn't be more like my brother, but that unease was lost in the greater anxiety over the house.

We resumed talking, once Billy went to bed. I asked if she really felt moving would be so awful. She said it was one thing to think about leaving the house because we were ready to, another to think of being kicked out, especially after what she'd done for Wilkie.

"Hasn't he paid you well?" I asked cautiously. She'd always been secretive about money, not just the accident settlement. At times she was generous. While I was in bed she'd brought me magazines or ice cream or some little present almost every day, though she was likely to remind me that she couldn't do this sort of thing all the time. Meaning, when I wasn't an invalid. She kept all her financial records in a locked file cabinet that she used as a nightstand in her room.

"Not really. Only if you figure in the house. Certainly not if you . . . Wait a minute!" She laughed, stood up, began walking around the room, gesticulating as though to some imaginary person. "There's something I'm forgetting, here. Mr. Wilkerson is talking about evicting his own son!"

I didn't know what to say. It wasn't a truth that had resonated in our daily lives. Billy and I both called Wilkie by that nickname. If there had been a period when Billy was encouraged to call him Papa, doing that very thing had become forbidden with Lion's entry into her life. Which had been fine with me. I'd minded Billy's having someone to call Papa when I didn't.

"He's on Billy's birth certificate!" she said triumphantly. "William Wilkerson Stern! There was never any question he was Billy's father. Billy's name is William Wilkerson Stern!" (I'd never heard this full name before, and thought it might not be true, but it was.) "I didn't know another soul in Santa Fe when I got pregnant." As she often did, my mother was answering an accusation nobody had made. "We were never just some business arrangement, and we're not now. This is his family he's talking about kicking out!"

I was uneasy. I thought she was furious and spoiling for a fight, didn't understand the fight would be legal. My mother and Wilkie had always been on-again, off-again but the *on* hadn't resembled a love affair since Billy's birth. When they got together it was about problems with a girlfriend or a boyfriend or a tenant. She, alone or with a lawyer, read new leases, then Wilkie signed them. Now she began pacing around the room, muttering. After a bit, she rummaged in the kitchen drawer under the phone, came up with a little pad and a ballpoint pen, handed them to me.

"Okay. Let's do a chronology. Madeleine born, February 13, 1971." She paced as she spoke. "Mother and Madeleine arrive Santa Fe December 1, 1976. Meet Mr. Wilkerson night of arrival. Billy born September 2, 1977." She looked up, grinned. "Nine months and one day. Can't be much clearer than that." She resumed. "Invited by Mr. Wilkerson to move into room on Canyon Road. Clean up room, move in. Begin dealing with tenants a few days later. Begin renovation of gallery, March 1978. Urge Mr. Wilkerson to buy this house . . ." She continued: Date of purchase of this house, then a hut, no hot water; dates of various improvements. Her memory for the names and dates was breathtaking and proved to be only occasionally wrong. In the meantime, they turned into something funny because she began singing her list to the tune of a song from *Pal Joey* that was one of her favorites, the one where every line begins with "ZIP" and goes on to something funny that happened or didn't happen, like Walter Lippmann's column wasn't brilliant that day. Her version went:

ZIP, *meet Mr. Wilkerson in January '77;*
ZIP, *son born nine months later, oh heaven!*

And so on. Eventually, she got me to join her in the melody, if not the making up of the words, or the way she'd begun dancing around the room. She was very high.

◗

She told Wilkie that she was looking for a place to live but needed a little time. The next day she saw the lawyer who read the Sky leases, whom she found insufficiently enthusiastic about righting the wrongs done her. She stayed high. She took a vengeful pleasure in thoughts of getting what was owed her, and I didn't blame her, although it made me nervous sometimes. She wasn't drinking at all during the daytime.

She hired Cyrus Jaffe, who was apparently known as the meanest son of a bitch in town. She told Wilkie she was trying desperately to find an apartment she could afford. She hid the Lion-family photograph and all other traces of Lion, as though Wilkie's lawyer were going to invade the house and snatch them to prove that another man had been important in her life. Wilkie hadn't the cunning, or the insanity, to think of things like that, but removing them had some effect on her. She began to say that she'd mourned Lion long enough. It was time to think about making another life. She talked about Jaffe a lot. Jaffe liked her. If only he were a little taller and better looking. He looked just like my father. And Ellery. (She'd become visibly anti-Semitic since Ellery's departure, and made elaborate, seldom-funny jokes about how whoever circumcised him should have taken care of his nose, and so on.) Jaffe had told her not to buy a new car or anything else, just now. He had an excellent mechanic in Albuquerque, where he spent one day a week, but the logistics of her getting to and from Albuquerque were complicated, unless she wanted to go with him. She told me all this proudly, said he was trying to lure her there and she didn't think she'd let him succeed. Finally, I told her about a big garage on Rosina Street, off Cerillos, that was owned by the Chávez family. Gerry Chávez, one of the nephews, had graduated from my school two years earlier, and was said to be a car genius.

Gerry, called Geraldo by any Anglo who desired his goodwill, was right up there on the long list of crimes my mother never forgave me for, though, whatever she thought, he never wanted to have anything to do with her beyond fixing the car. I was sixteen when we began, and he was nineteen. My mother was thirty-eight, but she never acknowledged a significant gap between people my age and hers; she was equal-opportunity friendly, just one of the girls until she got mad at you, at which point she became your mother, boss, whatever, and you had better know it.

The word was, Geraldo would have dropped out of school if his uncle hadn't told him, No diploma, no job. The word was, you'd better call him Geraldo until you'd known him for a long time and he was sure you knew who he was. Fourth- or fifth-generation Santa Fe Spanish and proud of it. All the girls were turned-on by him; most of us were afraid he'd try to do something about it. The line was, Don't start because you won't be able to stop. He'd gotten a woman in Albuquerque pregnant, and a couple of girls from my school were said to have had sex with him. He was nearly your typical, swaggering macho jerk, except that he didn't lay it on too thick and it seemed real, not put-on. He had the physical presence of five other macho jerks and he was gorgeous, with big dark eyes, shiny black hair and the kind of powerful, though not tall, maybe five nine, body that gives you dreams you have to wake up from.

My mother took her car to the garage. Geraldo told her it wouldn't be safe to drive it out; she could use one of theirs. She came home asking why I hadn't told her that Geraldo Chávez was a movie star.

On the Saturday morning when Geraldo brought back the car, Jaffe had phoned to say he wanted to see my mother in town. Geraldo didn't make a warning call, though he normally would have, because my mother had asked him to, and he had an allergy to following any direction from a female. Also, he thought she was a hippie, and the Spanish despised anyone they classified as hippie, maybe because the hippies were always trying to be Indians.

I was still using the crutches some, although the doctor had told me I didn't need to. He'd given me exercises but I didn't want to do them and my mother had gotten too busy to oversee them. She drove me to the school-bus stop every morning, the driver helped me on and off the bus, and one of the mothers drove me to my door after school. I wore jeans all the time except in bed because my leg looked all white and soft and disgusting. I had no energy. Not that I was ever such a ball of fire as my mother, but I'd always had the vigor to get up and move, if only out of her vicinity. Maybe that was the trouble. Instead of escaping, I was always waiting for her to come home and tell me the latest developments. Everything was on hold because we didn't know yet whether we'd have to move.

I heard a car pull into the driveway and assumed it was my mother until there was a knock at the door. I asked who it was, and when he said it was Geraldo with the car, I called that the door was open. I didn't know if he remembered me from school, nor could I picture how I looked, lying with my head on pillows at one end of the sofa, leg up against the back as though it were still in the cast. He opened the door and my breath caught. I'd forgotten the way the air around him seemed to get riled up. I might have blushed. I brought down my leg and tried to stand up, but I didn't quite make it.

He smiled, said, "Hi."

I said, "Hi. I'm sorry. My mother's not here."

He said, "I got her car in good shape."

Thinking she must have known he was coming, I explained that she'd been called into town.

He smiled. Devastation. He knew it. He knew everything that worked and everything that didn't work. I can't give him special credit for knowing I was nervous; anyone could've seen that.

I said, "I'm sorry I don't move around easily. My leg."

He said, "D'you mind if I take a drink of water?"

I said, "No. There's some coffee left . . . if you want it." My voice trembled as though he'd asked to take a drink of me.

He poured the coffee, came over to the sofa, sat on the wooden arm, facing me.

I said, "I was in an accident. The cast just came off."

He nodded, flashed a mischievous smile. "I heard you walked right in front of that car."

I was disconcerted by his knowing anything, much

less that. My face got hot again. What would my mother say if she heard him?

"Hey, Hon," he said, moving down to the sofa, putting a hand on my foot, which could have been my breast, for the shock of excitement it sent through me. "I didn't mean to upset you."

I said, trying to steady my voice and be stiff and righteous, "I just don't know where you get your information from."

He shrugged. "The accident was in the papers. But, you know, we see a lot of people . . ." Another, more devastating, smile. "Most of the ones with cars, anyway."

His hand was still on my foot.

My voice trembling, I said, "I don't like to be talked about."

He said, soft and winsome, "They only talk about the good-looking girls."

Meltdown.

He moved from the arm to the end of the sofa, not letting go of my foot, but lifting it, so that when he was settled, it was in his lap. I waited to see what he would do to me next.

He smiled. I couldn't have smiled back if I'd tried.

He slid his hand under the bottom of my jeans leg as easily as though my hood were open and my insides waiting to be checked out.

I said, voice still shaky, "My leg was in a cast for six weeks. It got all white and yucky."

He sidled-pushed-slid his body under the leg, toward me, said softly, "You should wear shorts, or a skirt. Let the air get to it."

I was almost on his lap. I stared at him helplessly. I would have let him take me to bed right then, but the phone rang. It was on a table at one end of the sofa, not in the kitchen, like most people's.

He said, very softly, "Let it go."

I whispered, "I can't. It might be my mother."

He sidled out from under me, got the receiver from the table and handed it to me. She'd called the garage and been told that Geraldo was out with her car. By this time I was sitting up, both feet on the floor, as though she might sense something was going on.

I said, "He's here."

She said, "Good. Keep him there. I'll be right back."

I said, "Okay," handed him the phone. He hung it up and began inching back under me, but I was too nervous.

I said, "She's coming back. She wants you to wait."

He laughed. "I have to wait. To switch cars."

I nodded, flushed. I was embarrassed.

"Boy," he said, "she's really got you coming and going, doesn't she."

I stared at him. I didn't know what to say. I was too full of longing to be angry, but I didn't know how else to be. I pulled away when he reached around me. He didn't get mad. He asked if I wanted to go to the movies that night. I said yes. No hesitation. He said he'd pick me up after the garage closed at seven, grinned.

I said, "Maybe you should wait outside for my mother."

"What for?"

I didn't answer.

He said, "She's not going to give you a hard time about me taking you out, is she?"

I said, very much on my dignity—and hers, "I don't know why she would. She's never given me a hard time about where I go. Or who I go with."

He went to the bathroom, took a while, so that by the time he came out, my mother was walking in the front door. She looked from him to me. Her antennae were up, but there was something else going on, too. I could remember the times she'd come upon Ellery and me talking, and acted as though there were a conspiracy. Her manner was the same now, but also different when she faced Geraldo. Coy.

"You were supposed to tell me when you were bringing the car, Gerry." A playful reprimand. "I could've saved you the trip."

He shrugged. "My name's Geraldo. I had to take it for a test run, anyway. It's working real good." He took the bill from his pants pocket, held it out to her, brought it to her when she didn't move toward him.

"Well, thank you very much, Mr. Geraldo. Why don't you stay and have a sandwich with us?"

Now there was no mistaking the flirtatiousness. He saw it, of course, but it just made him uneasy. She never stopped doing it with him, and he never stopped being uneasy.

"Thank you very much." Extremely polite. Not looking in my direction. "I have to get back to the garage. Keys in the Chevy?"

She nodded.

He said, "I think you're going to be very happy with the car, Mrs. Stern."

She said, "Cars don't make me happy."

He forced a small laugh, as though he thought it was just a joke, raised his hand in a goodbye gesture, winked at me, and left. He knew better than to say anything about seeing me later. Unfortunately, I had no way of knowing where she'd be when he picked me up, and I couldn't take a chance on being secretive.

She watched him go, hands on her hips, then, the moment the door was closed, whistled softly.

"That's quite a piece of work, Señor Geraldo. If Jaffe looked like that, I wouldn't be stringing him along." She made a José, took the bread, some cheese and bologna from the refrigerator, asked if I wanted a sandwich. I told her I'd have whatever she was having. Then, thinking I'd better get it over with fast, I said, "He's taking me to the movies tonight."

"Well, now I know why you sent me there, anyway!" She made one sandwich. She put her hand under it and sliced it in half, cutting into the heel of her

thumb sharply enough to yell out, then denying anything had happened when I asked her. I kept silent
while she set the sandwich on her plate, brought it to
the table and sat down, her left hand holding a crumpled dish towel.

"I sent you there because they call him Car Doc.
He's supposed to be better than anyone."

"Oh, my goodness!" Super-sweet, ignoring my
words. "I forgot your sandwich, Maddy!"

It was that edgy hostility I knew from before my
accident, more likely to go over the edge and explode,
the more comfortable I got. I made myself a sandwich,
got a Coke, hesitated because my inclination was to
take it to my room but that might offend her further.

She said, "Siddown." Like an army sergeant in the
movies. "I want to talk to you." Her left hand remained in the dish towel in her lap.

I sat catercorner to her. I didn't want to see her
staring at me.

"I hope you're protecting yourself, hanging out
with Mr. Babymaker."

So she'd found out about him. I had no idea of
what to say. It was a while since I'd had to be prepared
for surprises.

I said, "I just met him."

"Oh, well, that's different," she said mockingly.
"Nobody ever got pregnant by someone she just met."

"He's taking me to a movie."

"Hah!"

"You don't even know him!"

"I know that every time I see him in town, he's coming out of a bar with someone."

"What has that got to do with making babies?" I was disgusted. "Anyway, there're probably plenty of people who say the same thing about you."

She reached across the corner of the table and smacked my face so hard that my breath was taken away. Then she did what she'd always done before my accident, when she was mad at me. She got her bag and walked out of the house.

❿

*I* was asleep on the sofa when Geraldo came for me. I woke up when he and Billy were talking about the Dallas Cowboys and the Houston Oilers (I forget which one of them was for which team). In the car, he asked about the bruise on my cheek but I wouldn't tell him, and he didn't push me. He moved to the matter of our not having a TV. The kid needed it for ball games, if nothing else. He never said a word about my mother's insanity, but, a few weeks later, he acquired a secondhand one of those tiny portable television sets that someone didn't want because you could hardly see its three-inch picture. He got it into working condition and gave it to Billy, who kept it in his room for a long time before my mother knew it wasn't a radio he was always playing very low in there. Billy, naturally, admired and adored him. It was probably because of Billy, as well as her absorption in her suit against Wilkie, that my mother didn't make more trouble for Geraldo and me.

Geraldo's two older brothers had finished college and were engineers. He was no student, but he was as talented with females as with cars, if not as patient, once the honeymoon was over. In our early weeks, I was in heaven. Sex with him was so different from what had happened with Arnold, it should have had another name. It wasn't coming to him brand-new, wrapped up in a package that might have a bomb in it. He was a breathtaking combination of energy and skill, performer and pleasure-giver, couldn't rest until you were tired and as contented as he was—and he seemed never to tire. On that first night, he took me to the back of his uncle's garage, where there was a couch. (And a poker game, on Wednesdays.) There was no heat but I was too warm for it to matter by the time he helped me off with my sweater and my tangled brassiere, opened my jeans and kissed my belly, pulled them down along with my bikini underpants, all the while fondling me, purring lovely words at me. I could hardly bear to let go of him while he took off his own clothes. He was as warm as a stove (a great, potbellied stove; he already had a round, soft spread of a stomach that didn't show in his jeans) and I just kept my hands on whatever part of him I could reach until he began to play with me, getting me almost unbearably excited before he came into me.

"There we are," he murmured when he found the deepest, wettest part of me. None of those comments men make because they find it astonishing that someone's body is ready for them.

I didn't come. Not the first time or the second or third or fourth. He tried to bring me around, but I was frightened. I didn't know what would happen later. I didn't think he'd be like Arnold, but I didn't know what the possibilities were. Most of the stories you heard were, after all, about girls he wasn't with anymore. I fell asleep and dreamed that my eyes opened and the garage was dark and freezing cold and I was alone. I awakened to find him still stretched out against the front of me, but my back toward the room, which was icy cold. There was no light on, but I could see him as I dressed. I could tell when his eyes opened.

"*Querida.* Come here, *Querida.*"

I hesitated.

"I was freezing."

"Okay." He jumped out of bed. "I'll tell you what we're going to do. I'm going to get on my clothes." As he spoke, he did it. I put on my socks and sneakers as he did his. "And I'm going to take you for coffee, and some good, hot food."

I smiled. "I won't sleep if I drink coffee, now."

"Sure you will," he said.

He told me the plot of a movie he'd seen recently to tell my mother, if she asked, but she knew we hadn't gone to the movies.

And I slept.

# Chapter 3

In those few months with Gerry, I had extraordinary pleasure and no pain to speak of, body or soul. After a while, I stopped being afraid that each time was the last, and I began to come. Until I did, he drove himself crazy trying to make me do it. He was offended that I didn't. As though it were something about him.

My mother didn't mention him and seemed to make it a point to be out of the house, or, at least, out of the living room, when he might be picking me up or bringing me home. She was absorbed in every detail of the battle with Wilkie. When she talked to me, it was about that, but she didn't talk to me a lot. She grew more intense about the suit when my accident settlement turned out to be something less than she'd hoped for, or so she said. She got me to sign the settlement papers without letting me see the amount. She kept all specifics about money from me, even when she liked me.

Cy Jaffe caught Wilkie by surprise and scared him to death before he ever spoke to a lawyer. I think just seeing the chronology must have thrown poor Wilkie —this dated list of what he had done or was trying to do *to* my mother as opposed to what she had done and was still doing *for* him: ZIP, took this chunk of rotting real estate and turned it into one of the biggest money-makers on Canyon Drive; ZIP, raised and was still raising his child without asking him for support beyond her salary; ZIP, found and renovated this home he was now ejecting her from. (Jaffe dismissed the fact of our having lived in it rent-free for all those years, which was just about my mother's being too trusting a soul to have doubted Wilkie's assurances that we could live in it forever.) And so on. She had collected statements from more than twenty people—contractors, laborers, men and women who'd worked on the store or the house—to the effect that the first time they met Wilkie, they didn't know who he was, much less that they were working for him. Some were willing to testify to that effect in court. At least one of the others did it because my mother threatened to notify the IRS about what she'd paid him in cash if he didn't.

At some point, Wilkie's lawyer offered to have him sign over the house to her in exchange for her relinquishing any claims on the Sky. She laughed. She said that now they wanted to give her someplace to come home to but take away her workplace to leave. By this time, she was going for half of the Sky. She told Jaffe that there was too much bitterness attached to the house, now; if he got it for her, she'd probably sell it. She was looking at some new condos that were going up just outside of town. I'm not sure she meant it, yet, but she said it was time for us to be in town, not out there in the sticks.

Jaffe ordered her not to look at any more apartments until the case was settled and not to mention the possibility of moving to *anybody*. He was concerned that *I'd* heard her say it, but she told him I never carried tales from home. She repeated this to me, said she trusted me more than anyone, at least . . . heavy pause . . . as far as family business was concerned. The person in the real world whom she trusted most, these days, was Jaffe. She talked about him all the time, about how smart he was, about how she had to play him along until the lawsuit was settled.

By now, she'd sold herself on the notion that she had been Wilkie's much-abused common-law wife all these years. A couple of times she referred to Wilkie as "your father" when she was talking to Billy. When Billy said, "Don't call him that," she promised it was just until the lawsuit was over. I couldn't guess when her focus would change, whether she'd be worse to me if she didn't do as well as she hoped with the lawsuit, or whether she'd need to find some other reason she wasn't happy if she won everything she asked for.

At some point, when Jaffe had "very reluctantly" agreed to consider giving up the house in exchange for a greater percentage of the Sky, the negotiations changed in tone. I think about two seconds after Wilkie told Courtney they might get the house, she announced she was missing her family and wanted to go there for a visit. He wanted to go with her but she said they'd throw fits if she showed up with "some old guy" she'd been living with. Wilkie pictured himself alone on Cerro Gordo, without even my mother to comfort him, and he became frantic to settle without alienating her.

She got higher and higher as she and Jaffe closed in for the kill. Wilkie's lawyer wanted to go to court, but Wilkie didn't. Toward the end, when she was close to getting half of the Sky's real estate and everything on it, my mother said that for an even half, she'd let Wilkie and his sweetie have the house. He agreed, over his lawyer's protests, and made a sweet peace with my mother. He said she hadn't, after all, claimed anything that wasn't true. His lawyer, still trying to save Wilkie against his will, pointed out that if she was a half-owner rather than an employee, a salary would no longer be appropriate. My mother said that she'd actu-

ally need more money than before, since she'd be paying rent. Wilkie agreed.

◐

She was higher than the Sierras when she came home
that Friday night and described all this to Billy and
me. She said Jaffe and Wilkie's lawyer were still arguing when she and Wilkie left to celebrate. Now, Wilkie was taking his little baby Courtney to dinner, and
she wanted to take her babies, too. Something special.

"If you're supposed to see Ramones Cojones, he
can come along."

I was supposed to see him, but I hesitated. It wasn't
about my mother. Geraldo had become restless,
though I wouldn't have understood it that way at the
time. I was working at Sheila's full-time through Labor Day (it would be part-time, once my senior year
began), seeing him most nights. But I think he had
picked up that needy-boring streak in me, that dull
creature who only wanted to be with him, to stay
home, make love, read, listen to music, and it contrib-
uted to his natural restlessness. Even if we had the
house to ourselves, he'd tell me, after one or two regu-
lation screws, to get dressed, he wanted to play poker,
or head south to one of the clubs near Route 284. At
some point, I'd asked him, thinking I was being
funny, if I knew him well enough to call him Gerry.
He told me, straight-faced, that he would let me know

when. Once or twice, he'd failed to show up when he said he was coming. I missed that signal the way I missed the others.

Now, I called him at the garage to tell him my mother wanted to take us all to dinner. He said to tell her no, thank you. I said that it was a celebration; my mother and Wilkie had concluded their lawsuit amicably. I was afraid that an outright *no* would trigger a change in her mood. My mother, wandering around not far from the phone, drink in hand, heard me and asked if I was telling someone her business.

I said, "No. It's Geraldo. I was explaining why we're having dinner out."

Her gear switched. She danced over to the phone, grabbed it from me, looking as though she were going to chew it up. But when she spoke, her voice was controlled. Cute.

"Señor Geraldo? Is that who this is? Are you saying that I need an excuse to take my own kids to dinner, Señor Geraldo?"

I don't know what he said to her, but she told him the restaurant where we'd be and the time, said he was welcome to join us, if he so pleased. Then, she slammed down the phone and went for the tequila.

"You must have been telling him some great stories about me," she said.

I said, "I never talk about you. Anyway, he's been funny with me, lately."

She yawned. "You're full of shit. Anyway, I'm

changing for dinner. This is supposed to be a *celebration*."

Her voice had taken on the edge she was going to crash off in a couple of hours. As soon as she closed the door to her room, I called Geraldo at the garage and told him I really needed to see him.

He said he'd try to make it to my house, but after dinner.

I got frightened. Maybe I knew something I didn't know I knew.

I said, "I really need you, Geraldo. There's a lot going on here."

He heard me, as he always did at such times, and promised he'd be at the house.

❍

*T*he announcement of Ellery's wedding had noted that the groom was setting up his practice in psychiatry at the couple's new home on Acequia Madre, and I'd prayed that my mother wouldn't read it and/or make the connection to my accident. I hadn't seen Ellery since I'd been in the cast. Now, as Billy and my mother and I finally reached Rivera, he and Cona the Barbarian were coming out of it with a very skinny kid —young man—who turned out to be Ellery's son, Keith. Ellery and Cona greeted us with strained smiles. I thought Ellery looked miserable. And fat. When he asked my mother, in his pleasant, sort of professional way, how the suit against Wilkie was going, my mother, who'd cautioned us that we weren't to say a word about it to *anyone* until the agreement was signed, blurted out the whole story of how she'd come to get half of the Sky and remain friends with Wilkie, as well.

Billy stood there, shuffling from one foot to the other, until my mother told him to go in and get a table and a Coke.

Sweet, pacific Ellery told my mother how delighted he was that she was finally getting what she deserved from Wilkie, and Cona, having learned that the predecessor she hated and despised was about to become half-owner of one of the best pieces of commercial real estate in Santa Fe, initiated a friendly chat with my mother. It made me nervous but there was nothing I could do about it. Meanwhile, Keith came around and tried to chat me up. He said that his father had talked about me a lot, which just made me uneasy. I didn't know anything about him, beyond his wanting to be a painter, and that he'd been hostile to my mother. Keith said Taos was getting a little boring and he was thinking of moving down to Santa Fe . . . or someplace. It finally dawned on me that he was looking for some encouragement, but that just made me more uncomfortable. I asked if it wouldn't be difficult, moving to a place where he didn't know anybody.

He flashed this sort of stupid grin at me and said, "I know *you*," which made me want to tell him he didn't

and probably wouldn't. But my mother and Cona had
suddenly become best friends, and Ellery came over to
talk to us. He asked how I was doing and I began
telling him everything at once—leg recovery, job, colleges. Not Geraldo, although I mentioned having a
sort of boyfriend, not because I wanted Ellery to
know, but because I was signaling Keith to back off.
Also, for the first time I was thinking I missed Ellery,
wishing I could really talk to him. He said he was
settled in his office and would love for me to visit. I
nodded eagerly, promised I'd call very soon. We
parted, everyone saying how nice it was that we'd met,
and my mother and I went into Rivera, where we
found Billy and she proceeded to do serial margaritas
and hop tables to tell anybody she knew at all how
virtue had triumphed in her lawsuit. By the time we
left Rivera, she was so drunk that only Billy's being
with us made me get in the car with her. I asked if
maybe she'd like me to drive, once we got out of town.
I didn't have a license, but I could manage well
enough with an automatic, and I was frightened.

Her response was that maybe we should stop at the
Pink.

Billy, nearly asleep in the back of the car, said he
didn't feel good, he wanted to go home, so she headed
out of town, but she was muttering at me as though it
were my fault she couldn't go to the Pink. She drove
too fast, made an occasional dip toward a parked car
out of what I was certain was the simple desire to

terrify me. After we'd passed the plaza and were on the highway, she got crazier, went off the road at one point, but quickly veered back on. She laughed, began to hum, then to sing, a song with only a few words:

> *My, my, Acequia Madre*
> *My, my, Acequia Padre*

So, she'd finally made the connection.

I thought about trying to open the car door and fall onto the road, but I didn't want to leave Billy alone with her. I made my seat belt so tight that it hurt my legs and shoulder, but then I realized her belt wasn't on, at all. I told her to buckle it but she just kept singing the damn song, and finally, barely able to get out the words, I yelled, "I wasn't hiding anything from you, I just didn't know how you'd feel . . . I would've told you if you'd asked me."

"Told me what?" But she sang it, she didn't ask it, made it part of her mad song.

> *Tell me what, Acequia Madre?*
> *Tell me what, Acequia Padre?*

"That I was there because Ellery was showing me the house. Telling me they were getting married."

She began repeating my words, incorporating them into the song, mocking me as she sang them, making a liar of me. She must have been doing eighty miles an hour, in the left lane of 84, telling me what a great job Charlie Cojones had done on her car, it was still running perfectly, *Acequia Madre,* she just hoped I was protecting myself, *Acequia Padre.* When we reached our exit, she made her right turn from the left lane. Nobody was on our right, so nobody hit us, but Billy fell off the backseat to the floor. There was no sound, he appeared not even to have awakened, but I wasn't sure. I held my breath the whole way as we mounted Cerro Gordo. I think I've said that our house was on the left-hand side of the narrow, curvy road, past where the paved part ends. The road slopes off steeply to the right at many points. There were some farmhouses, the playground, and, by then, one or two newer homes, but there wasn't any kind of barrier along the right side, except at spots where people had made their own walls. I was convinced at every moment that the car was about to go off the road and tumble sideways down one of the open hills. But what happened instead was that my mother careened crazily to our house, then lurched off the road, not into our driveway but onto the narrow hill beside it, next to where Geraldo's old Lincoln was parked in the driveway, and then—I'm pretty sure I saw her actually turn the wheel hard to the right—pitching into the Lincoln, smashing into its rear left fender with our right front one.

We were jolted forward and for a moment I thought we'd smash through the windshield, but we were going uphill. She held on to the steering wheel, managing not to be thrown, and I crouched sideways in the front seat so that only my right shoulder and arm were hurt. Billy screamed and began to cry. A moment later, Geraldo came out of the house and ran toward us. Billy, seeing him, opened the door and scrambled out of the car and up into the house, lest he be caught, at the ripe old age of ten, crying. Geraldo saw that we were unharmed, then went to look at the damage to his car. He was grim. He didn't speak to me.

I began to cry.

My mother, quickly ascertaining that I had no good (physical) reason to be crying, tried to get out of the car, fighting with her door as though it had just tried to kill her. She hadn't crashed out of her drunkenness, but its hard edge had softened to a point where, when she finally managed to open the door and get out, she was able to go around to where Geraldo stood staring at the two fenders locked together in unholy matrimony.

She said, "Let's all go inside and have a drink."

He stared at her, disbelieving.

She shrugged. "Then we can figure out what to do."

Geraldo turned to me. "Leave the cars alone. We'll get them in the morning. You don't have to report anything. Private property."

And as I waited for him to make some gesture to

suggest that he knew I wasn't responsible for my mother's insanities, he slid, feet sideways, down the dirt hill onto Cerro Gordo, then loped down toward Palace Avenue.

○

*H*e and his uncle came with the tow truck the next morning. My mother sent me out to deal with them. His uncle told me to tell my mother they weren't reporting the accident. She could call his garage if she wanted someone to pick up her car and fix it. He didn't meet my eyes. Geraldo didn't come anywhere near me. He hitched the tow truck to the rear of the station wagon and held up the bumper, directing his uncle as they disengaged it from the Lincoln. Then he unhooked the truck from the station wagon and hooked it to the Lincoln and his uncle slowly drove-pulled it down the driveway. Until the moment when the Lincoln was on the road and he was walking toward it, I could tell myself he was preoccupied. But when he got into the tow truck without looking at me, I ran up to him and asked why he was acting mad at *me*.

He said, "I'm not mad at anybody."

I asked, "Then why aren't you talking to me?"

He shrugged. "Nothing to say." A wall.

I asked if he would call me later.

He said, "We're pretty busy," and got into the

truck, which moved slowly down Cerro Gordo, towing the Lincoln behind it.

◑

*K*eith called me once before he left Santa Fe and a couple of times from Taos, "just to talk," but I was always busy and I didn't think about him, once I'd hung up.

◑

*S*hortly before the fall term began, my mother found a little house on Delgado Street, close to the center of town. It was a one-year furnished sublet and cheaper than any of the new apartments she'd looked at. It was just several blocks from the Sky and Billy would be able to walk to school, though I'd still have to take the bus to the high school, which was outside of town. The owners of the house were going abroad, and there was a chance they would stay a second year. Actually, it wasn't my mother who found the sublet but a broker I cannot bear to name. The two had taken a great liking to one another, although the broker's husband, my mother told me, giggling, clearly was not thrilled with the friendship.

Billy was furious at having to leave the only house he'd ever lived in, and no amount of talk about how he would be able to walk to school and to many of his friends' houses swayed him. Hearing Wilkie's name was enough to make him leave the room.

Hearing Jaffe's name was enough to make my mother leave. He'd presented her with a staggering bill as soon as it became clear that she wasn't going to bed with him. She seems to have believed, until then, that she would get away with her teasing game.

We moved into the house on Delgado the following week, and she began almost immediately to complain about money. She'd had no idea how difficult paying a real rent would be, on top of outrages like Jaffe's bill. We'd had to leave most of our furniture in the old house, it was part of the deal, and she couldn't afford to replace or cover up some of the uglier stuff: a white leather sofa and chair that looked like something gangsters might buy; hideous copper tables with glass tops; orangey wall-to-wall carpeting. There was a big television console in the living room, but no TV by the time we saw it; she must have had them take it away. There was a tiny kitchen off the living-dining room. She complained about its distance from the sofas as though the owners had arranged to make it difficult for her to reach the tequila bottle. We were very close to the houses on either side. She cautioned me not to be so nice to the neighbors that they tried to get friendly. She was in a foul mood all the time. I kept out of her way as much as I could.

*A* few weeks into the term I had a reprieve when Wilkie came to her in tears because Courtney had gone back to Long Beach. He'd offered to drive her, but then she'd vanished in the middle of the night. No note. Left half the clothes he'd bought her. She didn't even care about the clothes! He couldn't bear to be in the house alone. My mother took him in. He shared her bedroom, which had a very wide bed, maybe king. I didn't get the impression they were having sex; booze was their sex.

There was nothing that cost money that Courtney hadn't liked, and Wilkie was broke. My mother got his/our house rented to one of her gallery customers for the winter months, so he'd have some cash.

Billy, still furious at having had to move on Wilkie's account, wouldn't talk to him. Wilkie, that great pile of refried beans, seemed not to notice. The first time my mother went back to calling him "your father," Billy gave her a dirty look, but Wilkie smiled benignly.

"It makes him feel good," my mother whispered. "He feels as if he has no one but us."

"He doesn't have *me*," Billy whispered back fiercely. "And you *promised*."

Which was the end of it, for the time being.

I felt like talking to Ellery but I was afraid that if my mother found out I'd been there, it would set her off. Occasionally I strolled along Cerillos, past the garage, pretending I wasn't looking for Geraldo. I can't explain why I needed one or the other when they were utterly different and made me content in nearly opposite ways.

I couldn't tell if Geraldo saw me; he never came out.

I began dating a boy named Steven who was president of the senior class. We made out, and he was perfectly okay, there was nothing wrong with him, I liked him, but he didn't press me to go to bed and I didn't encourage him. It just didn't happen. When I finally ran into Geraldo one day, where Cerillos meets Guadalupe, he was friendly, but I acted cool. I couldn't bear for him to think I'd been longing for him. When he asked what I was doing these days, I said I was trying to figure out which colleges to apply to. When he asked whether I wasn't going to UNM with my girlfriends, I said I was thinking more and more of going East, where my father was. He looked as if he knew what I was saying as far as he was concerned, but it wasn't true, of course. I kept wanting to run into him so I could give him another chance to come back to me, but it didn't happen.

I wrote to my father in care of the history department at Dartmouth. I told him I was in my senior year of high school, beginning to think about college applications, and Dartmouth seemed like one of the places I should apply to, especially if there was scholarship money available for faculty "family." I asked how he felt about this, said I wouldn't do it if he'd rather I didn't. I told him I was an excellent student and had many choices, but I wanted to be on the East Coast, in a place with green. I quoted Georgia O'Keeffe and said I felt exactly the opposite. I asked him to write me, if he wanted to, in care of my college adviser at school.

I got a response in a few days. He said that he would be pleased to see me at Dartmouth and was certain I'd be covered as a faculty child. He didn't know why I'd put family in quotation marks. He'd thought about me often, over the years, but had felt there was no point trying to be in contact when my mother was so determined that we not be. This was sufficiently unlike anything I'd ever heard from her that I knew Dartmouth would be a touchy subject, even before we talked about money. But in December I needed the checks to accompany my applications. I tried waiting until she was in a good mood, but that didn't happen, either.

Wilkie called Billy "my boy" one night at dinner, and Billy lit into him, punched him in the stomach and kicked his knees. Wilkie certainly wasn't going to hang around and try to convince Billy he was his father; father was tops on the list of all the jobs he'd never applied for. So he found himself another little Courtney who was dying to give up her waitress job and he moved into her place until the time when his gorgeous house in the hills would be vacant.

I had no idea how my mother would be about the checks to accompany my other applications, and I was looking for signs. (I was always looking for signs. I'm still looking for them. It's just that nobody's making them.) When I finally had to ask for the checks, I advised Billy to stay out of the living room, then I waited until my mother had settled on the couch with her after-dinner José. (From the time we moved, I hardly ever saw her without a glass in her hand.) I told her I knew she had a lot on her mind, but I needed the checks for my college applications.

"You mean, you have to give the bastards money even if you never go there?"

I smiled nervously. "It's a fee for processing the application."

"Mmm. No wonder I never applied to college."

I smiled dutifully.

"Give me my bag." It irritated her, but not much. We weren't girlfriends since Acequia Madre and Cona, but she hadn't gone out of her way to be horrible.

I gave her the handbag, and she took out her pen and checkbook. I started to explain something about the fees, and she said, "Don't bother. Just tell me who to make out the checks to."

"The first one's for Albuquerque. University of New Mexico at."

I think the amounts were all somewhere between twenty-five and fifty dollars. She made that one out, handed it to me. The next was for Yale.

She frowned. "Doesn't it cost a fortune to go to a place like that?"

I smiled. It was a good introduction. "I'm thinking about places where I might get a scholarship."

She wrote the check, handed it to me.

I said, "There are different ways you can get a scholarship. You have to be a good student, of course, but also . . . There are other reasons." I was having trouble getting it out; her radar picked up my slow-down and she watched me suspiciously. "That's what the next one's about," I said, increasingly nervous. "Getting a scholarship."

"Cut the bullshit."

"It's not bullshit. It's about not paying tuition."

I'd done the reverse of what I intended. She looked as though she'd come upon a dead body and me with a gun, and was listening to me swear I hadn't shot the guy.

"And what school would that be?"

I had to force it out. "Faculty child. Dartmouth."

She bolted out of the seat, splashing her drink, dropping the pen and checkbook. She went for the tequila, poured some more into the glass. I sat there like a little kid who's playing statues and has been told to freeze. Finally, she sat down. Monumentally casual.

"So, you've been in touch with the sperm bank."

I stared at her, baffled.

"With this man," she continued, still deadly calm, "who deposited his sperm in my womb, and wanted me to have an abortion when I got pregnant, and never had a thing to do with you afterward."

That wasn't my memory, of course. My memory was of long, peaceful afternoons in his study, me looking at my picture books or playing with a toy, my father reading, working, answering if I asked him a question. I couldn't picture him kissing me, but I couldn't remember him hitting me, either. Of course, *she'd* never hit me in those days, while later she'd smack me more readily than she'd answer a simple question she wasn't in the mood for.

"You said money could be a problem. This is about free tuition."

"Well, I'm really touched. You just decided, in the interest of saving me money, to contact your father, who's had no interest in knowing whether you were dead or alive for the past twelve years. Who never gave a shit for you from the day you were born. Who . . ." She tossed off her drink, set the glass on the table. "I'll tell you what. I think you should go to his fucking Dartmouth and see what a wonderful place it is, and see what a fucking sweetie pie I took you away from and—"

"He says you didn't want him to have any contact with me."

She began walking around the room in a jerky rage, like a Frankenstein monster who's been stuck by the doctor's needle. She stumbled over the edge of the rug, turned to me, tried to say something but choked on it and began to cough. She poured some tequila, took the first gulp as though someone were threatening to snatch it.

"Well," she said in a strangled voice, "I think you should believe him. I think you should believe everything he says."

I was shrunk into myself in one corner of the sofa by this time, wishing I hadn't told her what my father had said as I tried to figure out how fast I could run, though I was seldom aware of my bad leg, anymore. It didn't normally hurt.

She picked up her pen and checkbook and her bag, stood over me, holding it all in one hand, the glass in the other.

"Can I ask,"—her voice was very low and tight, but shaking—"just what in fucking hell you have got to be crying about? *Answer me!* You just told me you're getting cozy with this man I went through some hell to get away from, mostly because he was such an ice cube with you, and you're—"

"I'm not cozy with him!" I was frantic to explain. "I just—Ellery's been telling me I should go to the East Coast, the schools are—"

"Ellery!" she shouted. "Now it's Ellery, is it?"

"If you can be friends with Cona," I shouted back, "why can't I be with Ellery?"

She pulled into her own body as though she were preparing to hurl all of herself at me, but instead she hurled the heavy glass, still with plenty of tequila in it, at my face. It hit my cheekbone, then fell into my lap, the tequila splashing in my eyes and then down on my legs. I screamed and started crying. My eyes stung and my cheek felt as if the bone had been broken. I didn't want to open my eyes because I was afraid to find out I couldn't see. I felt for the glass, pushed it off my lap onto the rug, then curled up like a worm in the corner of the sofa, my face in my sweater, legs folded under me, though the broken one hurt when I bent it that far. My face got wiped dry by my sweater sleeve, but my skin itched from the wool. I didn't care. I stayed that way for a long time.

When I opened my eyes, it was very quiet. I didn't know whether she was gone, couldn't tell what would happen when I sat up. My cheek was the only place that really hurt, though my leg was badly cramped and the rest of me was stiff. Slowly I uncurled myself, opened one eye. I could see, though the eye stung. I wiped it with my hand. My mother didn't seem to be around. I opened the other eye, went through the same routine. The door to her bedroom was open. I called Billy's name. He came out of his room. I asked where she was. He said she'd had to go back to the gallery. I told him I hadn't heard the car start. He said that it had. He came over to the sofa, but slowly. He was uncomfortable, he was that age, but he couldn't just walk out on me. When I calmed down a little, he asked what was wrong with my cheek.

I said, "Nothing."

He said, "It's all red and swollen."

I said, "I must've . . . When I opened the kitchen cabinet, the low one, it banged into me."

We both knew it hadn't happened, or at least I assumed Billy knew, but he kept quiet about it. Billy stayed under the radar. That was one of the differences between us. At home.

When I got up the next morning, my mother wasn't around but there was a blank check made out to Dartmouth on the kitchen counter, along with a note suggesting that maybe I should try to find someplace else to live sooner than September. I filled in the check and left her a note with the amount, saying that if she had any good ideas about where I could live, I'd listen. Then I mailed off my application. I knew for certain I was going to Dartmouth if they gave me a scholarship.

She often smacked me in the face or punched my arm, but this was the first time I'd showed up at school with a bruise I couldn't cover. Everyone wanted to know about it. A couple of kids teased me about having another accident so soon, asked what I was trying to do. Laya looked distressed. She and a couple of the other girls tried to get me to tell them what had happened. I practiced the cabinet routine on them, and thought, until Laya and her mother testified for me at the trial, that she believed my story. By lunchtime I was so tired of explaining that I made up an index card that said, EDGE KITCHEN CABINET and attached it to my sweater neck with a paper clip. Everyone who didn't really know me thought that was adorable, a riot, and accepted it as an explanation.

My mother didn't come home that night.

◑

*T*he next day, Geraldo drove up after school. I think he must have heard on the grapevine about my cheek.

He said, a hand on my arm, "Hey, Hon, if I knew that was what you liked, I could've done it for you."

I pulled away my arm and said it wasn't funny, and he apologized. But the thing I can't forget, and have to force myself to write, is the wave of excitement that flooded me. I shifted my weight to my good leg, but all that accomplished was to make me feel I had to get to the bathroom. He smiled. He knew. I felt ashamed. I can talk casually about having sex; it's the neediness in arousal that shames me. It's like being six years old and waiting in the cold darkness for your mother to come home and then, when she does, her arms are full. That's what Geraldo understood until he decided not to understand anymore.

He took me by the elbow, asked where I was going. I said to Ellery's, though I hadn't been thinking of Ellery.

Geraldo said. "Watch out for the traffic, now."

I said, "Go fuck yourself." My voice was shaking. I didn't feel all that tough and angry, but whether he understood that or not, he wasn't going to let me get away with saying it to him. He got into his Lincoln, which was now painted a startling blue, and drove away without another word. I decided to go on to Ellery's, but I was so full of fear of Geraldo, fear of *wanting* Geraldo, that I forgot about Cona and about my face and just walked to Ellery's house and quietly went in through the gate and around to the back and knocked on the door without thinking of what I looked like.

"Maddy, what happened?" he said when he opened his door.

I said, my throat as tight as though a copperhead were wrapped around it, "I banged into the kitchen cabinet."

"I don't think so."

I burst into you-know-what. An arm around me, he led me into his office, where I headed for the couch, thought of my mother and all her shit about me with Ellery, and sat on one of the chairs.

"Maddy, my dear, what's going on?"

He gave me a box of tissues and finally I stopped crying. I wiped my face around the bruise, blew my nose. But my brain kept making up fantastical scenes in which my mother happened to be driving by the house as I happened to walk out; or she barged into the office to confront Ellery about advising me to go away, only to hear me telling him how she'd thrown a glass at me. If she should find out I'd been there, my life wouldn't be worth a box of cat litter.

The room was a decent size but a little dark, and all gray. Gray carpeting, gray upholstery on the couch and two chairs. Nothing Santa Fe. I thought for the first time of the unfinished bead belt I'd put on a high shelf in my closet. I remembered Geraldo's getting mad one night when I braided my hair into a pigtail, asking if I was trying to look like an Indian. I'd come up here to be saved from Geraldo, but I was reluctant to talk about him, now.

I said, "I wrote to my father. He wants me to apply to Dartmouth. My mother . . . when I told her . . . That's when she . . ."

Ellery nodded, grimly.

Tears, stupid tears, began to roll again. I was wondering whether maybe I could sleep in Ellery's office after he went upstairs at night. I'd go home if Billy needed me. Or if my mother suddenly noticed she'd made a mistake. At least I'd have had a break. Would Ellery consider such a thing? Would Cona have anything to say about it? Everything? I hadn't actually thought about it, until that moment.

I said, "I don't think I can stand any more."

Ellery said, "Oh, God, Maddy, I wish I had a solution for you."

I can admit now that I didn't simply intuit that Cona was my enemy, but I was hers. Long before she betrayed my mother, she took out of my life the person who'd made it bearable. While Ellery was there, my mother hadn't ever smacked my face or socked me, much less thrown a heavy glass at my head. It wasn't that she was pretending. At least, I don't think so. But more that a man's presence served as a sort of brake on her. Like the hand brake on a car. You can make the car move when it's on, but only in a slow, grinding motion. No chance it'll run away with you. Now, the car was still there, but the hand brake was elsewhere.

"We knew she might not like it," he said.

I nodded. "I guess I just have to stay away from her as much as I can. Until I get out of Santa Fe altogether."

It took him a long time to ask whether Laya's family might not be happy to have me. We were such good friends, and I slept over there so often, anyway.

"It's very tricky," I said. "My mother could just show up and throw one of her fits."

"Would that be worse than what's going on?"

"Oh, yes!" I was startled at his even asking the question. "I couldn't bear it if anyone—it's none of their business."

He nodded slowly. "I see."

I said, smiling, trying to be cute-wistful, "What I need is to get out of my life. Be someplace she won't come after me . . . I don't suppose you know anyone who needs a live-in housekeeper, or baby-sitter, or something."

He didn't, of course. To make his long story short, the house near the plaza was now rented, and Cona was working out of this one, so that they no longer had the space he might have been able to offer me, he only wished blah blah blah. By the time he'd finished, all I could think about was that I never should have gone there in the first place. No, that's not all I could think about. I was thinking about finding Geraldo.

I walked past the garage a few times, but I didn't see him.

◐

When I told my mother that I had interviews scheduled for Dartmouth and Yale, she grumbled about the airfare but also said it would be worth it to have me that far away. As though she'd have to see me all the time if I were in Albuquerque. Between then and the time when I went to Hanover and New Haven for my interviews, every argument we had ended with her telling me how happy she would be if I managed to get into a school "on the other side of the continent."

◐

I'd never been on a plane. I hadn't slept the night before, and I didn't sleep during the long ride to Boston or the short one up to Hanover. The woman sitting next to me was very businesslike, with an attaché case and papers she shuffled the whole time, except when the movie was on. We didn't speak. I couldn't read, either. I just looked at the stewardesses, and the clouds, and flipped through a lot of magazines. I had the same fantasy over and over again: Arnold Taylor, having learned of my trip to Dartmouth, applied to transfer there from UCLA for his junior year, and sat down next to me on the plane. He said he'd thought about me every day since that awful night, had wanted to talk to me hundreds of times. He'd been such a baby, then; I had to forgive him. We had the same sexy conversation over and over until the plane landed in Boston. It always ended with his telling me that if I went to Dartmouth, he was going there, too.

It would be close to dinnertime when the plane arrived. Someone from the school would be there to pick up all the students coming for interviews. My father had given me his address (as though I didn't know it!), told me the way to walk over to his house when I was ready. There were dorm arrangements for everyone; he hadn't said anything about whether I would sleep at the dorm with the others, or at his house. The tour of the school and the interviews would be on Friday. I'd return to Santa Fe on Saturday, except I'd made up my mind that if my father should persuade me to stay through the weekend, I would make the change in my ticket and simply call home, preferably at a time when I'd reach Billy, and give him my new arrival time.

Everyone in the Dartmouth jitney was friendly, but I mostly looked out of the window, wanting things to be familiar, but not finding them so. It was the end of the day, and everything was pretty dark. Aside from the snow and some evergreens, it was as brown and drab as Santa Fe. Hanover, when we passed through it, was much smaller than I remembered, the general rule of returnees, I gather. The exception being when one is released from prison, and everything seems vast.

Back at the dorm, every time the phone rang, I thought it might be my father, checking to make sure I'd arrived, but it wasn't. I showered, washed my hair and blew it dry, then had an atypically difficult time deciding whether to leave it loose so I'd look so mature and beautiful that he couldn't believe it was his daughter, or to wear a ponytail and look as close as possible to the way I had when he'd last seen me. I made a ponytail, but combed it out just before leaving the dorm. I wore a black wool skirt and a white sweater. I kept my green parka open so I wouldn't look like a balloon.

But when he opened the door, I was the confused one. I didn't recognize him at all. My eyes went back to the brass nameplate on the door frame. Stern. It was my house. *His* house. He had straggly, light brown hair but his beard and mustache were gray. He was skinny; I remembered him as round. He looked very old. (He was fifty-six.)

I said, "I'm Madeleine."

He said, "My goodness, and I was expecting Minnie Mouse." He didn't give me a big hug and kiss, as

I'd pictured him doing, or move aside to let me in, and I still wasn't positive it was he.

I said, "You don't look the way I remember you."

He was smiling, but there was a grim edge to it; I didn't know, yet, that he always looked grim when he smiled.

"Well," he said, "*you* don't look the way *I* remember *you!*"

I said, I suppose because he still hadn't beckoned me in, "You *are* Rupert Stern?"

"I was the last time I looked."

I felt a tremendous surge of dislike for him, had a momentary urge to bolt, but then I thought of what a good story this would make for my mother, and I was able to take command of myself.

"Well," I said evenly, "are we going to have dinner on the doorstep, or do you mean to let me into the house?"

He was thrown. I'd cracked the joke–ice barrier.

"Oh, God, I'm so sorry, Maddy. Or do they call you Madeleine, now? Of course. Please. Come in."

I walked behind him into the hall, my heart beating as though I might run into the ghost of my mother's twenty-six-year-old self, or something even more frightening. I could see his study to my right. The glass doors were closed. I remembered them closed, but with me always on the inside. There was music coming from the room. There'd always been classical music in that room and the doors were always closed. My mother was never in there.

He remained terribly awkward, not at all happy to see me.

"Uh . . . Why don't you sit in the living room . . . here . . . and I'll get my coat."

I felt goddamned tears welling. He saw.

"Oh, dear, have I said something wrong again?"

I shook my head.

"Is it that . . . Perhaps you'd like to look around the house?"

I shook my head again. Without instructing myself to do so, I nodded toward his study.

He smiled. "My study? Of course. You remember my study." He opened the glass doors. "We spent a lot of time here. Whenever your mother was away, or busy, we'd just . . . I'd work, and you'd sit on the carpet, or on the sofa, and read. Before you could read, you just looked at pictures, but you knew the words from memory. I think that was why you started reading so early. You knew what the words were before you looked at them."

So he really was my father, not some bad joke of an imposter. I followed him into his room, which was as I remembered it—the huge desk, brown swivel chair, its leather now cracked in places; darker brown leather sofa; the Oriental rug with its maroon background, also worn but definitely the same rug; and the books, of course.

"Why don't I leave you here while I get ready," my father said. "Wash my face. Feed the cats."

I nodded.

He smiled. It's hard to describe my father's smile. Not just because of the beard. It's not that his mouth looked mean, but his smile was more an announcement that he was smiling than an expression of pleasure, the lips just pulled sideways at their ends, and nothing else changed.

I asked, "You have cats?"

He said, "The women who live with me always seem to have them."

So. There was a woman. Maybe I wouldn't have to meet her. My mother hated cats.

He went to do what he had to do. I sat down at the desk and began to swivel in the chair, very slowly, taking in every detail—the book wall, the three busts of Civil War generals on the windowsill at the desk's right, the small glass-fronted bookcase to the left that held the valuable editions I hadn't been allowed to touch—*The Artillerist's Manual* by (Civil War) General John Gibbon, an early copy of *Huckleberry Finn,* and so on. Cloth showed through the sofa leather in big patches. I felt like stretching out, but I was afraid I would fall asleep. I hadn't slept for more than an hour or so at a time for the last two nights. I swiveled slowly, might have dozed off for a bit. When he returned and said, "All set," I was startled.

He pulled back the edges of his mouth.

From now on I'll just say he smiled.

We walked diagonally across the green to the Hanover Inn, a pleasant, old Eastern sort of restaurant with the atmosphere of a place that has never heard of Los Alamos, or dope, or sex within marriage. The hostess in the Inn greeted him as Professor Stern, but he didn't think to introduce her to me. Not absolutely everyone in the dining room had white hair, and surely a couple of these men with young women had left their wives, as men did in Santa Fe, but it still felt like a different world. My father requested a quiet table, which was funny, because the whole dining room was cemetery-quiet. If you didn't look at people's lips, you weren't sure they were talking.

My father ordered a scotch and soda. I asked for a rum and Coke. It's not fair for me to make fun of the menu, which was ordinary, though not for Santa Fe— shrimp cocktail, lobster, halibut, steak and a couple of dishes that were easy on the gums. When we got our drinks, he raised his glass to me in a sort of toast, though he didn't make one, then took a couple of sips and said, sounding as though he were rehearsing me for my interview, "So, what do you think of Hanover?"

I said, "Well, it's very different from Santa Fe, of course."

He laughed. "That's for sure. I guess there're even fewer Jews in Santa Fe."

I was startled. "I don't know."

After a while, he said, "You do know you're half-Jewish, don't you?"

In a way, I didn't. It came up very seldom, though my mother, before this trip, had said she'd better give me a little extra cash because "your father's a real Jew about money." It had taken me by surprise. I knew he was Jewish and I knew my mother was somewhat anti-Semitic. Near their beginning, she'd told Ellery he didn't seem Jewish. He'd been amused, said he was the archetypal New York Jew, she just hadn't known any. He said maybe we'd all go to New York sometime, and he'd point out to her who was and who wasn't.

I said, "I don't normally think of myself as being Jewish."

He said, "Maybe it's just as well. Your mother doesn't like Jews."

Carefully, I asked why he said that. She'd married him, after all.

He laughed. "She divorced me, too."

*She divorces everybody* was what went through my mind, but I didn't say it. What is true, though, is that I never exactly thought of anyone as leaving *her;* I thought she got unpleasant when she wanted them to go.

"Anyway, I'm not sure she knew what a Jew was when she came down to the States. She had to marry me to find out." He finished his drink and signaled the waiter to bring another.

"You sound," I said cautiously, "as though you think all Jews are alike."

"More like one another than like a Gentile. I wasn't too much aware of it, until I settled in Hanover. Just the language, alone. The sounds of Hebrew and Yiddish. The inflection carries over into our English. Ugly. At least when you're speaking Yiddish, you have the pleasures of the language to make up for the sounds."

I was puzzled. To begin with, I was pretty sure he didn't have the inflection he was talking about. Beyond that, I was completely befuddled by the turn his conversation had taken. One thing to acknowledge that our daily concerns were different, another to understand why he'd encouraged me to come to Hanover if he had no interest in who I'd grown up to be or what was on my mind. I finished my drink and he ordered me another without asking if I wanted it.

I said. "I'm not even eighteen, you know."

"Oh, dear, that's true. Well, I don't have any grass on me, so we'll have to stay with the booze."

He said it straight-faced, so that for a moment I didn't realize it was supposed to be a joke. My drink came and I pushed it away so I wouldn't sip at it thoughtlessly. My head was already a little woozy.

"So," he said, "you'll be eighteen in—February, is it?"

"February 13."

"Of course. You were six in 1977. That was when I

made my first trip to Israel. Until then . . . I hadn't been much involved with the country. The people. Now . . . I don't actually go anyplace else. I don't know if you saw the new bookcase. I have quite a collection on Israel and the Arabs. It's a kind of civil war, you know, whatever anyone says to the contrary."

I felt a strong surge of distaste. *This is not my father. It can't be.* It was helpful to me, thinking that way. I encouraged myself to keep doing it. *This is definitely not my father.*

I smiled.

"Are you smiling because I'm so consistent in my interests? That's what my current house—uh—house-mate says. She's a psychologist. Works in the public schools. Schools don't have many teachers these days, but they have a lot of psychologists."

I shook my head.

He was mildly irritated. "Well, would you like to tell me what you *are* smiling about, or is that your little secret?"

I felt very free. I was far from home, with someone I'd been terribly anxious to impress and no longer cared about, in a place I'd never come back to, no matter what Dartmouth offered me.

I said, "You haven't seen me since I was five years old, and you're talking to me about Israel and public schools."

He nodded. He wasn't any more uncomfortable than he'd been all along.

"Well," he said, "it's difficult to talk to somebody you haven't seen since she was five." He waited, but I had nothing to say. "Perhaps you'd care to tell me what it's like to live in Santa Fe."

I shrugged. "What do you want to know? It's very different from here. Sometimes it's more like being in Mexico than the United States. There are three separate cultures, Anglo, Indian, Spanish. Some parts of them hardly mix. I'm an Anglo, of course."

He nodded. "A Jewish Anglo."

"No. Not if we're talking about Santa Fe. I don't think I've heard the word *Jewish* ten times, except in the years my mother had a Jewish boyfriend. You can't talk about Santa Fe as though it were Hanover."

"Okay." He was interested. "So, you're an Anglo."

"Mmm. But my boyfriends tend to be Spanish." I heard myself sounding as though there'd been a lot of them, decided not to correct me. "Very macho. It's a problem with their families, sometimes, if they date an Anglo girl."

He nodded. "And the Anglos are . . . pretty much what you'd find here in Hanover?"

"I don't know. I haven't been here long enough."

"Ah, yes. Of course. And the Indians? Where do they fit into the plan?"

"They don't. They mostly don't want to. They have their own schools, pueblos—little villages—and they're discouraged from mixing with the Spanish and the Anglos. If they marry someone from outside, they're likely

to live in a pueblo. The Spanish have some of that xen-
ophobia, too. There are Spanish villages where some of
the old women, their great-great-great-grandparents
came here, they don't speak English. And some of them
speak a Spanish the others don't understand."

"That's fascinating." He was really interested. He
wasn't faking it. "Tell me more about the Indians."

"I can tell you the names of some of the pueblos,
but not much more, because I've never been to any of
them."

"Why not?"

I shrugged. "They don't really want outsiders, except tourists who buy things. I pretty much stay
around town. This is the first time I've been on a
plane."

"Hm. Remarkable, in this day and age. Isn't your
mother still a real traveler?"

"I'm not sure what you mean." I wanted to hear
what he would say.

"Oh, you know . . ." He flubbed around for a bit,
finally said, "She likes to go places. At least, she used
to."

I decided to put him out of his misery, at least
briefly.

"You mean, she's restless."

He nodded.

I said, "Only when she doesn't have a boyfriend."
And waited.

He said, "I suppose it's time to order some food."

I said, "Or when she's not terribly busy at the Sky."

"The sky?"

I explained to him how she'd built up this shopping center named the Sky. I made it sound as though she was just working for Wilkie; she'd warned me not to tell him anything that might give him the idea she could pay my college expenses.

We ordered and then, while we waited for dinner to arrive, I sipped at my drink. It was lovely not to have to worry about saying the wrong thing, to know it wasn't going to matter. By the time the food came, I was more than a little drunk, but when he asked if I'd like some wine, I told him I'd prefer a beer. I said I'd become accustomed to drinking Mexican beer in Santa Fe. A lie. I wasn't accustomed to drinking anything except Coke. And when he said, a while later, that maybe now that I'd been on a plane, I'd become more adventurous, perhaps I'd want to go to Israel and find out that I was a Jew, I just laughed.

*God, you're such a prick!*

He sipped at his wine, but he looked pained.

"I understand that you're not tuned in to your Jewish history. But it's there, anyway."

"I'm not so sure. I'm not even sure you're my father." It just slipped out. I hadn't planned it.

He said, very stiff, "As far as I know, your mother didn't sleep with anyone else during the time when you were conceived. Besides, you bear a strong resemblance to me. To my mother. We all have the same coloring. Same eyes. I have some old pictures, if you're interested."

"Are any of them hanging in the house?"

He shook his head. "They're the last thing I'd want to look at every day."

I thanked him, ate my dull food, drank my beer. I understand my mother and anyone else who wants to be drunk, even if I don't get that way often. My brain was angry, hating him, wondering whether I couldn't pick up my clothes and get a cab to the bus terminal and sleep there until the bus left for Boston in the morning (from there, I'd go to New Haven) but I felt fine, because I was drunk.

I asked, "Do you ever get angry?"

He said, "Not really."

I said, "Me, neither. Maybe that's in the genes, too."

He said, "You sound pretty angry with me." When I didn't answer, he added, "I'm told that no matter who did the leaving, there's anger at both parents."

He looked as though he'd run over a dead skunk, but at least he was trying.

I said, "I never felt angry at you, that I can remember."

He said, "Oh?" But he'd traveled about as far into the land of feelings as his tank would take him. He ordered another glass of wine, checked to see that I still had some beer, inquired as to whether there was anything I wanted to know about Dartmouth or the interviews. I asked what he thought I should know and he chatted me up, just the way the interviewer would the next day. He inquired about school, extracurricular activities, about whether I'd ever been to the museum in Albuquerque. I said I could discourse upon it at length.

He smiled. "I thought you never left Santa Fe."

I smiled back. "I don't. I thought an interviewer might ask, so I talked with one of my teachers about it."

He whistled softly, stared at me with something resembling curiosity for the first time.

"You're quite a piece of work, aren't you, daughter mine."

I felt a brief, perverse satisfaction in his saying it, but then I got anxious. I thought of how—I don't know when it began, it was at some point after my mother came home from the hospital with Belly—I would awaken in the morning thinking I was back in my father's study. I would see the raw planks behind my bed and wonder where the books were, then decide my father must be angry with me, to have moved me out of his room. Finally, I'd remember.

I said, "I don't know what that means." A lie. I could tell, though I hadn't heard the expression before. "But I think, I think you have no idea what we have to do to survive." My voice wanted to tremble and I allowed it to.

"You and your mother?"

I shook my head. "My brother. I have a brother. He was born about nine months and two minutes after we got to Santa Fe." Then I got very uneasy. I'd never said even that much against my mother. One of the reasons it had been easy to stay close with Ellery was that I hadn't had to tell him anything; he knew.

"I see." He was a trifle grim. "And did your mother marry that lucky fellow, too?"

"Not exactly." I explained a little more about Wilkie and my mother and the origins of the Sky. He asked questions, listened carefully, grew thoughtful. He said my mother was extremely intelligent; there was no telling what she might have done with a good education.

I said, "But she did it without one. Except she doesn't make a lot of money."

He didn't argue with me, but clearly she'd done it in a world where it wasn't worthwhile to measure accomplishment. Anyway, he didn't bother to give me a speech on the value of higher education. My little story had done its job.

A couple he knew came by the table and I was my usual charming self. They were surprised Rupert had a daughter, stayed to have a brandy with us. They asked which subjects I liked best, were interested to hear that I loved English and math but didn't care for any of the sciences, though I'd gotten A's in all of them. I told them that I'd worked after school, and I expected to work if I got into Dartmouth. They said, as they got up to leave, that they were sure I'd make a wonderful impression on the interviewer.

By the time we left the restaurant, it was freezing cold.

My father said, "You do make a good impression, Maddy."

We walked across the green toward his house, not toward the dorm where I was supposed to sleep. I thought of how nice it would be to have breakfast in the kitchen. I could see my mother (looking the way she looked now) opening a cabinet to get down the Frosted Flakes. By the time we'd reached the other side of the green, I was beginning to feel more friendly to him.

Then he stopped, looked around, and said, "Oh, dear, I'm afraid I've walked you in the wrong direction." He turned and beckoned to me to follow him around the green. To the dorm.

It was fine, actually. I was exhausted and I was about to get one of my headaches. Maybe someone at the dorm would have aspirin.

At the building entrance, he stopped, took my hand as though he were going to put a diploma into it, and told me he looked forward to seeing me in the fall. Nothing about the next day, about when I was leaving, about whether we'd be in touch.

That was fine, too.

I asked, "Why did you want me to be named Madeleine?"

He smiled. "As a matter of fact, I didn't. It was the only name your mother would hear of."

I said, "Thanks for the dinner. It's been a pleasure, getting to know you a little."

And I walked into the dorm, thinking I'd kill myself before I ever went to Dartmouth.

◑

*I* liked the people who interviewed me at Yale more than I had the ones at Dartmouth, and there was a greater diversity to the student body. The girls didn't all look as if they'd just skied in off the slopes. But the buildings were stone, dark and depressing, and you could hardly see where there might be some green in the spring. The rooms we saw had beds that were practically cots, which a couple of the girls whispered over. The beds didn't bother me, but then a lot of the public places were paneled in a dark wood that someone said was magnificent, but that left the rooms so dreary that they must have required electric lights even on the brightest days. Where once there'd been a contrast in my mind between Santa Fe's red-to-dark browns and New Hampshire's greens, now the contrast was between the bright and varied clay and earth colors of home, and the drab stone and dark wood of the East. A couple of the kids asked more questions about the food than anything else.

When I went home, I told my mother some of the

kids didn't think about anything but food, and the
Yale buildings looked like medieval prisons. However
much she'd sworn that she was dying to be rid of me,
she loved it, loved even more the caricature of my
father, stiff-lipped, stiff-necked, saying, "I really do
have a mouth and all the organs other people have, I
just think it's more seemly to keep them covered with
this beard and mustache." I didn't tell her I'd vowed
not to go East to school, but I appear to have left her
with the impression that I was planning on going to
UNM.

In a burst of good feeling, she offered to drive four
of us down to Albuquerque for our interviews. I had
to tell her that one of the mothers had already arranged to do it. She was very suspicious: They didn't
think she was good enough to drive their precious
fucking daughters to Albuquerque. Well, if they'd
heard about her little accident, it was the kind of accident anyone could have had . . . late at night . . .
after a couple of drinks.

Dolly's mother took our crew to Albuquerque. I
breezed through the interviews—we all did—but I left
feeling miserable about the possibility of being there
for any length of time, my dream of grass and trees
reinforced by a place where nothing was green except
the tourist money in the fake Indian village near the
highway.

❿

*In* March, I got the big envelope from Dartmouth. Everyone in school was excited for me, but when I tried to tell my mother, she was too frantic to listen. I left the envelope on the coffee table, but she didn't express any interest in knowing what was in it. My brother was going to sleep-away camp and I thought that was what her hysteria was about. She kept telling him she didn't know what she was going to do without her man (sic) in the house, but my going away to college never came up. His absence would make him more precious to her, if that was possible; mine would simply mean I didn't exist anymore.

# Chapter 4

Like my mother, Cona had customers, not friends. I don't know if Ellery ever noticed this about his bride. What's the use of having all that wisdom for other people if your own brain's blindfolded by love? Need? Real estate? Whatever you want to call it, Ellery seemed miserable, and what appeared to be a real friendship between Cona and my mother must have made him more so. Especially when he found out what his charming wife was plotting.

Sometime during that spring, Wilkie began to join my mother and Ellery and Cona for drinks and/or dinner without his little girl—Doreen, I think this one was. Cona, my mother announced to me one day, thought Wilkie was "adorable." (Ellery had asked me once whether I'd ever heard Wilkie having a conversation with anyone. I'd laughed and Ellery had said, "Oh," and that was the end of it.) At first, my mother expressed pleased surprise at Ellery's willingness to sit around and relax and drink after dinner. This was clearly Cona's "good" influence on him. And it was important to poor Wilkie, who was depressed. Wilkie thought Doreen was drifting away from him and he didn't even care. My mother said it was because he was going to be fifty in June, and he was feeling bad that he hadn't done anything with his life. She offered to teach him about the Sky's workings, so he could become a more active partner, maybe do some simple bookkeeping, or sales. He gave it a couple of weeks but it was too difficult to wake up and get dressed when you knew there was something you had to do afterward.

My mother was going to be forty in September and said, whenever the occasion arose, that forty wasn't what it had once been for women, especially women of accomplishment. The thing I noticed she was doing that she'd never done before was, after a couple of drinks, she'd turn around the ring on her ring finger so it looked like a wedding band. Worse than that, I'd catch her looking at Wilkie as though he were human. Even lovable. When she'd been trying to get him interested in the Sky, she'd recalled its having been their first home. Now, she began to talk about turning the coffee shop into a real restaurant, with a bar. A place where pals like the four of them could hang out, feel at home. Once, when Wilkie was worrying aloud about money, she joked that they could always turn the storeroom in back of the gallery into a tiny apartment where Wilkie could live with her and Billy. She only made this joke to me, of course. Billy wouldn't have liked it, but why would I mind? It wasn't as though I actually existed, except when it was time in her cycle for that rage whose cause was most often found to be me.

But it became clear that something unusual was going on that even she couldn't imagine had anything to do with me. First, Wilkie disappeared. My mother said neither she nor Cona had any idea of where he was. Then the phone stopped ringing. Not even Cona! Cona stopped answering messages my mother left on the machine, and my mother couldn't find her or Ellery when she drove over to their house. Finally she found a house sitter there who said they'd had to go to New York to see Ellery's parents. But it was too weird, all of them leaving at the same time without a word to my mother. She kept saying something was going on, but she wouldn't speculate about what it might be. Her movements got jerky. She spoke, if at all, through clenched teeth. "Yes. No. Maybe. Leave me alone."

I asked Billy if he happened to know anything about what was troubling her, but he didn't understand the question. It was baseball season. His little

TV set had long since died, and when he wasn't playing down the hill, he was watching the game at a
friend's. He'd gone beyond taking things in his stride
to being this dopey kid who batted away what was
under his nose without even knowing he was doing it.

I left a message on Ellery's machine that he should
please call me at work if he picked up messages and if
he had any idea of what was going on with my mother
and Wilkie and Cona. He didn't call. Later, he said he
didn't know how much my mother suspected and
whether she would get worse if he told me when she
hadn't. She got worse anyway. So jumpy, I was afraid
to be in the room with her. She looked as though
she'd explode if touched, and nothing changed, even
briefly, when she drank. I didn't see her eating. When
she finally found out what was happening, she didn't
tell me—as though I might be part of the conspiracy.

Even before Wilkie's betrayal, my mother didn't
believe in coincidence. If two things happened at the
same time, it was a conspiracy. It wasn't that she
looked for explanations; they were ready for her.
When Ellery tried to explain how something she'd
done had caused something else—let's say, how con-
vincing some painter to move from another gallery to
hers might have incited the other gallery's owner, who
was on the Historical Review Board, to vote against
some proposal beneficial to her—she couldn't accept
this as a matter of emotion, politics, cause and effect,
that if she wanted the other guy's support, she

shouldn't have "stolen" his painter. She'd explain how
she hadn't stolen the painter, he'd been looking for
another gallery, and all she'd done was to point out,
etc. While if a painter left the Sky, it wasn't because
he'd been dissatisfied with his sales or his wall place-
ment or whatever, but because that fucking faggot Rinaldo, who'd been hot to steal the guy for years, must
have brought him to his astrologer, who Rinaldo practically owned outright, he'd sent so many people to
her, and he must have programmed her to tell the
painter it was time for a change. Furthermore, Rinaldo
was a friend of So-and-So, who she'd had a run-in
with years ago and who'd hated her ever since. And so
on.

I have the opposite habit of thought. When Steven,
the boy I'd been dating for a while, invited Laya to the
prom, I didn't think, Whoops, he's heard about Geraldo's turning up at school; I just figured he liked Laya
better. I was in no mood to go to the prom, anyway.
When Geraldo showed up at school again, I didn't
think of a reason beyond his wanting to see me. Or
somebody.

I was with my girlfriends, wishing it were one of my
work afternoons so I wouldn't have to think of another reason not to go home, when he pulled up to the
curb in some flashy car I'd never seen, leaned out of
the window and waved. He looked wondrously beautiful to me, and I wanted to cry.

Laya said, "I think he really thinks you're getting into that car with him."

I said, "I am. There's something we have to talk about." I didn't know it was true.

They looked at me, then at each other. Laya asked if I was sure. I nodded. I'd never talked about Geraldo with any of them. I had the impression they thought he might be responsible for my occasional visible bruise, but then my eye had happened when I wasn't seeing him anymore. They were curious but I think they admired me for not talking. They didn't know how easy it was for me. They'd figured I was having sex with him, but then they'd readmitted me to the Virgins Club without questions.

Laya took me aside. She said, "Maddy, I know you like to be private, but, you know, you don't have to go if you don't want to."

I came as close as I could to a laugh. "Of course I don't, Nutso. He never made me do anything." I kissed her cheek—Laya was a real sweetheart—waved to the others, went to the car and got in. I remember that I was sitting sideways, as the car drove away, and staring at him. I felt as though I loved him. Not exactly him, but someone who looked like him and made love to me the way he had and who'd understood that I needed him right now, however long I'd managed without him.

Someone had told him I'd gotten in to Dartmouth and he had decided to give me another chance to be nice, although he was the only one of everybody who knew me who didn't take it for granted that I would actually go. It didn't occur to him, as crazy as he thought my mother, that she wouldn't have told me what was going on. I thought—I know this sounds ridiculous—*Maybe I won't have to go to Dartmouth, after all.*

He got on the highway, as though toward the house on Cerro Gordo. I didn't talk. He asked how things were, and I just said, "Dunno," because I didn't. My mother might not matter so much if I had Geraldo again. I asked how he was and he shrugged.

"Okay. Missed you."

That made me cry a little.

"Hey, hey," he purred. He pulled over to the side of the highway to kiss me and comfort me, but I couldn't stop weeping. Finally, he said, very softly, as though he were getting me into bed for the first time, "Who's gonna make you feel better if you're way the hell up and gone in Nueva Hampshire?"

It hadn't occurred to me that he knew. Not only did he know, but he didn't want me to go. I stopped weeping. Someone wanted me to stay in Santa Fe. I longed to tell him my mother couldn't wait to be rid of me. I had to remind myself that he was the last person in the world I could tell. It wouldn't serve a purpose, anyway. It wasn't as though I could move in with him.

"Who's at home?" he asked.

I smiled. "You know we're not on Cerro Gordo, anymore?"

He nodded. "I know where you are, Sweetheart. I been keeping track." He was driving with just his left hand, his right arm around me. "Nobody's at the house?"

I said, "Probably. Unless Billy came home."

Then he asked, "Everything's cool with the new owner?"

I started to explain that Wilkie hadn't sold the house, just rented it.

He said, "I meant the stores."

I asked, "What stores?"

"You know," he said. "The shopping center." (He'd always refused to call it the Sky.)

"Same as ever, I guess." But I was getting nervous, or I imagine I wouldn't have added, "I don't know for sure, because my mother's not talking to me this week."

He said, "Mmm. She must be upset."

I moved away, looked at him. "Upset about *what?*" It was a bit of a screech. I was beginning to realize that Geraldo knew more about what was going on with my mother than I did.

He was just realizing it, too. Near Delgado, he pulled over to the side of the road and turned off the car's engine.

"She didn't—You didn't see the paper this morning?"

I shook my head.

"Wilkerson sold his half of the Sky."

My brain capsized. After a while, it began looking for a way to right itself, trying to make sense of what he'd said, or, even better, figure out what he might have gotten wrong. But every time it looked for a flaw, it found confirmation: in Wilkie's disappearance; in the silent telephone; in my mother's raging anguish.

I asked what else the article said.

"Not much. The usual shit. I can find it at the shop later."

"Now . . . Please." There was no way I could think about anything else.

He understood. He drove to the garage and I sat in the car while he fetched the *New Mexican* and brought it to me, with its late flash regarding the major real-estate deal orchestrated by the Cona Barbarian Queens Agency: Wilkie, the headless worm, the snake, the jerk-off jackal, had sold his half of the Sky to a consortium headed by a Japanese-American businessman named Tom Hana, who'd fallen in love with Santa Fe . . . blah blah blah. Mrs. Queens, who was married to the psychiatrist Ellery Queens, with whom she owned a house on Acequia Madre, had worked with Mr. Hana's lawyer, Cyrus Jaffe, to put together this deal. Mr. Wilkerson had gone to California for an extended visit with his family. He was sure he'd return to Santa Fe sometime, but "California is where my roots are, you know."

That son of a bitch Cy Jaffe had had his revenge on this woman who'd stretched out with half the scum that ever floated through Santa Fe and wouldn't do it with him.

Geraldo said, "It's not the end of the world."

I said, "Yes, it is."

He knew it was true and he shut up. He drove back to the house and came in with me. I found Ellery's bead belt in the plastic bag in my closet, cut it into small pieces and threw it in the garbage. Geraldo waited on the sofa, then let me sit with him quietly, holding his hand.

After a while, my mother came in. Geraldo rose from the sofa and greeted her, super-polite. She nodded, filled a glass with tequila and took it to her room.

Geraldo said he had to get back to the shop but he'd call me later, we'd go out for supper. He left, closing the door carefully behind him. Minutes later, she came out for more tequila—in her bra and bikini. I hadn't moved. She didn't look at me or seem to know I was there. She sat at the other end of the sofa, just one cushion between us. But it wasn't as though she were sitting *near* me, more as though I weren't there. She was humming to herself but she was only pretending to feel like humming, just as she was pretending I wasn't there. I was trying to figure out a way to make friends with her when I saw the horrible gash in her left arm that her shirt had covered. It was really awful-looking—deep, dried-blood lines, the first perhaps a quarter of an inch wide, then two thinner ones, running from her wrist to the crook of her arm.

A fearful chill went through me; it was worse than anything she'd ever done to me.

"What happened to your arm?"

She looked at me with an expression suggesting I knew damned well.

After a long time, I said, "I just found out about the Sky."

"Well," she replied, "good for you."

I was accustomed to pushing uphill, and I kept trying. "Have you talked to the people? Can you tell if you'll be able to . . . you know . . ." I trailed off, not only because of her sardonic expression, but because when I looked down from her face, I saw her arm again, and that same ghastly feeling swept through me.

"No," she said, "I don't know. Tell me." She finished her drink, got the tequila bottle, brought it to the sofa, swigging from it along the way.

I'd intended to ask whether she thought she could work with the new people, but I realized it was the wrong question. She'd never worked *with* anybody and didn't want to now, unless it was a piece of Silly Putty like Wilkie. If the stupid bastard had sold twenty-five percent of the Sky instead of fifty, she might have been all right.

I tried to be cute. A bad mistake.

"If you'll tell me what happened to your arm."

"What happened to my arm." She was calm. Away someplace. For a moment, I thought it was going to be okay. I must have not been looking at her eyes until she said it again, and then it was too late. "What happened to my arm. I'll tell you what happened to my arm."

She took my hand. I saw her eyes and stopped breathing; she was speaking, as though in her sleep, to someone in back of a hole in my head.

"Well, the first thing that happened was a messenger came from Mr. Jaffe's office with a letter, and I read the letter. Then I took my Sky mug, and I threw it against the bronze Indian smoking a peace pipe by Alan Allen. Then I picked up a piece of the mug, and I slashed the big Santa Fe sunset by Rusty Soames. Up. Down. Sideways. Then I took another piece of the cup, and I ran it down my arm. Like this." With her left hand, she scratched her long nails down my right arm so deep and hard that there were blood lines along it. "That's what happened to my arm."

I didn't cry but I lost my insides. I don't mean I just soiled my pants. I mean that until then, I think my expectations weren't entirely different from other people's. I carried on in the outside world and assumed, without thinking about it, that I would become an adult and move far enough from my mother to live like other people. Something told me I was going to Dartmouth, though I couldn't quite believe it. Occasionally I worried that before I ever left, she would drive her car off the side of a cliff, perhaps with me in it, but without even knowing she was willing to kill both of us. I knew she liked to hurt me when she was mad, but she'd never done it before without even being mad.

My mother sat there, a dreamy smile on her face. A couple of the lines on my arm were bleeding. The wet, dirty pants I was sitting in might as well have been cement. A minute or an hour or a year later, she raised her free hand toward her face. I was afraid she was going to scratch herself, too, so I grabbed her hand, but she pushed me away as though I were trying to hurt her. Then, all of a sudden, she collapsed into herself and said she wanted a drink.

I said, "I'll get it. I just want to wash myself."

She said, "You stink."

I said, "I know it. That's why I want to wash."

She said, "I want a drink."

I said, "In a minute."

She said, "Now." She stamped her foot.

I poured some tequila into a glass, set it in her right hand.

She drained it and said, sounding like a little girl, "She stinks, doesn't she, José."

"Where's Billy?" I asked.

"Dunno."

"Is he coming home?"

"Dunno."

I double-locked the front door. Then I led her to

her room, where she let me help her off with her brassiere but not her underpants, and cover her with a sheet when she lay down. She asked for some tequila, but she was asleep by the time I brought it. I took a lot of aspirin and showered and washed my underpants, then I cleaned up the living room as well as I could and took the top lock off the front door, so Billy would be able to get in.

○

*B*illy didn't appear to notice but Geraldo knew something was wrong when he came a little later, maybe from the detergent smell in the living room. I told him my mother wasn't feeling good and I wanted to give Billy dinner before we went out, but Billy was so happy to see him, dinner didn't matter for a while. Billy told Geraldo the detailed history of his attempts to salvage the little TV. Geraldo said he knew of an old black-and-white set that might still be around. He'd bring it over, if Billy wanted him to, but it was bigger than the other one and it'd be harder to, Billy knew, not see it. Billy told him my mother had seen the old one, anyway, and she was used to it. Then he polished off a couple of sandwiches and went back to the playground, which he now called the ballpark.

"What's been going on?" Geraldo asked.

I shrugged. "She's too upset about the Sky even to talk about it."

"Why does the place smell like this?"

"Detergent," I said. "I cleaned. Let's just go."

I started to get up, but as I did, he grabbed my hand to hold me back, and he saw the scratches on my arm. He whistled.

I said, too fast, "She didn't do it. I did." I tried to pull back my hand but he held on by the wrist.

"How?"

"She was trying to hurt herself, not me," I said.

He was looking at me, waiting for me to say something that made sense, when the door to my mother's room opened and she came out, very groggy, still in her underpants but with no brassiere on, the gashes on her arm very visible.

I stood up. "Geraldo's here."

She ignored me—us—and sauntered across the room toward the kitchen as though we weren't there. Geraldo staring at her, turned a deep red. Embarrassed, disbelieving and, I suppose, disgusted. In the kitchen, she got a fresh glass of tequila, came back into the living room.

Geraldo stood up. "I'll wait for you outside."

I said, "Maybe we'd better forget about tonight."

He said, "I don't think so. I'll just wait for you outside."

My mother didn't appear to notice when he left. She sat at the dining table, her beautiful breasts settling on its surface as though they were supposed to be there. It crossed my mind that she didn't know *I* was still there. I didn't know what to do.

The question that drove me craziest of all the dumb questions people asked is the one about why I didn't contact a social-service agency. What on earth do they think would have happened if I had? They'd have tried to get our fathers to take us? Both fathers were saner than my mother, but that's not saying either was terribly sane. Or wanted either of us. Would we be put up for adoption like a couple of adorable Indian babies? I was eighteen years old, and Billy wasn't yet twelve, and even if we'd been younger, it wouldn't have been done right, as you know if you've ever dealt with agencies full of well-meaning people. If it was accidentally done right, new regulations would have required them to change it. Take us back. Switch us around. Or let's say, just for the sake of argument, that I'd been adopted by Laya's family, the best and most likely one, and Billy had been taken by one of his friends'. What did they think would have happened then? Would I forget about my mother because I was a few hundred yards down the road? Or a few thousand miles, for that matter? If I couldn't get away from her by killing her, how, for Christ's sake, do they think they would have gotten her out of me alive? And Billy. She wasn't *in* Billy quite the same way, and he barely spent an hour a day in the same room with her, but that doesn't mean she'd have let go of him. Then there's, *They could have gotten her into a program.* That's the line I love. Programs solve everything. Alcoholics Anonymous. They would have cured her. First of all, she didn't think she was an alcoholic, she believed she could cut down or stop anytime she wanted to, so she'd have refused to go. But let's say she did go, and she didn't drink anymore. What, then? Would she be a different person? Not thirsty-angry all the time? She wasn't a drunk when she gave birth to Billy, and that was when she started being horrible to me. I don't think it makes sense to take children from their parents just because they're getting beaten up. Your parents are your parents, and if you don't have them anymore, you just go around looking for them.

She let me lead her back to the bedroom, where I helped her into white pants and a long-sleeved white cotton sweater as she held on to her drink, transferring it according to what I was doing. She didn't want a brassiere, said she was bound up enough, and I didn't argue, of course.

I wasn't thinking about Geraldo; I'd forgotten he was waiting outside. When the doorbell rang, I thought Billy must not have his key. I told her I'd be right back and went to the door. It was Geraldo. I told him he could come in. When he didn't move, I said in a low voice that my mother was dressed. But I was irritated that I had to say it. I would have liked it if he'd just left my mother and me to go out for supper. On the other hand, I still didn't have a driver's license and even if she could walk a few blocks to a restaurant, she probably wouldn't do it.

I told him I was afraid to leave her alone.

He looked at me to see if I meant what that sounded like. I didn't know whether I did. I just knew I was even more afraid than before. Of everything.

I invited her to come with us. She hesitated. She was gripping the sweater sleeve over the nightgown bandage.

I said, "Nothing shows."

She said, "It feels." She looked at me accusingly, as though I'd done it to her, and, at that moment, I felt as though I had.

I said, "I'm sorry. Do you want some aspirin?"

"No," she said. "I'll just have another drink before I go." She stood, a little rockily, made her way through the living room.

Geraldo was watching from just inside the front door. I was very nervous.

She called, "Good evening, Mr. Chávez." Very meek.

He nodded.

"Where're you taking us for dinner?"

"Wherever you want." Stiffly polite.

Somehow, we got her to the car. She was a little sleepy, by this time, but awake enough to know she didn't want to sit in the back. I let her sit in the front with Geraldo while I sat in the back and prayed that nothing terrible would happen. Neither of them would pick where we were going, Geraldo wasn't talking at all, so I chose a new place called the Crock, away from the center of town, thinking it would be just as well if we didn't run into a lot of people she knew. It didn't work, of course. A minute and a half after our drinks arrived, some wiseass came over to ask my mother if she was taking lessons in Japanese. She just looked up at him, her mouth trembling.

Geraldo stood up and suggested the guy try out for the *Late Show*, since he was such a comic. The guy looked as though he'd been hit by a truck—gee-whiz, all he'd wanted to do was make a cute little joke—then skulked off without another word. Geraldo sat down again.

My mother smiled at him sadly. "Who's going to protect me from these assholes when Maddy's halfway around the world in fucking Hanover?"

She probably wanted him to say he'd be there for her, but if there'd ever been a chance he would say it, there was none now. And I was thrown by this first acknowledgment that she knew what was in the big envelope.

I said, "I don't even know if I'm going there."

She said, "Sure you are. You applied, you got in and you're going." She gave the passing waiter her empty glass. There'd be no more trembly mouth tonight. My mother and Billy were both ashamed when they wanted to cry. She smiled. "Right, Geraldo?"

But he wasn't going to get pulled in again. She knew it, so she got worse, though it took a while to notice, the place was so crowded and noisy. Geraldo asked if we wanted to go someplace else to eat but she most emphatically didn't. We all ordered hamburgers. She was on her third drink by the time the food arrived. She had a few bites of her burger, then stood up with her empty glass and began wandering around the room as though she were looking for someone she knew.

Watching her, Geraldo said, "Let's get out of here fast."

I said, "I don't think I can leave her."

He said, "She can get a ride. She does it all the time."

I said, "You don't know what she does all the time."

He shrugged. "Whatever it is, she did it with one of my friends."

I was furious. Furiously ashamed. Too ashamed to stay with him, except that I couldn't just leave my mother. My head felt the way it had before my accident but there was no car, now, that was going to smash away the ache. My mother was near the front of the bar, talking to a couple of men, laughing the high laugh she had sometimes that made me uncomfortable because it had nothing to do with thinking something was funny. I started to get up but Geraldo put his hand on mine to stop me.

"I have to pay the bill."

I shrugged. "So, you stay."

He said, "Cut it out."

I said, "I have to make sure she has a way to get home."

He stared at me for a minute and I thought it was a toss-up whether he was going to walk out on me, but he didn't. When he could see what my mother was doing to me, Geraldo was always wonderful. He paid the bill while I went over to her. I didn't call her *mother*, of course. I just said Geraldo was ready to go and asked if she felt like coming. Or we could meet her later.

"Oh, I dunno," she drawled. "Fellas, this is my friend Maddy. I came with her and another friend."

They were pleased to meet me; one of them was eager for me to join them but I said we were leaving. The other one said it'd be no problem at all to give Anita a lift . . . he rolled his eyes . . . to wherever she wanted to go.

I told Geraldo she was staying and walked out ahead of him.

He stayed with me for the night because I was sleeping so lightly that every time he started to get out of bed, I began to cry. But he left very early in the morning. He didn't want to see my mother.

❍

*A*fter that night I was never not frightened. It wasn't the opposite from the way I'd always lived—when I opened my bedroom door, would I face the lady or the tiger—but it had grown much more intense. My brain was always walking around land mines. The simplest thing was enough to make my mother explode.

I reminded her that she still had her half of the Sky and the Hana people wouldn't be able to do anything without her consent.

"Consent!" she screamed at me as though I were the one threatening her. "Thanks a lot! Just like when I was in school and I needed my mother's consent to go someplace!"

But she didn't hurt me. She knew she wanted something.

The next morning she was up very early and made coffee at home for maybe the third or sixth time in my memory. When I came out of my bedroom, knapsack on, prepared to dash for the school bus, Billy had left already. She told me to sit down, she needed to talk to me. She was wearing a long-sleeved blouse.

I was flustered. I didn't know how late she'd come in, how much sleep she'd had, whether she'd heard Geraldo tiptoe out of my room when it was getting light outside. There was no way I'd make the bus if I didn't leave then, and it was the last week before finals.

I said, "I'm going to miss the bus."

For a moment she just looked angry. Then she said she'd drive me to school in a few minutes—unless only Ellery was allowed to do that. I sat down.

"Chiang Kai-shek wants to take me to lunch next week."

That had to be Tom Hana. I would have thought it a good sign that he wanted to have lunch with her, except for the expression on her face. I waited.

"He's bought a house. One of the high spots on Tano Road. Overlooking Tesuque. They can see Colorado when it's clear." She sounded certain he'd be watching her with a spyglass from that spot. "He's not going to be an absent partner. He's really going to be here."

I pointed out that a lot of rich people who owned big houses just spent a few weeks of the year in them.

She said, "It's a fucking palace."

"You think he'll be a nuisance?" I asked cautiously.

"He is already. I don't have help. I can't afford to close up the gallery and waste a lot of time with him."

I said, "You mean lunch? You can do it on Tuesday, when you're closed."

She said, "Oh, my God, that's brilliant!"

I got increasingly uneasy as she did a riff on my brilliance, on how she'd ever manage without me, and so on. It was clear that she wanted something.

She said, "I don't know what's going to happen. I need somebody there I can trust."

I waited.

"I need you more than Sheila does. I need you to work at the gallery."

So, that was it. I felt as though she'd slipped a plastic bag over my head. I stood up, brushed an arm across my face as though it were a simple cobweb instead of a sticky plastic bag trying to smother me. She began to cry.

"Please don't cry," I begged. "Just let me think for a minute."

"Never mind!" she yelled. "If you have to think, I don't want you!"

Instantly, I calmed down. I told her that was silly. It was my last week of high school, and I was supposed to begin at Sheila's full-time. I wanted to help but I needed to figure things out.

She said, her voice the little-girl one again, "I don't know what's going to happen, and I can trust you. I can't trust just any kid I hire off the street who doesn't know the merchandise, or the people in the other shops. Who doesn't . . . you know."

I knew.

●

*K*eith called me that week to congratulate me; Ellery had told him about my getting into Dartmouth. Keith just said his first name, as though I knew him, but it took me a moment to remember who he was. He told me he was coming down to Santa Fe for a couple of days, then going to visit his mother in New York. I was as polite as I could be, but it felt as though some Martian had touched earth in New Mexico and, thinking I was somebody important, was advising me of his plans to see the rest of the States.

I didn't think about him again until he showed up at the prison.

◑

*T*here was no point in telling Geraldo about quitting Sheila's until I'd done it. He would refuse to believe I had to. Sheila was another matter. I had dreams in which I was wearing the nightgown she'd given me but it was all cut up and bloody because I'd had to use it to bandage my mother's arm. Sheila had no children of her own and she was nice to all the girls unless they were real fuckups, though she liked some of us more than others and trusted me the most. I worked the cash register when she wasn't there. We were almost in July, the height of the season, and I knew she'd be horrendously upset when I told her . . . *if* I told her. I made up my mind to wait until after my mother's lunch with Mr. Hana.

◑

*T*he following Tuesday she woke up at about eleven-thirty and said, "Lunch is at one," as though it were about me. I was studying for my history final the following day, but I didn't think I had to mention that. Then she said she wanted me to go with her.

At first, I thought I hadn't heard her correctly. I asked where she wanted me to go.

She said, "Bolero. At one."

I asked, "Why?"

She said, as though it were an answer to my question, "Ho Chi Minh is bringing his wife. They paid two million bucks for that house."

I said, "Fine. If you ever decide to sell your half of the Sky, they can pay a good price."

She said, "That's not funny."

I said, "I meant, if you—"

She said, "I don't want to hear it." She went into the kitchen and poured herself a drink—as though I'd forced her to start early. But when she came back, she was apologetic. "Don't pay attention to me. I'm as nervous as hell about talking to these idiots. I just need someone there with me. For balance. I suppose I should've taken a fast course in Japanese."

I didn't bother to tell her Ho Chi Minh was Vietnamese, any more than I'd told her that Chiang Kai-shek was Chinese. I just asked if they were Japanese-American or Japanese-Japanese. She waved away the question. She thought he'd been born in California; the wife was a Japanese wife, no matter where she was born. Maybe if HoJo wanted to talk business, I could keep the wife busy. Maybe I could ask if binding up your feet had any effect on the growth of your brain. She began to get carried away with anti-Japanese stuff, so I just interrupted to say I'd go with her. There was no point in arguing; if she got hysterical, I wouldn't be able to work, anyway.

◐

*F*or the lunch, we dressed nicely in light cottons, she in her white pants, me in a skirt, both of us in cotton sweaters that would be okay outside or in air-conditioning. She put on too much makeup, and when I said she didn't need that much, she announced, not as though it were a joke, that soon she'd be forty and she'd use even more, and then more every year after that. She tossed off a fast drink before putting on a redder lipstick than I'd ever seen her wear.

Walking to Bolero, we giggled like best friends, wondered whether we were dressed well enough for the fanciest restaurant in town. But when my mother gave the maître d' Tom Hana's name, we were treated with a deference beyond his first polite greeting, and escorted to the nicest four in the room, next to the big front window.

A large blond woman sat in the seat that commanded the best view of the big room. The host's seat. She wasn't especially pretty, but she was a real blond. A huge gold cross on a heavy gold chain rested on her white linen dress, between her breasts. There was a bottle of designer water in front of her on the table.

Confused, my mother turned to question the maître d' just as the blond woman said, "You must be Anita Stern. I'm Tom's wife, Hope Smith. Please sit down."

My mother had been thrown too far to answer. This woman wasn't just self-possessed, she acted as if she also owned everything else in sight.

I said, "I'm Madeleine Stern, and this is my mother, Anita Stern."

She smiled, beckoned us to the seats on either side of her, said, "How nice that you were able to join us, Madeleine."

My mother, still in shock, was just staring at the gold cross, so I explained that I'd been at another gallery, but I would be working at the Sky with her all summer, before I went off to college. I hadn't been certain until that moment that I would be.

"How lovely for your mother," Hope Smith said. "Where are you going?" I think she saw the effect she'd had on my mother, which only made everything worse.

I said, "Dartmouth."

"My goodness," she said. "You must be an excellent student."

"My father teaches there." I was showing off our credentials, but then I cursed myself lest she believe it was the only reason I'd been accepted. My mother wasn't even listening.

The maître d' returned, followed by a slender Japanese businessman in a beige linen suit. My first impression was that he was about half his wife's size. (I turned out to be wrong; he was close to two thirds.) By this time, my mother was sufficiently recovered to say, when his wife introduced us, that she was pleased to meet him. He said we needed some champagne to celebrate this new partnership, and asked the waiter for a bottle of Moët & Chandon.

The white wine he ordered during the meal was California, as was the red. As was Tom Hana. Very California, very breezy, but extraordinarily deferential to his wife. He had an ex-wife who'd gone to live with her parents in Kyoto, taking their children with her. He referred to her in passing, as he referred to Hope's having swum in the Olympics—as though there were no way in the world we didn't already know.

Each time my mother seemed almost to get back herself, something was said that knocked her off balance.

Tom Hana raised his glass of champagne to propose a smiling toast, "To the partners!"

I didn't know why it sounded odd until I realized he was toasting two *other* people, my mother and his wife.

And it became increasingly clear, as we proceeded through lunch, that he didn't expect to share in the everyday operations of the Sky, that he'd bought it for Hope to play with. My mother tried to keep up a front but she was pulling at the crewneck of her sweater, as though it were a turtleneck—or a noose tightening around her. Then, as our main courses were being set before us, she summoned the politesse to ask if they had any questions about the Sky, and Hope replied that they had the figures, but of course there'd be all sorts of decisions of taste, decoration, merchandise and so on.

My mother startled in a way that reminded me of Belly when he was an infant in the car bed. I'd be sitting on the floor, just watching him sleep, not,—I repeat, *not*—touching him, and it was as though a little shock had gone through his body, someone had switched his dream on him, jolted him into a different world. She looked at me; I tried to smile reassuringly, but whatever she saw didn't help at all. She looked at Tom, but he was looking at Hope. She looked at Hope, but then her eyes went instantly down to the cross. Hope had been playing with the cross, feeling it, fondling it, whenever that hand wasn't holding her fork. It wasn't an ordinary gold cross; there were slender golden branches twining around its center in a way that made them seem like arms.

Hope smiled at my mother. "I see you're admiring my crucifix."

My mother looked up at her wonderingly.

"It was made for me by Walter Robles, a superb

goldsmith who goes to our church in Los Angeles." She smiled again. "We don't go to the one in Beverly Hills."

"Oh?"

Hope shook her head emphatically. "Too many, you know . . . movie types."

"You don't say."

She was doing better. If she stayed sober enough to hold up her end of a conversation, we'd be all right.

Hope Smith was radiant. "I'm hoping to lure Walter to Santa Fe, once we have room for him in the Sky."

My mother stared at her as though she'd said she wanted to raze the whole place to make space for an office building. I tried to find her leg under the table so I could squeeze it, get her to say something, anything, but I couldn't reach it without leaning in too far.

"Well," Hana said jovially, "I have a meeting. I'm afraid I don't even have time for coffee. Should we all adjourn? Or should I leave you girls here to talk?"

"I think you might as well leave us, Tom," his wife said. "Don't you think so, Anita?"

My mother nodded. She was licking her lips as though they were very dry. The wine was gone. She drank some water. Thinking to save her, to get her out of there, I said I had finals the next day and I really had to get home.

"Why don't you just go along, Honey, and your mother and I will stay here and talk."

It had a condescending tone I wasn't accustomed to. As though I were some little kid my mother had dragged along because she couldn't find a sitter. It made me feel stubborn. I said it was okay, I'd stay. From that moment on, Hope didn't look at me or speak to me, except to ask if I drank coffee when the waiter came for our dessert orders. As though she thought I'd want milk. All this made me even more certain that I shouldn't leave my mother alone with her, but, in fact, *I* was the one who couldn't be left alone with her, because Pope Hope seems to have decided already that contrary to anything she had heard, my mother was a perfectly amiable human being, and I was a pain in the ass.

We were there long past the time when everyone else had gone. The host was not about to suggest that Hope leave before she was ready. At one point, she stood to go to the bathroom. I watched her in amazement. I had realized she was a large person, but her butt dwarfed the rest of her; it might have belonged to somebody three times her size. It was significant that with a rear end that size, she didn't worry about wearing a white dress; any part of her was beautiful because it was hers.

I said to my mother, "That's a lethal weapon she has there. Imagine if she sat on you."

My mother didn't laugh. She just stared at me. In a

trance. I didn't understand, yet, what was happening, so I simply told her that if she was okay, I'd go home.

She nodded.

I gave her a peck on the cheek, collected my stuff, and left the restaurant before I had to say goodbye to Hope. Hope the Pope. Pope Hope. My mother was going to love that.

Once in the apartment, though, I didn't even open a book. I felt *deeply* unsettled. I'd told Geraldo I had to study and he shouldn't even call, but now I needed badly to be with him. I started to phone the garage but then decided to walk there, instead. I meant to be casual, just ask him to come over after work. But when I reached there and he saw me and started across the street, I suddenly realized I couldn't call her Pope Hope in front of Geraldo, and for some reason that made me cry.

Geraldo asked what was wrong, why wasn't I home, studying?

I said, "I had to go to lunch with my mother and the new owner."

"So?"

"And his wife."

He nodded.

"She's the one who'll be in charge. With my mother, I mean. She's a beast. I don't know how . . ."

He was waiting. Finally, he asked if she and my mother had argued. I shook my head, said, "Not yet," but I didn't know what else to say, in view of the way he was about my mother. Two men were watching us from the garage. He signaled to them to go back in.

"Look," he said, "I get out in maybe two hours. Should I come over?"

I nodded. I was embarrassed that I needed him when I'd made such a big deal about studying, but there it was. He said he had the TV set for Billy and we agreed he should bring it but leave it in the car until we saw what was going on with my mother. He smoothed back my hair, gave me a kiss on the cheek, went back across the street and into the garage. I watched him, feeling like a deflated balloon. I forced myself to walk a block or so away from the garage, just so nobody in there would see me, but I felt as though I'd never get home. I was on a strange road with no signs. I finally made my feet go in the right direction by reminding myself that my mother was probably home.

But when I got there, the house was empty. I stretched out on the sofa with my American-history textbook and began to think of how I would tell Sheila that I was leaving. Then I fell asleep. I dreamed that we were in the house on Cerro Gordo. Three of us, but I couldn't identify the other two. It was dark outside and there were animals running around. Someone was telling me I had to go to school and I protested because there weren't just dogs and cats, there were lions and cougars, and I was afraid of getting eaten alive. I might have been thrashing around in my sleep.

When I awakened, my mother was on the other sofa with her José, eyeing me in a strange way. Not exactly argumentative. Besides, I couldn't think of what she might want to fight about. Then I remembered the lunch. And Pope Hope. That would be enough reason for her to be wound up alarm-clock tight.

Billy was at the dining table, eating a sandwich, reading a comic.

My mother said, "We picked up Billy at school and Hope took us to see the house."

I smiled, complicitous. "Oh? A visit to the Vatican with Pope Hope?" And waited for a loud laugh, an acknowledgment that I'd come up with a really good name.

She said, "That's not very funny. Hope's deeply religious, you know. You wouldn't want to say it accidentally and—"

I stood up, dropping my history book. "I'm not the one who says things accidentally."

For a moment she froze, and I half-expected her drink or some magazine to come flying at me, but then she became supercomposed. "We need to talk."

I sat down again. She made herself another drink, returned to the sofa. I assumed she was waiting for questions. My assumptions were seldom correct, after Pope Hope entered our lives.

"What was the house like?" I finally asked.

Billy said, "It's unbelievable, Maddy. A double tennis court and two pools, indoors and outdoors. She said they'll teach me to play tennis, and I can come swim any time, long as somebody's watching me."

I smiled. "You hardly have to go to camp." Two of his best friends were going to the same camp.

"I know it. But Mom paid already, and she says . . . Anyhow, it'll be there when I get back."

My mother smiled. "It's like being in a museum, only comfortable. Huge. Everything's gorgeous, very low-key. All the furniture. White, but not crappy, like this. White linen or something. It must get cleaned every other day. The rugs are unbelievable. Navajo. Huge. They must've cost twenty thousand apiece. She's got the best collection of Pueblo pottery I've seen outside of the museum. And baskets. Gorgeous." She paused. The air was heavy. "But the most extraordinary collection, you'd have to see it to believe it . . . There's a room that's like a chapel. The feeling, I mean."

Here it was, but what was it?

"She's had the niches made all around the walls, and there's a collection of *relicarios* . . . *nichos* . . . and of course the sculptures. The saints. Jesus. Mary. The holy family. It's the best of that stuff I've ever seen, and she's got much more, put away. She's got a great eye. And the money, of course."

I waited. Her whole body was insisting that she was being casual.

"Did you talk about the Sky?" I finally asked.

"Mm. She wants to turn part of the gallery . . . She says there's hardly anyone selling real quality devotional items. She wants to use part of the gallery to . . . you know . . . sell them."

"No."

"Maybe when one of the leases is up, we'll take over another store. For that. Or for the gallery."

I said, "Jesus Christ."

My mother said, "She's a very good person, Maddy."

I said, "I don't believe it."

My mother said, "She's really religious. She's not just putting it on."

"So, let her buy a church."

My mother started to say something, stopped herself. I thought she was just being careful because I hadn't told Sheila, yet, that I was leaving.

"You really didn't like her, did you," my mother said in a sort of wondering tone, as though it were beyond belief that someone could fail to appreciate this magnificent human being. I waited. I'd been thrown back into my dreamworld, where people weren't who you thought they were and you didn't know why they did anything.

She sighed a distinctly theatrical sigh. "Well, sometimes people just don't have the right chemistry."

There it was again. It wasn't so much that I was in a dream as that *she* was and didn't know it. Her worst fears had been realized, and she didn't seem to know it, yet. Could she really believe that she and Pope Hope had the right chemistry? She sounded tolerant of stuff she'd hated all her life. Really tolerant, as opposed to trying to get along. I was at a loss, but she needed support now, even more than before, and I had to be patient.

"I think she's very special," my mother said. "But if you don't . . ." She shrugged. "Maybe it'll be best for you to stay with Sheila, after all."

I was jolted to some other place. I stared at her, as though from a great distance.

She smiled sweetly. "I know you must be relieved. Sheila would've hit the roof."

She was serious. She looked down into her drink, as though for further directions. I couldn't understand how this had happened. Nor could I be purely happy about it. Something about my life had been decided between Pope Hope and my mother, without consultation with me. I'd been erased.

I asked, "Who'll work in the gallery with you?"

She smiled that same beatific smile, got up in a slow, floaty way to pour some more tequila.

"We figured it all out. Hope *wants* to spend a lot of time there, really get to know it. Get a feel for the traffic, the kinds of customers, and so on. When she can't be there, she's got a Japanese girl staying with her. A Californian. No money. She's going to Harvard, Tom went to Harvard, and she's staying with Tom and Hope until the fall term begins, baby-sitting and so on. She'll work at the gallery whenever we need her. We can pay her minimum wage, because she gets room and board from the Hanas. She's perfectly lovely. Carolee. I met her and the two babies Tom and Hope have together. Twins. A boy and a girl. Two years old. They're adorable. They look Japanese, but Hope doesn't seem to mind."

Wisecracks were way beyond me.

"There's a regular nursemaid for the children. It's all too perfect." My mother settled back onto the sofa in a pose intended to convey her relief and satisfaction at the way the world was spinning. I couldn't tell how much of her brain bought what she was saying. Whether she thought she was serious when she said it was perfect.

"It sounds as though they're really moving in on you."

My mother nodded vigorously. "And I'm glad of it."

I didn't say anything.

"You know, I'll be forty years old in September, Maddy."

She never mentioned it without saying it wasn't going to make any difference in her life. Forty was nothing, these days. And so on.

"I've been working hard for a long time. I can use some real help."

Again, that smile. She was enjoying the fact that for once she was getting along with a female who didn't like me, and vice versa. I suppose it was part of Hope's plan to get full control of the Sky that she separated me from my mother and convinced my mother that they were best friends. She did quite a job, and, of course, my poor mother needed to think it was real. Her whole life was tied up in that place. She didn't believe she had options.

My brother, the little genius of timing, said, "Geraldo's trying to get me another TV. So I can see the games."

"Fine, fine," my mother said. "The last one didn't bother me, this one won't, either."

He grinned at me. I didn't grin back.

I said, "Geraldo'll be here later. I don't seem to be able to study."

She said, "Geraldo won't bother me. I have work to do."

Nothing bothered her. No nasty jokes about Mr. Cojones' being back in my life.

Billy went out to see if anybody was at the playground, and my mother went to her room. She came out with papers that she set on the dining table in a way that conveyed seriousness. I just sat and watched as she got her pocketbook, took out a package of paper and some markers.

"We should have a copying machine," she announced.

"What for?" I asked, astonished.

"Oh, come on," she said, impatient if benign. "I don't want to walk to a store every time I need a copy."

I had no idea how to reply. Fortunately, Geraldo rang the doorbell at that moment. I opened the door and he came in, followed by Billy. I told him, straight-faced, that my mother thought it was wonderful he'd been able to find Billy another TV, and he, straight-faced, led Billy back to the car to get it. I sat on a chair watching my mother, and waited. It was graph paper in the package. She opened it, kept fussing with things, as though she didn't want to work while I was there. Nor did she move the tequila bottle and salt closer, though her glass was empty. Geraldo and Billy came in with the television set, which was much bigger than the old one, and carried it into Billy's room. Billy said he could hook it up himself, but then he came out and said there wasn't going to be room for the record player, anymore.

My mother said, "Put it out here, Sweetie. In the cabinet."

Billy and I looked at each other in astonishment, but then he quickly looked back to her.

He said, "I'll tape your records for you, so you can play the stuff whenever you feel like it."

"Fine," my mother said gaily. "Just don't talk to me, now, because I have to figure things out."

In the car, Geraldo wanted to know why my mother was in such a good mood. I said I guessed that was it, she was just in a good mood. But he took me to a tavern south of Santa Fe that I didn't know, and I let him talk me into having a beer before I ate, and I found myself talking about Pope Hope.

He wanted to know, if my mother got along with her, what was the problem?

I said, "First of all, it can't last."

He said, "So?"

"So, what do you think'll happen when it ends?"

He asked why I should worry about it now, which made me so mad I started to get to my feet and walk out—just the way my mother had when we were all together. But he came around to my side of the booth and sat down, wedging me in. I was still angry, but I knew I had no good reason, and besides, I was aroused.

He smiled, leaned forward to kiss my lips very lightly.

"Let's have some supper and get out of here."

It worked for as long as it worked. I had another beer with my food and I was high enough to have put Pope Hope at a distance before we left. He asked if my mother was still at the apartment. I said no, because I wanted to go back there, but I thought she probably was. She'd looked settled in. I couldn't remember seeing her look that way, drunk or sober.

When we got there, she was still at the table, but her head was resting on it and she was snoring. One clenched hand rested on the table, the other was at her neck—the struggle with the noose, again. Papers were spread out on the table, except for a few that had been crumpled and thrown on the floor. I looked at the ones on the table, first.

On the graph paper, my mother had done several outlines of the Sky, one showing the shops as they were, except that Wilkie's was now called the Sky Coffee Shop; another with the jewelry store turned into a place she'd labeled Santos de Santa Fe—Santos y Retablos. She was losing no time trying to please her new friend. On yet another sheet of paper were the names of each store; the volumes they'd done for the past two years; the dates when their leases were up.

Geraldo came up behind me as I was standing over her, trying to figure out if I could get her to bed without waking her all the way. He kissed my neck, hugged me, fondled my breasts, played with my nipples, made me terribly excited. I held on to him tightly, torn between trying to do something about my mother and just going into the bedroom with him.

Geraldo had a *weight* to balance my mother's. Very few people I've ever known have had that. More inside prison than out of it. Some of the guards, just because they were so strong. Or had weapons. But there were women who were that way without weapons. There was my friend Lucille, who'd been a big drug dealer. There was a quiet, dangerous thing in her that didn't need threats or weapons. She would kill you if she had to. That sounds funny, in view of what's happened, but I don't really see myself the same way. I see myself as having killed my mother out of weakness, not strength.

Anyway, Geraldo led me to my bedroom and we made love for the first time in a very long time. I was almost unbearably excited, cried when I came. Not just a little snuffling. Everything in me let go. I cried and I moaned and I heaved with him and clung to him as though I were falling through space and he was the only solid object to stop me. Then I fell asleep. No dreams. I awakened because Billy was knocking on my door.

He called, "Mom needs us to help her."

I said, "Geraldo's here. We tried to move her, but she was out too . . . She didn't want to." And then I was embarrassed because I'd told a sort of lie in front of Geraldo.

We got dressed and went out but Billy was uneasy with Geraldo in a way I'd never seen. He let Geraldo put an arm around my mother under her arms to get her up from the chair. He put an arm around her waist and together they walked her into her bedroom. But then he mumbled something and practically ran into his own room.

Geraldo said that when he'd last been with me, Billy hadn't exactly known what we were doing, but now he was old enough to not like anybody messing with his sister.

I laughed. "That's silly. He likes you more than he likes me."

Geraldo shook his head. "He talks to me more. It's not the same."

I didn't believe him, but in the next few days, I began to think he must be right. Billy wouldn't stay in a room with the two of us and he was distant, or at least awkward, when he was alone with me. I got a kick out of the *idea* that he was jealous of Geraldo. In theory it was adorable. But he was the one in the house who'd talked to me as though I were human, and I couldn't enjoy his avoiding me.

It was a relief when my mother finally drove him to camp. (One of the other mothers took his two friends, but my mother wanted to drive Billy herself, and he let her.) That night she wept that she didn't think she could make it, having her baby away for two months.

When I asked, "Make *what?*"—I was the one, after all, whom she'd thought she needed help from—she looked at me as though I'd set a trap.

She said I wouldn't understand if I didn't have a son.

"*M*y mother's crying about Billy going away," I said to Geraldo. "She misses him already."

He said, "Don't worry about it."

Nothing about my mother touched him because he cared for me and he thought she was purely my enemy.

"She says I don't understand because I don't have a son."

We were in the car. I don't remember where we were supposed to be going. He opened his window, spat out, then glanced at me guiltily—as though he'd spat on my mother.

He said, "My mother misses my sister if she doesn't see her every Sunday. She talks to her on the phone practically every day."

"Is that true?" I asked.

"Sure," he said. "You think women only love their sons?"

It was more or less what I did think, although in my friends' houses, I saw the kids being treated in a manner less skewed than in ours.

I said, "I don't want to have a son *or* a daughter."

He said, "You will."

I said, "No, I won't."

He said, "Don't say that."

I asked, "Why not?"

"It's bad luck," he said. "And when you have one, you'll feel different."

I said, "I'm not going to have one."

He said, "You're not supposed to take the pill for a long time."

I said, "I never took the pill."

After a while, he began to laugh. "You're not kidding, are you."

"No. Why would I kid?"

"All this time, you never been doing anything to not get pregnant, and you not Catholic?"

"That's right."

He whistled. He wasn't at all angry, he was getting a kick out of it. "*Querida*, you're whacked!"

I wasn't deeply offended because he'd used the affectionate word, but I didn't like it, either.

"Well," I said irritably, "the fact is, I've never used anything and I've never gotten pregnant, have I! And if I did, I'd take care of it, so you wouldn't have to worry."

"I'm not worried, *Querida*. You have my baby, I'll marry you in a minute!"

I was startled, then upset. We'd never talked about marriage. I never thought that far ahead, and it hadn't occurred to me that he did. I didn't know what to say and so I didn't say anything, but the feeling in the car changed. We drove some distance in silence. Then, after a while, he pulled over to the side of the road and turned to me.

"Maybe you think a Spanish guy is just good for fucking?"

I said, "You know that's not what I think."

He said, "What, then?"

"I don't even know what you're asking me," I said, getting frightened that he'd leave me again. I couldn't bear that, not right then, when I had nobody else. My girlfriends were as nice as ever, when I saw them, but when they weren't discussing boyfriends or clothes and makeup, they talked about Albuquerque; the assumption that I was going to Hanover had already created a gulf between us. I had *no one.* "I don't want to get married. I swear to you, I never think about marrying *anyone.* I just want to go to school. I mean, I don't even want to go to school, especially, but I need to get away from . . . You know."

He thought he did, and he softened.

I put my hand on his arm, which felt wonderfully warm, for all the air-conditioning.

I said, "I would love it if you came with me."

He turned to look at me. He wanted to see if I meant it, and he could tell that I did.

"You know I can't do that. My job's here. Everything. It would be different if we were married."

"I don't know if it would be different in a good way." I heard my voice quivering. That was fine.

He said, "You don't know what anything is until you get there."

I said, "I won't believe I'm getting out of here alive until I do it."

He said, in a very low voice, "Mother of God."

I wanted to make a joke about where the Mother of

God was when I needed her, but I never made jokes like that with Geraldo.

When we'd driven back to the house, I asked if he felt like coming in. He wanted to know if my mother was still there. I said I couldn't tell, though I was pretty sure she was.

"When you're married, *Querida*," he said, "you never have to worry about who's home."

I didn't really understand what he was telling me. It was outside of my understanding that the male in a couple, for whatever reason, should be the one determined to marry.

# Chapter 5

At the end of July, my mother went to Billy's camp for visiting day. When she came back, she babbled endlessly about how he'd grown at least three inches and looked like a movie star. When she wasn't raving on about Billy, she talked about Pope Hope. It was as though I were living in that house with the three of them. At one point, trying to get her off Hope, I asked whether the owner of our house was going to renew our lease or whether we had to find another place. She said I'd have no finding to do because I'd be gone.

My working hours were supposed to be from two to ten, but I began staying to lock up for Sheila on nights when Geraldo hadn't come for me by ten. I was the only one she trusted to do it. Afterward, walking home, I would try to get my brain into a place where it could deal with my mother. She had entered her terminally crazy stage and I was too occupied with her to think about what Geraldo was doing when I didn't see him.

She might or might not be at the house when I got there. She might or might not be drunk already, might nod at me, might ignore me, might want to tell me the current status of "our"—hers and Hopey's—plans. Someone observing might have believed she wanted my opinion, but she didn't. Any reaction or suggestion was brushed off with a remark about how *I, she* or *we,* most often the last of those, had already thought of it and it wouldn't work. Or it wouldn't make any difference. She carried the rolled-up plans around with her, including to her bedroom at night. The phone rang for her or didn't, according to whether Tom was out of town and "Hopey can work as much as she wants to," or he was home and had to be catered to by "Poor Hopey." (I'm not making this up.) Once I told her she made this big, fat, rich broad with a bunch of servants sound like an orphaned papoose. She stared at me for a long time, then said, calmly, "Maybe you can find a class that teaches you to have some human feeling, while you're at Dartmouth," and went on, as though she hadn't wasted me, to detail the difficulties she and Poor Hope were having, getting the architect or designer to understand what they had in mind. "We finally had to make detailed sketches, they just couldn't get it. Hope says I draw better plans than either of them."

When I told her I'd like to see the plans, she said they were in the bedroom—as though that were an answer.

On this night, she came home even later than I did, and, doing an unconvincing imitation of a herald triumphant, announced they'd finally settled on their plan. She was exhausted. Half-plastered. Tom was around, so she and Hope hadn't even been able to have a fast one before Hope "had to go home." (Increasingly, Tom had appeared to be in the way of her and Hopey's plans.) Would I join her in a celebratory drink? I said I would; she was edgy-high and it seemed better not to give her an excuse to go over the edge. As she prepared proper margaritas, she hummed one of her tunes. And when she carried over the drinks and her bag, she also brought the plans. She sat right next to me and said, in a way that might have sounded happy to someone brain-deaf, that it was all settled.

"Next Monday we do the work. We won't lose more than a couple of days. Maybe not that, unless it's damp and the plaster doesn't dry."

I sipped at my drink so that when she asked if I wanted another, I wouldn't have to point to a full glass.

"Okay," she announced, "here they are. The last

two plans. See if you can guess which one . . ." She unrolled two large sheets of graph paper, securing them on the coffee table with her bag, her glass, my glass, the ashtray. I had to look at them for a while before I understood what I was seeing.

In the first drawing, one of the narrow end walls had been divided in three, with some sort of frame around the entire wall. Each section had niches and shelves appropriate for religious relics. In the second plan, the long back wall, up to the corner where there was a narrow entrance to the storage room, was full of niches and shelves and the pictures were confined to the small side walls. The cash register was beside the front door.

I knew which plan would make my mother crazy if her brain were not occupied by some lunatic acolyte of Pope Hope's, but as things were, I didn't know what to say. She didn't speak, but watched me, as though from a great distance, with a radiantly false smile that remained fixed as she took some more tequila and came back to sit next to me.

I said, "They're very different."

She agreed, pointed to the short-wall drawing, holding down the corner that had curled up when she took her glass.

"This one's too much like a church. A little much for a gallery, we decided."

I wasn't certain what she'd convinced herself of, so I waited.

She picked up the short-wall drawing, rolled it up, happily sent it sailing across the living room.

"And . . . here's the one we're going with! It'll make a spectacular entrance. Most of the pieces are small. People'll have to come in to see them, not just look from outside."

She appeared to be letting her gallery be annihilated as thoroughly as she had been in this new friendship. A gallery that sold paintings and statues would become one that sold religious art and a few paintings. I warned myself to keep my mouth shut. But when she turned to me, a sort of blind-ecstatic smile on her face, like somebody in the terminal stages of cancer who's just been to Lourdes and thinks she was cured, and asked what I thought, I had to say *something*.

I kept my eyes on the drawing and tried to look casual, unchallenging, as I asked, "Where will the big paintings go?"

I could feel her turn to stone beside me. She finished her drink but then she choked on it and began coughing. When she couldn't stop coughing, I took the glass with one hand and tried to pat her back with the other, but she shoved me away and stood up, began circling the living room, waving one arm, as though she were casting a spell to chase away the choking. I knew she wouldn't take water, so I refilled her glass with tequila and offered it to her. She knocked it out of my hand. I vowed that I wasn't going to clean it up. Soon I was going to be two thousand miles away; she'd have to get used to cleaning up her own messes.

When she could speak, she said, "There's plenty of room on the end walls."

"Mmm." I was thinking of a painting she'd shown the previous summer, done by a hippie-would-be-Indian named Marilyn Brownbread. Marilyn had talent, but she was as dumb as her chosen name suggested. In the style of Frederic Remington, she had portrayed a battle for the center of Santa Fe between the hippie-Indians and the Spanish. In the background, the rich WASPs they should have been united against sat on the veranda of a colonial mansion, drinking mint juleps and watching as though the action were on television. The title of the painting was *Friends Acting Like Enemies.* It was four feet high, and perhaps ten feet wide. My mother had priced it at fifteen thousand dollars, saying she'd reduce it to ten the following week. But the first Texas divorcée who'd walked into the gallery with her decorator had snapped it up; it was just the right size and shape for her new living room. After the check cleared, my mother gave her Marilyn's written explanation of what the picture was about, but the woman couldn't have cared less; the size and the colors were perfect.

The long back wall was where my mother had always hung paintings that were so big they would have filled either short one.

"What's the shrug about?" my mother asked.

There was a menacing tone to her voice, so I didn't answer. But she wouldn't let it go. She was determined to make me say what she was thinking.

I said, trying to sound matter-of-fact, "If it were up to me, I'd put that stuff on the short wall and leave the long one—"

"Well, it isn't up to you!" she shouted. She was *savage*.

I shrugged. "That's why I wasn't going to—"

"You weren't going to do anything but sit there and make faces at me!"

Where was Geraldo? Suddenly it felt ominous that I was seeing less of him since our conversation about babies. I stood up. I hadn't been making faces before, not knowingly, at least, but now, between being puzzled about making faces (my mother was the only person who ever claimed I did that) and feeling uneasy about Geraldo, I must have made a face even as I told her I wasn't aware of doing any such thing. She leaped at me like a cougar, claws out, aiming at my face. I met her with my own hands, gripped her wrists, screamed at her that *I* wasn't the one she should be mad at, *I* wasn't the one who was wrecking the Sky, the witch who owned half was doing it, and why was she letting her? This only gave her the energy to knock me down to the floor, and she fell with me, on top of me, so that her whole body was keeping me down, her hands holding my wrists, her knees squeezing my sides. When she could get the leverage, she kicked me in the legs. I think I liked being under her because I could fight hard without doing much damage. But suddenly she stopped. I remember she had my hair pinned under one of my hands and it was hurting so much as it pulled that I screamed, and then, suddenly, her weight on my hair lightened so that it didn't hurt as much. She let go of me and I stopped screaming.

After a moment, she rolled off me, slowly pulled herself up to her knees. She looked very tired. Old. The way she had after Lion died. All the energy went out of me, too. For a long time, she just knelt there. Then she sat back and moved to beside me on the floor and began to cry. I sat up, put a hand on her white cotton pants leg, but I had no idea of what to say.

After a long time, my mother said, "She's not a bad person, Maddy. She's just . . . very sure. She's always sure she's right."

I said, "That's bad."

She smiled. Her eyes were still brimming. "I wish I could be that way."

I tried to smile back. I'd thought of her as very much that way, before Pope Hope.

Finally, picking each word with the utmost caution, I said, "What I don't understand is, you still have equal say, don't you? Don't you still have fifty percent?"

She shrugged. "It doesn't matter. They can buy me and sell me."

"Not unless you want them to."

"It changes everything. You don't know." She went to get herself some tequila, came back to sit facing me, cross-legged, on the floor. I didn't move or speak. Finally, she said, "A few weeks ago, after the contractor was there, and we had the estimates, I asked if maybe we should wait until Alma's lease came up next year and set up the santos, all that crap, in there without losing the . . . you know." Her voice was quivering.

I smiled to acknowledge that I did know, and that I also knew she hadn't spoken to Pope Hope that way.

"D'y'know what she said to me? She said she understood if I didn't love the santos as much as she did, and she'd understand if I wanted to sell her my half of the Sky and get another place." She began to weep again. Very soft. Helpless.

"Maybe you should. Maybe you could sell them part, and use the money to—"

"The Sky is *mine*! I made it up!"

"All right. I'm sorry. Don't get angry with me. I'm trying to help." But I stood up, not knowing what would come next.

"It's not helping to say I should throw my whole life away!"

"I meant you could do the same thing all over again someplace else, if you got the money. Taos. Some other town."

"I'd have to pay off the mortgage. There wouldn't

be that much left. I'm almost forty years old. I can't start all over again."

"That's not old," I said, although I didn't believe it.

She shook her head. Her tears came back. "It's mine. My Sky." She was not, thank God, mad at me. "Hope is thirty-four years old."

"You're kidding. She looks ten years older than you."

A tiny smile.

"Maybe," I said, "if you gave them a hard time, they'd let you buy them out. They could start all over again easily. Maybe you could get the money to buy her out."

She shook her head. "It was the Sky she wanted. Do you know why? The name. Aside from its being so beautiful, she loved the name. I should've named it Shit City, he'd have bought her a different shopping center."

I smiled.

She went to the dining table for more tequila, returned and sat on the sofa.

She said, "Santa Fe is *my place*. It's the first place I was ever comfortable. It's the first place I ever knew what it was about, when I had an argument with somebody."

I asked what she meant but she ignored me.

"Where would I go? Taos? Nasty little Keith is in Taos."

"So're a lot of other people."

"California? Fucking Wilkie's in California." She sipped at her tequila. Reflective. If you weren't listening to the words, you'd have thought she was making sense. "Texas? I don't know anybody in Texas. I don't even know Lion's family's real name. I never wanted to know. Chicago? Seattle? It rains all the time in Seattle. It's the opposite of Santa Fe. I love Santa Fe." She began to cry in earnest.

I went over to sit on the sofa arm, but she got up and began pacing the room. I let myself collapse onto the sofa.

"D'y'know what she said to me, Maddy? When she saw I wasn't about to cash it in? She said she was glad I was staying, we were destined to be partners. She said just the chances of her finding a white, Catholic partner in this town . . . Don't tell me who she's married to. He's pale. Anyway, if you have enough money, you're white. Everybody wants to adopt you, and you get to be white . . . I didn't lie about going to church, I just . . . He converted because she'd only marry a Catholic. He's really wild about her, you know. He still does anything she asks him to." A wry smile. "Why can't I find a man like that?" She finished off her tequila. "She wants me to go to church with them. As soon as the first work on the Sky is done. When I look unhappy, she says I'm missing the God connection."

"First work?" I picked it up, though she'd rushed past it.

She shrugged. Super-casual. "There's always going to be work. She's that way about the house. No matter how beautiful it is, she never thinks it's finished."

"Have you told any of the artists?"

"What do you mean?"

I was disconcerted. So much of my mother's life, not just her sex life, had revolved around the Sky's artists, it was hard to believe she hadn't thought about what would happen when she had less than half, maybe a quarter, of the space she now had to show them. She had to be worried about which of her perennials she'd let go.

I said—cautiously, not understanding, yet, how far her brain had removed itself from the realities, or how little good caution would do me—"I was thinking about guys like Mel Watson, and Dick Rathbone." Both did big paintings, each worse than the last. She had two or three of each man's at a time, always on the long wall because she couldn't have fit more than one on a short wall. She'd fucked both of them when they first came to the Sky.

She nodded very slowly, as though she were getting the point, but what she said made me realize she hadn't. "The desk is going to be sideways, so there'll still be most of that wall. Except for the windows."

Three windows, one to the left of the door, and two to the right. They chopped up the entire wall.

I laughed. "Maybe you can find some sexy guys who do miniatures."

Her eyes narrowed. She said, "Every time I think you're turning into a human I can talk to . . ."

I was puzzled, then angry. She'd trapped me into talking, then turned on me. I wasn't even certain what I'd said wrong. It had been taken for granted in our house, the extent to which her sex life revolved around artists who showed at the Sky. She'd never made any attempt to conceal it. Even her bar pickups hadn't had the same meaning for us as they might for other people, although she'd been more selective, in recent years, about which ones she brought home, especially if Billy might see them. Actually, it was a while since she'd stayed in town or brought anyone back.

I said, "You *can* talk to me. We were having a conversation, and I wanted to know how you were going to manage about the space."

She said, "Get out."

I was startled. "Why?"

She said, "You never could stand it when I found a woman to talk to."

This was one I hadn't heard, since there hadn't been any except, briefly, Cona, nor did I believe she had one now. I said I hadn't meant to get her more upset, and she said she hadn't been upset until I started in. I tried to tell her I'd been asking a practical question, but she wouldn't let me finish.

"Just get out." Flat.

I said, "I can't. It's too late."

Maybe I could talk Geraldo into living with us for

this last month that I was home. She'd behave if he was around. Dartmouth classes began later than UNM's, September 20, but I was supposed to report there two weeks earlier. Meanwhile, I had to live, and I had to go to work, and I had to do things like shopping for clothes. I had to broach to my mother the subject of getting a computer. On the Sundays when I was with my girlfriends, they were talking about clothes and school supplies. I was the only one who hadn't done most of it. Everything had seemed too far off to worry about, but now I wanted to do what I needed to do.

*"Get out!"* As she screamed it, she threw her open pocketbook at me. It didn't hurt all that much, but the stuff scattered around me. The compact opened as it dropped and its powder dusted the air. Change from her wallet spilled around it. She was still screaming at me when I ran out of the house without stopping for my bag or the keys.

It was only when I was a couple of blocks away that I realized I didn't have change to call Geraldo. I was going to tell him that he had to let me phone him in emergencies. This was an emergency. I needed him to get me away from there. I would tell him that if I couldn't call him in an emergency, he wasn't my friend. I doubled back to our driveway and opened the door on the driver's side of the car, looked in the little compartment between the seats and then in the glove compartment, hoping to find some change. Nothing. I rummaged around on the floor, where I found two dimes and five nickels. It was a few blocks to a pay phone, but I was still determined to talk to Geraldo.

I had to ask information for his number, which I had never called. That was one of the things I was going to point out to him, that after all this time . . . A very sleepy woman's voice answered and I thanked God, or whomever, that Geraldo's family didn't know me.

I said, "I'm very sorry to bother you at this hour, but it's an emergency. I have to talk to Geraldo."

The woman said, "I'm sorry you have an emergency. Geraldo doesn't live here. He lives with his wife." She hung up fast.

I set down the receiver, opened the booth door so I wouldn't suffocate, and stared at the phone as though I were going to wake up and see that it was my alarm clock. After a long time I began to walk in the general direction of my house. I didn't want to go home but I couldn't think of anyplace else to go at that hour. Laya was on the other side of town, now, and the others weren't accustomed to emergency visits. I might end up talking more than I should. I had to go home. I'd had to go all along, I'd just wanted help. Not only wasn't I going to have help, it seemed I wasn't going to have Geraldo.

Except . . . except it was Thursday night and I'd seen him on Tuesday. Surely he hadn't gotten married on Wednesday. He'd been married before I saw him.

It wasn't quite the end of the world, then. He was married, but he hadn't forgotten about me. I would be all right as long as Geraldo didn't leave me before I went to Dartmouth. If he took me shopping for clothes, and maybe to the airport. I wasn't going to be able to ask my mother.

Things weren't so different, then. It was peculiar for Geraldo to be living with someone his mother called a wife. But it also seemed as though, if she were a *real* wife, he'd have told me about her. Told me *something*. In a way, it was good that he had her. Especially if it meant that he wouldn't be angry with me about not wanting to get married.

By the time I reached our driveway, I was quite certain that Geraldo's getting married was a good thing for both of us.

The front and back doors to the house were both locked and nothing happened when I rang the bell. I was cold. Finally I settled into the backseat of the car. It took me a long time to fall asleep, but I did. I awakened in the early morning, before there was action on the block. When I heard my mother moving around inside, I rang the bell. She didn't answer. I sat down and leaned against the door so she couldn't slam it on me when she saw me there. I kept very quiet. When I finally heard her undoing the latch, I leaned hard into the door, and when she opened it, I rolled over and into the house, so that when she tried to push it hard and get me out, she couldn't, though she hurt me badly, of course, leaning hard against the door so that it squeezed my legs like a vise until I could get them out and pull them into the house.

After that day I carried both keys on a chain around my neck. She could still lock me out if she was determined to, by fastening the chain, but I made up my mind that if she did that, I would ask for help. The police, if necessary, since I didn't know any neighbors.

◐

*I* didn't hear from Geraldo on Friday and I arranged to go to Laya's for the weekend. She said she was glad I was coming, I did it so much less often now that I didn't live on Cerro Gordo. But there was another reason. Steven had become her boyfriend after the prom. They were one of a few couples who'd had no interest in each other during our four years in school but had suddenly decided that parting would be too awful to bear. Steven was going to St. John's, right in Santa Fe, and Laya was acting as though she were going to New Hampshire. Laya told me they were supposed to go to the movies, Saturday night, unless there was a party. Either way, I was welcome to go with them. I wasn't sure it was true; she was just being nice. Anyway, I didn't know when I would hear from Geraldo. It was possible he'd come by Sheila's. He liked Sheila. She'd always acted ladylike with him.

But I didn't see him until Monday, when I went to

the garage and waited across the street until he came
out to the lifts. Then I waved. He looked around as
though someone might see him, then wiped his hands
and came across.

"How you doing?" he asked, still holding the oily
rag.

I shrugged. "Okay, but I've been missing you."

He was uneasy. "I have to talk to you, but I been
very busy."

"I know all about it," I said. "I don't care. I still
miss you."

He searched my face for a minute to see if I was
telling him what he thought I was telling him, decided
I was, broke out in a big grin.

"I hear you, *Querida*. I maybe . . . I'll try and
pick you up after work tonight. At around nine.
Okay?"

I just nodded. I was too relieved to talk.

He blew me a kiss and went back to the garage.

❂

Geraldo and his wife, Loretta, were living on the
Tesuque pueblo, where she'd grown up. This suited
him fine because it was "far away from work and everything else." Loretta was pregnant. Did I know that,
or just that he'd married her? I shook my head but I
smiled to tell him it was just fine with me. He gave me
a kiss. Loretta would have the women in her family

right there when she needed them. He liked babies, wanted to have plenty of kids. That was one of the differences between us, he reminded me. He thought I had the right idea: The two of us should never get married but we should always be friends. I asked him what his wife called him, and when he said Geraldo, I told him I was going to call him Gerry from now on. He laughed, said it was a deal.

He acted a little guilty, as though I were his wife and he was cheating on me with Loretta.

He promised to take me shopping soon. The bargain places were too far to walk home with a lot of packages.

◐

*I* steered clear of my mother and she didn't do or say anything that would prove she was on the warpath, but it was as though screws had been tightened into both sides of her head. She couldn't even open her mouth in a normal way when she spoke to me, which wasn't often. And she no longer bought one or two bottles of tequila at a time. She bought three or four, left a couple open. When she sat in the living room, she had one of them with her. I was afraid I'd say the wrong thing if we talked about what was going on at the Sky. I was afraid if I asked about charging my clothes and my airline ticket, she'd change her mind about letting me do it. I was afraid to assume there was any money left from my accident settlement. I decided if I had to, I'd pay for the clothes I absolutely needed out of my summer salary. And I had to get her a birthday present. I wanted to get a ring or a bracelet but I hadn't begun looking. I finally told her I was going to have to buy a couple of pieces of luggage. She gave me her Visa card without a question. I looked at some luggage in Santa Fe, but I didn't see anything halfway reasonable. I'd never owned a piece of luggage. I gave her back the card, saying I couldn't tell when Gerry would have time to take me to the mall. She didn't answer me. The screws in her head just kept getting tighter; her eyes were more starey, and there were very dark patches under them. I was frightened all the time. I began actually to wish for my brother to be home.

Sheila was being even nicer to me than usual since she'd asked what was going on and I'd begun to cry.

◑

*T*his day was so hot and beautiful that everyone who had a pool or a way to get to water wanted to be there. The center of town was empty. There were three of us, including Sheila, and no customers. She said I'd been working terribly hard all summer, and I should take the rest of the day off. I must have things to do for college. Gerry had promised to come by that night.

I thanked her and left. It occurred to me that I

should stop at the Sky and ask my mother for her Visa card and maybe buy some clothes. Even in Santa Fe there were bargains by this time in August. The trouble was, I knew the work on the Sky was finished, and I was afraid to see it. I was having dreams about going to Dartmouth but the place I was leaving was the real Sky, the old one, even before the gallery. Before it had a name. When it was just our home. The thing that had been great about living at the Sky before it became the Sky was, there were always people around, even late at night. In my dreams, now, it was always empty.

I started to cry, then kept walking because I hadn't a tissue and I wasn't going into the Sky with a wet face. Not that it would matter. Pope Hope would doubtless be up at her pool on a day like this. Maybe even my mother wouldn't be working. I had no particular destination in mind, but after a few minutes I realized that I was very close to Ellery's. For the first time in a long time, I missed him. For the first time, I felt I'd been a little hard on him. What had happened wasn't his fault. He was almost as much a victim of Cona's conspiracies as I was. I kept walking up Acequia Madre, thinking I could turn and run if I saw Cona. But I didn't see her. Outside of the house, I saw a fat, little man in a visored hat, holding some gardening tools. He turned as I approached. It was Ellery. He'd gained even more weight, so much that I hadn't recognized his back.

"How *are* you, Maddy?" he asked, as warm as though nothing had happened.

I hesitated.

He asked whether I'd like to come in, have a cold drink and chat for a bit. We'd be alone. We'd go into his office, because it was air-conditioned. I followed him in, where we settled down and he congratulated me about Dartmouth, then asked whether I was preparing to go.

I said, though it wasn't what I'd planned to say, at all, "You don't blame my mother for not speaking to her, do you?" I couldn't say her name.

He looked down at the table, and after a long time, he shook his head. I didn't say anything and finally he looked up.

"They were determined to get it," he said, "and somebody else would have figured out how to get to Wilkie. He wanted to sell. I still wish it hadn't been . . . hadn't been . . ." He couldn't finish. He was suffering, which made it a little bit more all right.

I said, "I don't think my mother's handling everything very well."

He asked what was going on.

I told him about Pope Hope's turning the Sky Gallery into a church, and he asked a lot of questions about how my mother was acting, things she'd said, and so on.

Finally, looking like someone who's been hired to tell somebody else she's dead but she might like the way it feels, he said, "Well, Maddy, it does sound as though she's been dealt a difficult hand, and she's doing the best she can with it."

I said, "She's buying tequila a few bottles at a time and she's always drinking. Mornings. Always."

He said, "Oh dear."

I said, "Our lease'll be up at the end of September, and she hasn't said a word about it. And I won't be here to help."

He smiled. "Maybe Pope Hope—I love your name for her—maybe she'll let your mother go back to the house."

It took him a moment to be certain I didn't know what he was talking about. Then he sighed deeply, *theatrically,* and delivered a little speech of self-justification that puzzled me more with each word. *Now* maybe I could see why he thought he'd better stay out of things. He never knew what my mother was aware of or what she'd told me. There were things that were public knowledge that she didn't know because she spoke to so few people in town; other things that were supposedly secrets that she managed to find out. He had no good idea when my mother had learned it, though she doubtless knew, by now, that when the Hanas bought Wilkie's half of the Sky, they'd also bought the house. Wilkie's house. *Our house.*

Even before I understood precisely what he'd told me, I bolted for the door. Ellery tried to stop me by grabbing my arm, but I pulled off his hand and he didn't follow when I opened the door and ran down the path, out to the street. I headed for the Sky without even thinking about it, but then, when I was just a couple of blocks from it, I stopped, momentarily uncertain that it would be there. The Sky had fallen. The person who'd brought it down owned my mother. She owned all of us. I didn't know what would happen to us. She could push us off the edge or let us back. Rent us our own house. Which was no longer our house. It had still been ours, in some way, when Wilkie owned it, but it wasn't ours anymore.

But before I'd reached the Sky, it occurred to me that there was one good thing about the whole macabre transaction. Or, one thing that *might* be good. It might have made my mother realize she had to mobilize to protect herself. I reminded myself not to say that too soon. First, I had to find out what she knew and when she'd known it. Comfort her if she'd just found out and was finally disillusioned with Hope Hitler. Or a little crazy.

That was what I was thinking when I opened the gallery door and, for a split second, thought I'd come to the wrong place.

The entire long wall facing me was framed in the dark wood that the drawing had indicated on the short wall. You barely noticed the narrow doorway that led to the storeroom at the wall's end. The niches were full of her fucking saints and relics. But the short walls were framed, too, which left even less space than there would have been. One short wall held a few small paintings, the other, two medium ones. Our wonderful tree trunk hadn't survived; the cash register was on a tiny stand next to the front door. Minuscule paintings by artists I didn't know hung between the windows.

It was an entirely different place.

I went to the back room, where some of the large paintings had been stored vertically in the old racks. The girl—I couldn't remember her name at the moment, but it was Carolee—sat in a chair near the back window that provided the room's only direct light, reading. I coughed and she started.

"I'm so sorry," she said, soft and bouncy at the same time, like a detergent commercial. "I didn't know someone was here." She closed her book, stood, set it on the chair.

I said, "I'm looking for a very large painting."

She was suspicious, because I was too young, but she was polite. She started to explain that I was free to go through these standing in the racks back here, but—

"Never mind," I interrupted. "I was really looking for my mother."

"Your mother?" She had no idea.

"Anita Stern."

She was startled, embarrassed. "I'm sorry. I didn't know. I just know Billy." She didn't move.

"Well, now that you know, would you mind telling me where she is?"

She hesitated.

I said, "If you know where she is, maybe you'd like to check to make sure I exist."

She smiled brightly, the idiot, and said that was an excellent idea. She went to the wall phone near the entrance, dialed a number, said it was Carolee for Mrs. Hana, please, and a moment later she was explaining that a young lady had come into the gallery who appeared to be Mrs. Stern's daughter, looking for her mother. A lengthier pause, a thank you, and then she hung up.

"I'm so sorry," she said. "You know, in the Hanas' position, we have to be very careful."

I wanted to smack her. It's the first time I remember having a violent impulse toward somebody. Ever. I'd never wanted to hit my mother, only to keep her from hurting me. Instead, I just asked Carolee, in the pleasantest manner I could muster, whether I was going to have to listen to a speech on the difficulty of having a zillion dollars, or was I going to find out where my mother was. She got extremely, disgustingly, apologetic.

"I'm *so* sorry . . . I really . . . I . . . They're in the pool. I mean, they're at the house. They wanted to take a swim. You know. The weather."

My mother couldn't swim and never went near a pool. Or a tub, for that matter. We only had showers in our house. But at least Carolee had gotten uncomfortable. I tried to stop thinking about her and the Sky and to focus on getting to my mother.

"Yes." I nodded. I was embarrassed to ask outright whether my mother had told her I should walk up to the Hanas'. I wouldn't have gone, anyway. I just needed some idea of when I could talk to her. "Did you speak to my mother, or just to your boss?"

"Mrs. Hana had a message from your mother. Your mother said if she wasn't home in time to make dinner, there was plenty of food in the refrigerator."

I stared at her for a while, trying to figure out if it could be a joke, then I began to laugh and couldn't stop—as though it *were* one. Carolee must have thought I was crazy. If I didn't exist, why should my mother ever worry about making me dinner?

**◑**

*I* awakened because I was cold in the air-conditioning, with only the bath towel over me. For a moment, I thought Billy was home. I think it was because he'd been in my dream. He and my mother and a more reasonable Lion, in an old-fashioned boxer-shorts bathing suit, and with his stupid blond hair cut too short for a ponytail. All swimming in Hope's pool. I was just watching.

It was close to eight. Gerry was supposed to pick me up but I never knew, anymore, whether he'd come before or after supper. I got under the covers, but then I felt hungry. I put on a long T-shirt. There was classical music playing. My mother never played classical music. I opened my door, half-expecting to see Pope Hope with her, but there was just my mother, sitting in the small upholstered armchair that had become her favorite. The little table was next to it instead of in front of it, like the table at the sofa, so she could reach her glass more easily. The drink was there but the bottle wasn't. She was reading some brochures. She didn't look up.

She said, "You got Carolee very upset. Maybe you'd better stay away from the Sky."

I said, "She was just upset because you didn't tell her I existed. I was upset, too."

"Oh, for Christ's sake," my mother said. "Maybe you should make a list of things I have to tell every Chink kid who works for somebody I know."

It embarrasses me to admit it, but I was reassured instead of being pained by her language.

I said, "I was just looking for you to ask for the Visa card. To get the stuff for school."

Wearily, she got up, went to her room for her bag, returned with it, handed me the card, went back to whatever she'd been reading.

"What's my limit?"

I'd expected irritation, expletives, maybe a speech about how I knew she wasn't a rich woman, but there was something else going on. A challenge.

"No limit. It's your money. The Madeleine Stern Fund for Leaving Home." She was enjoying herself. "Did you think I spent the accident money on myself?"

"Not exactly. I just thought—How much is it?"

"Fifty thousand dollars." She was still enjoying herself, but at my expense—as though she were telling me something awful. My mother could turn anything bad. "We'll get you your own Visa card. I'll probably have to sign for it, but I don't mind. I always trust you about money. As a matter of fact, I'll have it all transferred into your account right away."

I felt destroyed. I don't know if anyone can understand that. I don't know if anyone can understand anything that went on between my mother and me. It was too crazy. Even as my brain was telling me I was rich, that I'd be able to fly home from New Hampshire as often as I liked, I was getting confirmation of the fact that she wouldn't want me back, that she'd just as leave I disappeared off the face of her earth. There was a knock at the door but I couldn't go to it. I had to try to climb back into the real world—even if she stepped on my hands as I was doing it.

I said, "You're in such a sweet mood. Maybe you're just happy because your friend the Pope is going to be your landlord, too."

It took her a moment, but she stood, yawned and said, "I haven't actually made a decision about that, yet. Why don't you get the door, Smart-ass. I'm going to take a shower."

It hadn't worked. I had to find a different way to make contact, no matter how scared I was.

I called after her, "Why didn't you tell me about the house?"

She didn't look back. "Why? What difference does it make to you?"

"What do you mean, *what difference does it make to me?* You're talking about my home! The place where I grew up!"

At her bedroom entrance, she looked back, her expression as calm as though she were stoned.

"But you'll be gone."

I would be gone. Erased.

"Don't you think I'm ever coming home?"

She shrugged, went into her room and closed the door.

More knocking, then the doorbell sounded. I opened the door for Geraldo, but told him I couldn't leave right away. I began to cry. He asked what was going on. I said, in a very low voice, that she was being so horrible, I didn't know what to do.

"We get out of here," he said. "That's what we do."

But I couldn't.

"I can't go out, looking like this," I said. "Crying." But I could feel him getting impatient with me. "Could we just go into my room for a minute? Until I can get myself together?"

"Where is she?"

"She's taking a shower."

"Okay," he said. "But we get out before she finishes."

He let me lead him to my room by one hand. I turned on the night-table light and automatically locked the door behind me. He went to the window and he was peering through the blinds, but then, when he turned around, something crazy happened. It was as though he were bathed in some sort of celestial light. I know what that sounds like, but I can't help it. I'd always thought him handsome, but now he seemed incredibly beautiful. His hair was shinier than it had ever been, his eyes, darker, his olivey skin looked as soft as velvet. I went to him and hugged him and was overwhelmed by desire for him. He always excited me but this was different, way beyond what I usually felt in its strength. He was excited, too, of course, but not the way I was.

"So, what now, *Querida?*" he asked.

"Make love to me," I said.

"We won't get to the mall. If you have to shop . . ."

I kissed his ear, licked its insides, played with the hairs at the back of his neck. "I can't shop this way."

"You're sure, Madelena? I can't promise I'll have another night."

"I don't care." I didn't. I wanted him in me, as urgently, more urgently, than I ever wanted anything

in my life—before or since. Including the moment
when I wanted to keep my mother from killing me. I
couldn't let go of him. I held him around the neck
and stood on his feet as he walked us back to the bed,
and pulled at his clothes with him as he tried to get
them off, hindering as much as I helped. He didn't
know what to make of it but he didn't try to stop me;
he was too turned-on by this time. When his shirt was
off and his pants were down around his ankles, I stood
on his shoes again and wrapped my arms around his
neck and pulled him to the bed. It seemed to take
forever for him to be in me, but then it felt as though
he were in my head, my torso, all through me. When I
came, the feeling was so intense that his mouth and
his tongue had to bury mine to keep me from screaming. When I fell asleep, he was still inside me.

◐

"*H*ey, *Amiga.* Time to wake up."

*Amiga.* Pal. I tried keeping my eyes closed until he
called me by the right name, but instead he said that if
I wanted to sleep, he'd go home. I opened my eyes.
He'd rolled off me and was on his side, resting on one
elbow, gently shaking me.

"It's seven-thirty. If we don't go to the mall fast, we
don't go."

I got frightened. He sounded businesslike.

"I really do need to shop."

"Okay. Then let's go. Pronto."

I jumped out of bed, wiped myself off with my T-shirt and gave it to him. I couldn't tell whether my mother was still in the bathroom, or even in the house. He was dressed in ten seconds. I didn't take much longer. I combed my hair, trying not to look at myself in the mirror, because the one time I did, my face looked as though the parts didn't belong together.

I said, "I think I hear somebody outside."

He said, "What difference does it make? We're going."

I nodded. I wasn't really awake, and I was uneasy because he seemed distant from me. He had to remind me to take my bag. Then I turned the lock and opened the door.

My mother and Pope Hope, whom I'd never seen in that house, were sitting at the dining table, Pope Hope at the head of the table, the chair transformed by her presence into a throne. She wore a huge orange caftan, and acres of gold jewelry. Her hair was braided in a crown on top of her head.

My mother must have asked her to come down so they could stare at us together. Two women who'd never even known anyone who got laid.

Behind me, Gerry pushed gently at my back, said, in a low voice, "Say hello and keep going."

So I did, though I could barely get out the hello. He did the same. We walked past them to the front door, and out of the house. We were at the mall before

I realized that I hadn't brought my list, but I knew what I needed for the colder weather where I was supposed to be going. A new parka. Boots. Gerry waited in the car because we were too close to Tesuque to take a chance on his being seen.

He was pleased at how fast I'd been when I brought out my first purchases but I ran back in for two sweaters and a pair of woolen slacks, and this time when I came out, he was just in a hurry to get me home. Drop me off. Drop me off the face of the earth. Just like my mother.

I kept talking about Dartmouth to remind him that I was leaving. That he'd be rid of me soon. But he didn't talk.

When he stopped the car in our driveway, I reached around to hug him and got excited all over again.

He said, "I'll call you when I can." Very cool.

I said, "Billy's coming home on Saturday."

He said, "So?"

I said, "I don't know. Nothing. I'll be gone soon."

He kissed me on the cheek. "I'll call you as soon as I can, *Amiga.*"

There it was again. He could have sounded closer on a long-distance call.

I got my stuff out of the backseat and went upstairs without closing the back door of the car.

My mother was asleep at the table again, her head cradled in her arms, which rested on the pile of paper. The glass and bottle nearby. I put the stuff I'd bought

in my room and came back to her. I slid out the top
page. It was covered with crude sketches of daggers
with blood dripping from them, of guns with blasts of
fire coming out of them. Best of all was one of a big,
fat woman, sitting in what was clearly an electric chair.
The chair wires were plugged into her crown but there
were also knives sticking out of her in different places.

I couldn't rouse my mother so I just went to sleep.
Sleeping was still more of a pleasure than being awake.
I liked dreams, even though I sometimes didn't enjoy
what happened in them. One of my dreams that night
was that Gerry and I were having an argument about
whether I should call him Gerry or Geraldo. When I
woke up, I couldn't even remember which side he'd
been on. I couldn't even remember whether one of us
got hurt. It certainly never occurred to me to worry
about hurting my mother. Everything in me was
geared toward my own survival during the week between the time Billy came home and the day I left for
Dartmouth.

◑

*T*hat Sunday my girlfriends had a farewell pajama
party for me. I sat on a quilt on the floor at Laya's, and
listened to them talking about clothes and reading
from the UNM catalog, pretending to make fun of it
by reading in mock-serious voices . . . *If you wish to
consider several possible areas of study or are unsure of*

*your academic interests, you are encouraged to devise a
first-year program* . . . da da da da . . . They could
have been inquiring politely about outer space when
they asked questions about Dartmouth. It made things
worse, not better, that I mostly didn't have the an-
swers. I couldn't remember even the things I did
know; when I pictured my father's study, I couldn't
find him in it.

Laya told me when she visited me at the holding
pen that the girls thought I'd forgotten about them
even before I left, that I no longer cared about anything to do with them or with New Mexico.

Sheila did realize I was distraught and she was even
nicer to me than usual. But I was afraid to talk to her.
I felt like an upside-down sack of flour: Once I allowed the smallest leak, all my insides would spill out.
Sheila got a friend of hers right in Santa Fe who han-
dled all kinds of handbags and luggage to sell me a
huge suitcase and an overnight bag, at cost. I put my
new clothes in the big suitcase without taking off the
labels.

My mother was in a fever of activity, with ledgers
I'd never seen and phone calls during which she lowered her voice as though the enemy were listening.
After one of these practically whispered conversations,
I heard her say goodbye to Belly Darling, which drove
me crazy, of course, not only because she was telling
this kid what she wouldn't tell me, but because she'd

gone back to my baby name for him that he wouldn't
let me use.

The next morning I called the garage. The man
who answered said Gerry was out. I hung up, though I
didn't believe him. Then, a little while later, I gave a
customer who bought a Santa Fe mug change of a
twenty when she'd given me a ten, and the customer
told Sheila instead of me. Sheila asked me if something was wrong. I said no, but she knew I was lying.
When she told me what I'd done, I got more frightened than I'd been. I had no idea of what I might do
next. I almost explained what was going on at home,
but I stopped myself. If I agreed with Sheila's view of
me as my mother's victim, she failed to understand the
other side to it, didn't understand our closeness. Furthermore, I couldn't trust her not to repeat what I told
her, especially about my mother and Pope Hope.
Sheila couldn't keep anything to herself. There wasn't
anything she heard while I worked for her, except
maybe some stuff about my mother, that she didn't
tell me. She was the one who reported that the contractors who did all the work for the Hanas hated
Hope. One of them had told her that Hope was in
charge of everything that went on at the house. The
guy who owned the contracting business had told his
men that Tom Hana had said to him, "Listen, it's hard
for a man as rich as I am to find someone to boss him
around, make the tough decisions."

Sheila said, "Maybe I'll just stay at the cash register today. While you're upset."

I thanked her and asked if I could take a little walk to clear my head. She let me, of course.

I walked down to the garage. Gerry was outside with one of the other men, looking at a car engine. He saw me, but pretended not to. He turned his back to me.

I returned to Sheila's but I didn't do much there. I was in a trance.

I felt as though I didn't know a soul in Santa Fe.

It was Thursday. On Saturday my mother was driving to Billy's camp to pick up him and his baggage. I was supposed to be in Hanover a week later. I'd packed my big suitcase and it was ready for the UPS man to pick up on Tuesday, along with the small one, which was not yet packed. They took up so much of the floor of my room that when I was in there, I felt as though I were suffocating. When I wasn't sleeping, I lay on Billy's bed and watched his television. At least, my eyes were trained on the screen. Nothing went from my eyes to my brain.

I let myself into the apartment. She wasn't there. That was just as well. I needed to sleep. I wheeled the suitcase out to near the front door and put the empty satchel on top of it. Then I stretched out on my bed and closed my eyes.

I dreamed that everything was all right. My mother and Billy were stretched out on some kind of couches at a gallery that wasn't the Sky. Maybe she'd started a new place. There were a lot of people; it might have been an opening. Everyone was drinking and talking and laughing. But even before I was awake, I realized that the reason they were all happy was that I wasn't there.

Awake, I began to consider whether it might not be sensible to commit suicide. I didn't mind the idea of not being alive. My pleasures in life were few and specific. I could see no reason to live, if I was going to be deprived of them. If it was going to be a struggle to see Gerry. If my mother and I weren't going to be friends. Not only was it unlikely that she or my brother would miss me, but it was possible that without me around, she would mobilize herself to deal with her real enemy.

I tried to think intelligently about the various ways I might kill myself. If she needed to be sure I was dead in order to get on with her life, then my just disappearing wouldn't work. Nor would pretending to go to school, when she would be afraid I might come back at any time. Besides, it was harder for me to imagine where or how I'd disappear than it was to picture myself taking a lot of pills and lying down and going to sleep. Though my imagination balked in strange ways. It wouldn't picture me lying down in any bed but my own after I took them, and, if I did that, there would be too great a danger of my being found there before the pills had done their work. You could put the end of a rifle in your mouth and shoot yourself and know you were doing the job, although the thought of tasting that cold metal wasn't appealing. Lion had had a rifle, but I had no idea of where it was now. Besides, who would clean up the blood and gore if I wasn't there? My mother wasn't going to do it, and it wouldn't be nice to leave the job to Billy. The other ways—slashing my wrists with a razor blade, sticking the bread knife into myself and so on— were all too painful, too slow, too chancy.

I was still thinking about the possibilities when my mother came into the apartment and shrieked something unintelligible. She was already drunk. I decided I'd better stay where I was but I called that I was in the bedroom and a second later she opened the door.

"What's that crap doing out there?" she asked, as though I'd scattered luggage all over the apartment. As though she'd care if I had. (*What's* sounded like *wuz* because she was already drunk.)

I called back, "If you mean my suitcases, I'm getting them ready for UPS."

"When are they coming?"

"Tuesday."

"Why do they have to shtay out here all that time?"

As though it were months away. She was looking for a fight and I was even less in the mood than usual. I wasn't in the mood for anything, aside from a painless way to erase myself from her picture so she could find out who she was really angry at.

"They don't," I said. "I'll take them back."

That left her at a loss. She went to the kitchen to get her homecoming José, then sat in her favorite chair while I brought the suitcases back to my bedroom. Then, thirsty, I went into the kitchen. I got some cubes and filled a glass with water, took four or five aspirin, then sat down opposite her in the living room. I was hoping she'd have one of her mood changes and talk to me as though I were a human for the day and a half before she brought Billy home. But she eyed me as though I were trying to trap her.

She said, "Shtop making faces at me."

I said, "It's not at you. I have a headache."

After a while, she said, "I haven't sheen Sheñor Geraldo around, lately."

(The rest of her sounds were almost as messed up as the *s*'s, but it's harder to show them.)

I made a fast decision. "He got married."

It had worked. The hostile aura dissolved.

"Are you sshhreeus?"

I nodded. "He didn't tell me. I heard it from other people."

"The bashtard. The lousy bashtard."

For a second, pride tempted me to tell her I didn't care that much. That he'd wanted me to have his baby. I could have married him. But I needed her to feel sorry for me more than I needed my pride.

I said, not trying to control the tremor in my voice, "I wanted him to last long enough for me to go to school. Drive me to shopping, the airport, all that. I know you're too busy."

She said, "I'm not busy. I'll drive you. I have nothing to do at the Shky, anymore." Her eyes were half-closed.

I asked what she meant, being careful not to seem eager to find out. She finished her drink, poured another. I realized it was a while since I'd seen her bother with anything but the tequila.

She said, her eyes still closed. "They want me to take the house in exchange for a bigger percentage of the Sky. Or all of my half. Then there'd be money, too, but I'd need a lot of it to pay off the mortgage."

"Oh, my God," I said. "If she can't get what she wants one way, she tries another."

"It's not her, it's him," my mother said. "We had a long talk. She's very upset. She keeps apologizing. She can't budge him." My mother sounded like one of her old 78's, her voice veiled and remote, words running into each other, slurred and without inflection. Her eyes remained closed. "The Sky's worth more than a million, so my share's at least half, except most of that is mortgage. They could get three hundred thousand or so for the house. He's got it all worked out. Very neat. The house plus they take over my mortgage on the Sky. They've improved the offer. They saw I really didn't want to do it." She finished her drink, poured another, sipped at it. "Hopey says, if she was me, she'd get out, because once Tom sets his mind on something, he keeps at it until he gets it." She tossed off that drink, smiled sadly.

I said, "The talk in town is, he does whatever she tells him to. You said yourself, he likes doing—"

My mother's eyes opened unnaturally wide as she cut me off. "The talk in town! Are you talking about my business to everyone in town?"

"Not to anyone, I swear it. There's just a lot of talk about them because of the house, and Sheila told me—"

"Oh, my God, Sheila! Please, God, save me from this one and Sheila!"

"You don't need to be saved from Sheila!" I said. I heard myself saying *shaved* as though I were drunk too, I was so upset by her words. "You don't even need to be saved from *them,* if you just take care of yourself. You still own fifty per—"

She stood up, then, and threw her glass at me. She missed by a wide mark, but that was when I should have gotten out, of course. Gone to my room. Left the apartment, if necessary. It didn't matter that I had no place to go. I could have wandered the streets, called up Laya. Anybody. Even Sheila. It would have been better to spill everything, no matter whether my mother beat me up or kicked me out forever or anything else. It would have been better to start hitching toward Dartmouth and get myself killed. Much better. It was what I actually wanted to accomplish. But I couldn't let go of her. It wasn't just that I wanted to help; I needed her to *understand* that I was helping. I couldn't leave while she thought *I* was the enemy.

She headed toward the kitchen, came back drinking from the tequila bottle.

I yelled, trying to force her to hear me, "Tom Hana tells people he's so rich, it was hard for him to find a woman to boss him around!"

That was the first time she came at me with the bottle, but then she stopped abruptly, began looking around the room desperately.

"Mother, please! I don't want to upset you! I just want to talk about it!"

She stared at me for a long time, as though I'd threatened her with something horrible, then she said, "Where's my knapsack? I'm going to get Billy!"

I screamed, "No! Not now!" I didn't say anything about being drunk because I knew it would enrage her further, but I was terrified. I just said, "It's Thursday night. You're not supposed to get him 'til Saturday."

"Are you telling me when I can get my own Billy?" she screamed. "My baby?" She waved the bottle in the air, splashing tequila all over the place. "You don't let me live or breathe, and now you're telling me when I can get my baby?"

"No!" I yelled back. "I'm—asking you not to drive now!" I could picture her getting on the highway for just long enough to smash into another car.

She ignored me. "Where's my knapsack?" She took

a slug from the bottle and began to laugh. A ghastly, cackling laugh I still can't shut out of my dreams.

I was at my wit's end and finally I shouted that if she had to go, I would drive her.

She headed toward the bedroom to look for her knapsack. I tried blocking the way, said, "It won't be any worse if they stop me for no license than if they get you for—"

She shoved the bottle into my stomach, very hard, to get past me. She was going to do whatever she had to do to get hold of the knapsack. It had to be in her bedroom. If I found it, I could hide the car keys, and at least keep her from driving for a while. Maybe I'd throw them into the bushes outside the window, if I could open it fast enough. In her condition, it would be hard to find them, and maybe somebody outside would hear us and help me.

I turned and ran to get into the room ahead of her, saw the knapsack on the dresser and grabbed it, then whipped around because I heard smashing, shattering glass.

She was standing at the bedroom entrance, her feet planted on the sill, her left hand pressed against the doorjamb. The jagged bottom of the tequila bottle's neck was in her right hand, aimed at me.

I reached into the knapsack for the keys.

She screamed, "Give me my knapsack!"

I screamed back, "Not with the car keys!"

I was groping for them in the bag but I couldn't find them.

For a moment she stared at me, her eyes bulging wildly out of their sockets, her face red, her whole body shaking with rage. Then she came at me, the jagged glass aimed at my eyes. Something in me still fights believing that she meant to kill me, but I believed it then and I was terrified as she came at me, that jagged glass bottom aimed at my face. At my eyes. I threw the knapsack back over my shoulder and tried to set my feet wider and more firmly on the floor so that I could wrestle the broken bottle away from her. She stopped for a second and grinned, so that for a split second I thought maybe it was a horrible, drunken joke, not something she meant to do, but then her left hand grabbed a handful of my hair and she brought the bottle neck toward my face with her right hand, screaming at me that I was a shit and she was going to flush me down the toilet. I was afraid to grab the bottle by its jagged edge but I managed to grab her right wrist. I tried to pry the glass out of her hand with my other one, but she wouldn't let go, so finally, still clutching the hand with the glass, I bit into it so hard that I felt as though I was going through bone, and she loosened her grip enough so I could grab it. By this time I had no question she was trying to kill me. I lunged at her with it. I wasn't aiming for her neck. I wasn't aiming at anything. I just lunged. Once. My eyes closed. But then I opened them. Blood was already gushing out of her neck. A thick, red, spurting fountain of blood. As I write this, I'm seeing a fountain in the park in Hanover that she took me to when I was little, though I'm not certain there was a fountain there. It doesn't matter, does it. By this time, I was crazy. Crazy with rage because my mother had tried to kill me. It's absolutely true that by this time, it wasn't self-defense. I was in a crazy rage and I couldn't stop. When I saw her eyes close, it didn't matter. When I felt the life draining out of her, it didn't matter. When she had no struggle left and I had to hold her up, it didn't matter. I couldn't stop. I smashed the broken glass into her face and the top of her head, her arms, her stomach, her breasts. Her beautiful breasts, under her white T-shirt. It was when the T-shirt was sopping wet with her blood that I stopped and sank all the way to the floor with her. Her head was on my chest. Her arms were almost around me. We were at the entrance to her room. There was blood all around us.

# Chapter 6

When I awakened, we were stuck together with dried blood. It hurt when I unstuck myself from her, but I had to do it, of course, so I could call the police. I let her down very gently to the floor and got a bed pillow to put under her head without exactly looking at her. Her face looked too awful, all bloody and twisted, and her mouth open.

When I called the police, I just said, "My mother tried to kill me," and told them the address.

Later, the district attorney suggested I was setting up an alibi, but that's absurd, of course. In my mind, it was still the most important thing that had hap-

pened. When I'd hung up, I opened the front door
and wedged it with a sofa pillow, so they wouldn't
have to make a lot of noise, coming in. I sat in her
chair.

Soon cars pulled up and they were all in the house
—policemen, ambulance attendants carrying a
stretcher, a medical attendant. They burst in and then
stopped short, because I hadn't told them there was a
dead person, only that she had tried to kill me. The
ambulance people went over to her but the cops came
to me. One of them asked me what had happened.

I said, "She tried to kill me but I got the bottle
away from her and I killed her." I said it quietly and I
sounded rational, which was also held against me later.

They asked if I was hurt. I said I was scratched up
and shaken, bloody but not bleeding. It sounded peculiar and I looked to make sure it was true. She'd
never gotten the bottle back from me, so I was
scratched and bruised under the blood, but I had no
deep cuts.

I recognized the paramedic with the ambulance
crew and I said, "Hello. I don't know if you remember
me. You came when I broke my leg on Acequia Madre."

He looked at me as though I were crazy, but my
craziness had passed. I just ached all over and I was
exhausted, or in a state I thought was exhaustion. I
suppose it was. An exhaustion past the possibility of
sleep.

One said they wanted a statement. I started to tell him what had happened, but he said I should wait until someone got a pen and paper. He told me to talk slowly. I offered to write it. The two men looked at each other, and then the one with the paper and pen handed it to me. My handwriting was shaky, but you could still read it.

*My mother said she was going to drive to my brother's camp to get him two days before he was supposed to come home. She was very drunk, and I didn't want her to drive, so I got her bag with the car keys to keep it from her, but she was furious that I was trying to stop her. She broke off the neck of the bottle and came at me, at my face, with it. I managed to get it out of her hands and we were struggling, and I slashed at her with it, and I cut something big in her neck. Blood started coming out. I went a little crazy after that, and I kept slashing at her. I couldn't stop. Someone has to get my brother at camp.*

I signed it, and then somebody told me to stand up, we had to go to the detention center, and he held out handcuffs. I asked if he didn't want me to wash off the blood, first. He said I could do that at the detention center, after I was booked.

I said, "My brother's at Camp Lahomee; somebody has to bring him home. If I'm not going to be here, somebody has to watch out for him."

There were people, most notably that cop, who reported this as a sign that I was a really cool customer who knew what I was doing all along, had made up the whole story after deciding to kill my mother. Some more or less stuck with that belief no matter what they heard. Others, most particularly Ellery, claimed it was proof my feelings had gotten split right down the middle, and half of me had been left insane. I hated both arguments, of course. But when they said I could make one phone call, Ellery was the only person I could think of.

It wasn't even eleven o'clock, and he was awake.

I said, "Ellery, there's an emergency and Billy has to be picked up at camp."

Ellery asked where my mother was.

I said, "She's dead."

He yelled, *"What?"* and then I could hear fucking Cona in the background, trying to find out what was going on.

I said, "She tried to kill me with a broken bottle and I got it away from her and I slashed her neck and I killed her and she's dead." My voice trembled but it didn't break, another bad sign on the police guiltometer.

He said, "Oh, my God, Maddy! Oh, my God! Where are you?"

I asked the policemen where I was and one of the them got on the phone and asked who he was speaking to, then told Ellery I was at the detention center on Airport Road and he was my phone call. The policeman listened, then he said I couldn't see anyone right then, sir, but he could come in the morning, and he might want to get me a lawyer. He took Ellery's name and phone number, then he let me have the phone back and I told Ellery where Billy was, and that he was supposed to come home on Saturday.

Ellery said, "I'll get him tomorrow."

I said, "Maybe you should leave him 'til the last minute."

That wasn't sensible, of course, but I was thinking, the longer Billy didn't know, the better.

Ellery said, "I'll take care of it, Maddy. I promise. And I'll see you as soon as I can."

I gave the phone back to the policeman.

After that, they took photographs and some finger-prints, and then they tried to talk to me. I shook my head and smiled politely. They asked why I'd smiled and I said I didn't know, that my face wasn't actually connected to the rest of me, and one of them said to the other that I was quite a wise guy, for a kid who just murdered her mother. I told him I hadn't mur-dered her, I'd killed her in self-defense. He was irri-tated, but I looked it up later on, and I was right. A murder is malicious and/or premeditated. I didn't murder my mother. I killed her in self-defense.

Most of the time I've thought I would have been just as well off letting her murder me.

I didn't sleep, of course. I lay on my back on the mattress with my eyes open that night and for I don't know how many nights, reliving—no, just *seeing*—what had happened in every detail. That was when I figured out that my mother probably wanted me to kill her. She knew I was stronger than she was and she knew what I was saying about the Hanas was true. But she was feeling too old to start again. She really couldn't bear the thought of going on.

After a number of days I began sleeping for a few minutes at a time, but I didn't have dreams. Or, I should say, my dreams didn't have pictures. I knew what was happening, but it was a story in my brain, I couldn't *see* any of it. The worst part was, I couldn't see my mother. I wanted to see her when she looked happy, maybe when we were traveling cross-country, or when we'd just reached Hanover. But I couldn't get a good likeness of her in front of my eyes, even during the day. That was frightening. Or would have been, if I had feelings.

In the morning, they gave me a message from Ellery that he'd gone to get Billy and was hoping to reach my brother before Billy heard from someone else. (SANTA FE TEEN MURDERS MOM was on the morning TV news.) Ellery came to see me as soon as they'd returned. He left Billy with Cona.

Somewhere in a corner of my brain there was a small, unimportant person who was surprised that Ellery hadn't remembered that my brother couldn't stand him or Cona and asked one of Billy's friend's parents to get him. That small person was out of touch, as it turned out. Not only did Billy stay with Ellery and Cona, but he didn't want to see anyone else. Especially me. That was painful for the small person somewhere inside me who had feelings. That person needed badly to see my brother and had tried to remember every last detail of the truth so she could explain it to him. But Ellery came without Billy.

My cell was crowded (the whole detention center was crowded) and they brought me into a small, quiet room to talk to him. A guard stood nearby so Ellery wouldn't pass me a machine gun or a hand grenade. Ellery looked very somber, as you would expect.

He said, "Hello, Maddy." His voice was shaky but mine was steady, if dull, by this time.

I said, "Hello, Ellery. Where's my brother?"

Ellery said, "He's at the house."

"At the house? Who's with him?"

"My house. Our house. Cona's with him."

I stared at Ellery but my voice remained as flat as a dead person's. "Cona? You mean, the same Cona who sold the Sky and made my mother crazy?"

Ellery said, "I told you, Maddy. Every broker in town knew the Hanas wanted it. It made me uncomfortable that she was the one who closed the deal, but somebody would have done it, and she—we—needed the money."

That was the end of that. Period. Nothing to talk about. But he was my connection to Billy and I needed him too badly to argue, so I just told him I needed to see my brother. I needed to explain. I didn't want Billy to think it was my fault.

Ellery said, "I'm afraid he's not ready to see you. He just heard, a few hours ago."

I just stared at him.

Ellery said, "He doesn't care whose fault it was, yet. He only knows his mother's dead."

The small person told me I was too upset to speak with Ellery, but I really had no choice. He was the only one taking care of things that had to be done. He said he was looking for a good lawyer and I could talk to him, Ellery, if I wanted to, or I could wait for the lawyer. I told him I had nothing to say, but he pointed out that if I explained exactly what had happened, he could pass it on to Billy, and to the extent that it would make a difference in Billy's feelings . . . maybe not right away . . . but when the shock had passed . . .

So I told him exactly what had happened. When I was finished, I stopped. He didn't ask me any questions.

He said, "I'm going to talk to a couple of lawyers now, Maddy. I'll be back as soon as they let me."

Ellery was a good soul. Doubtless he still is. He just has his priorities. Like other people.

If I could have cried about anything, I guess it would have been because I couldn't see my brother. Billy was being a zombie, just like me, and Ellery had to help him get out his feelings, and the biggest feeling was, he hated me for killing my mother.

When Ellery kept visiting me and kept explaining

why Billy still didn't want to come with him, I said, "Thanks, Ellery, for helping my brother with his feelings."

Ellery said, "Some of the anger might pass, Maddy. It's part of the healing process."

It was a while after that before I could bear to speak to Ellery.

**o**

When Keith and I got together later on, Ellery said I was getting even for Billy. When I asked what Keith was getting even for—after all, *he* was the one who'd come after *me*—Ellery shrugged and said, "His life. Real and imagined." Whatever that meant.

Ellery was a little like my mother, in that way. In Ellery's system of thought, other people didn't have accidents or coincidences. Nothing ever happened unless someone meant it to. Later, when we were having an argument about Keith, he said that when Keith and I were together, he was always there with us, in some way, which sounded so nutty, I asked him if he was taking his medication. A line I heard often in the joint. In prison.

In the meantime, more sympathy poured in than the small person in me could bear; you'd have thought she was the one who'd been murdered. People like Sheila, who wanted to be on television, told stories about what an angel Madeleine was, and how her mother was a devil. Laya visited me once in the holding pen. She cried. After that I told them to tell everyone except Ellery and my brother that I'd left for Dartmouth and wasn't available. One of the stations had a nauseating interview with Cona, who allowed as how Billy had brought her and her husband closer together. Ellery was embarrassed when I told him I'd seen the interview on TV at the detention center. I'm pretty sure he hated that she'd talked to those people.

Geraldo cooled it. He didn't visit me but he refused to talk to anyone, though they found out about his being my boyfriend and followed him around for a while, used him for filler when they ran out of people who talked. When they had a few seconds to spare, they stuck in a clip of Geraldo leaving Loretta's pueblo (strangers weren't let into the pueblo, even to buy bread or jewelry, normally large sources of income, until a couple of weeks after the trial was over), or walking into the garage. One of the reporters faked a highway breakdown, but when he started a conversation with the man on the tow truck, the man got back into the truck and drove away. After that, Geraldo's uncle refused to take new customers for a while and the reporters had to find another gruesome story to drool over. Geraldo never came to the holding pen, but he volunteered to testify for me at the trial.

When Ellery asked if I wanted him to write to my father, I did an imitation of a laugh. I never heard from my father and couldn't tell when or if he knew. I

suppose he learned something when I didn't show up
for school. It didn't matter to me.

I had my nineteenth birthday while I was still at the
detention center. My mother would have been forty,
by that time. I wanted badly to see her. My dreams
still weren't having pictures. I told Ellery that for my
birthday I wanted the photograph of my mother with
Billy and Lion that hung on the living room wall.
Ellery said that all our stuff had been packed in cartons and brought to his house. Billy had taken that
picture and refused to let go of it now, even for long
enough to have it duplicated. I asked Ellery if he
thought that was reasonable. He said he wasn't sure
reasonable had anything to do with the situation but
he hoped Billy would let him copy the photo, sooner
or later.

❂

*F*or anyone who doesn't know how these things
work, at least, how they work in Santa Fe, the defense
and the state have to agree together to waive the right
to a jury trial. The state has to be careful not to leave
itself open to the charge of avoiding a trial, and so they
go to great lengths to assure defendants the choice.
Still, ninety-five percent of all trials are pleas negoti-
ated with a judge. No jury. Evan Keilly, the lawyer
Ellery hired for me, thought I should go for a jury. He
agreed with Ellery that I was such a sympathetic fig-

ure, I might get off entirely with a jury; a judge would be tougher. I told them I couldn't face the idea of a jury. I didn't bother to explain that I had no desire to "do better." I couldn't imagine what I would do if I were set free. Finally, we waived the jury trial and went before Judge Tavarez.

The district attorney's main witness was Pope Hope, who said Madeleine was a nasty, sullen adolescent who hated her mother to a point where she, Saint Hope, had felt Anita's health and well-being were threatened by the girl. That was enough to make the small person inside me vomit, though I just smiled a little. Hope said that Madeleine's mother had talked to her a great deal about the girl, had feared she might not survive until Madeleine left for school.

Carolee testified that I seemed like a very angry person, told the story of my showing up at the gallery that day. She didn't appear to comprehend why the denial of my existence might irritate me.

It was Ellery's telling my brother about Hope's testimony that persuaded Billy to testify, though he wouldn't do it in my presence. I had to be kept out of the courtroom. I said that if I couldn't be there, I didn't want him to testify, but they had him do it, anyway. Apparently, he testified to my mother's torment at being squeezed out of the Sky by the Hanas; about her sounding drunk, after that, when she called him at camp; and, when the judge insisted he answer the question, about her being nicer to him than to me.

He didn't claim that I started some of the fights, as he had to me. I asked Ellery.

The DA tried to get Ellery to say that I started fights with my mother, but Ellery never said even the little he'd said to me at the house. He told the judge my mother was very nice to him during their first year, extremely loving to Billy, routinely unpleasant to me. After the first year, she was drunk a lot of the time, abusive to me and almost as nasty to him. I didn't mind when he told them about her drinking, because not only was it true, but I knew it had nothing to do with me. But when he talked about the stress I was under all the time, he still made it sound as though the stress came from inside my brain, which was ridiculous.

Leslie, the girl who'd been working for my mother at the Sky when she got Jaffe's letter, also testified on my behalf. She told the story how, when the messenger came from Jaffe's office, he asked my mother to sign for the letter, and left, and how my mother stood still as death for a long time, then broke the mug and began slashing things. She said she'd been too afraid of my mother ever to go back. Her father had collected her paycheck.

Geraldo was even better, in terms of making my case, but he said things about my mother I'd rather he not have said. He told the judge my mother flirted with him, had seduced one of his friends who "wasn't looking for it," and was so awful to me that he couldn't stand to be around her. When he was asked for an example, he told about her being drunk already one night when he came to get me. I was taking a shower. She sat next to him on the sofa, leaned all over him, asked how come he was the only man in Santa Fe who didn't know she was sexier than her daughter. When I came out of the shower, she made fun of the way I looked, said I could be a ten-year-old going to Catholic school. I couldn't forgive Geraldo for telling that story, but Evan Keilly loved it because Judge Tavarez was a Catholic.

Geraldo never looked at me the whole time he was in the courtroom.

Keith showed up at the trial a couple of times, but I barely noticed him.

The DA tried to get most of the testimony disallowed as having no bearing on the brutal manner in which I'd killed my mother. But Evan Keilly said that my mother's behavior toward me had a great deal to do with whether I'd believed she would murder me when she came toward me as though she were going to do it; with the fact that she was competitive rather than nurturing; etc.

Good coaching, Ellery.

The judge said that while he believed that my mother had abused me, and that I'd had to wrestle the bottle away from her, and that this had made me furious enough to hit her with it, the kind of damage I'd done suggested a rage that had been waiting for its reason. He felt it would be unwise to tell every teenager who was angry with a parent, even with real justification, that it was okay to kill the parent instead of finding help. He sentenced me to four years in the New Mexico Women's Correctional Facility at Grants, which was likely to be cut in half for good behavior.

Evan Keilly was upset; he'd been certain that two years was the longest I'd get. I told him not to worry about it. I wouldn't let him appeal. I told him I'd behave badly in the courtroom if he did.

I had to convince myself that it didn't matter if my sentence was short; I could misbehave and get my time in jail extended, or kill myself as soon as I got out.

◊

Grants was just this tiny, dry and dusty little town in western New Mexico until uranium was found there. Jobs and motels and the rest of it followed. When the uranium was used up, it became a nothing little town again. There were a couple of prisons there already. Some rich men persuaded the government to buy their land for the women's prison, which opened not long before I got there, and which is run for profit by a private corporation called Corrections Corporation of America, that's licensed by the state. CCA. The state makes us follow certain guidelines—in theory. In practice, they delay doing things they don't want to do, like writing reports that would get prisoners released when there aren't others to replace them, since that would cut into their profits, and/or providing legal assistance to that portion of the population that might benefit from it. Among the supervisors and guards, the percentage of lice and sadists to decent human beings is probably greater than it is on the outside, but there are humans who are just there because they need a job, and who are decent as long as you don't cross them. I had no desire to cross anyone.

They brought me from the detention center to Grants in a small bus. In handcuffs. With two guards. It was odd that they thought I needed handcuffs. They could have begged me to run away and I'd have refused. I was the only prisoner in the bus until Albuquerque, where two other women were picked up. Spanish. One tall and attractive, with beautiful wavy brown hair almost down to her waist. She radiated hostility toward me as well as toward the guards. I couldn't have cared less. The other woman, darker skinned, just looked frightened. When I picture her now, it seems to me I'd have guessed it was the first time she'd ever been to jail, but I would have been wrong, though it was the first time she'd ever been in for manslaughter. They'd killed her husband together after he beat her up once too often. They were going to one of the other prisons.

The prison is a sprawling, one-story, precast-cement building in desert country. I was unloaded in a small yard with high metal fences topped by coils of barbed wire. At the time, I didn't think about the wire, but when I finally fell into a real sleep, I dreamed I was sleeping on it, like a fakir on a bed of nails. It wasn't a nightmare; it was a relatively good dream.

For the first month everyone goes to R&D (receiving and diagnosis) while they decided whether you're a danger to yourself or others. Apparently, my answering questions and following orders in a matter-of-fact way made them think I might be a real nut. When they asked why I was there, I said I'd slashed my mother's carotid artery. When they asked if I'd aimed for the carotid artery, I said no, that I hadn't even known about it at the time. Somebody who was a little smarter than the others decided that I might kill myself next, so they kept me in a cell in ad seg (administrative segregation) for an extra month. The fact that being in a cell for most of every day made me think of killing myself all the time instead of just some of it did not affect matters, though they did put me on an antidepressant that, combined with a lack of reasonable means, kept me from making any reasonable progress toward death.

Looked at rationally, the cells weren't terrible. Six by eight feet, with a window, white walls, a teensy stainless-steel toilet—which accommodated my rear end more comfortably when I entered Grants than when I left it, because meals are the big events of the day and you eat quantities of sweet, starchy food, and I did finally begin eating more than a few bites at a meal—and a minuscule sink attached to the top of the toilet tank. The place was so new that things were very clean.

Every few weeks, they give you a test, ask you questions to see if you and/or your attitude and/or their view of you and/or your behavior have altered so markedly as to justify your moving out with other inmates. Finally, I went into medium security. There was no maximum security, at the time, which is why the Serious Murderers, as opposed to a Young Recreational Murderer like me, were taken elsewhere.

I was in a bunk in a big room called the E unit. Every two bunks have a wall about three feet high between them and the next set of beds. Some of the cells and bunks were decorated like a fourteen-year-old's, a fourteen-year-old who read decorating magazines . . . cutesy, fluffy. One had a lace curtain taped to the end of the bunk and a pink and blue quilt on the bed. I was vaguely relieved to notice, when they led me to my bunk, that there was no decoration except a couple of photos of the woman's children over her bed. My bunkmate, Lucille, was reading and didn't look up except to nod at me. That was good, too. There were a few who needed to be so friendly, they would have driven me out of my mind. At that point, just friendly could have done it.

Prisoners wear navy blue pants all the time. (Except at night. Pajamas are pink or peach. Issued or store-bought.) The tops are different. I had to wear a red

T-shirt while I was in R&D. I hated red, still do, and was glad to get into medium security. Yellow. The guards were mostly low-class Anglos, like the warden, who'd once been a guard, or Spanish. The women, some transferred from other prisons when Grants opened the year before, were mistrustful of anyone and everyone, but some were particularly hostile to me because I'd had the great good fortune to be on television. And that was only because I was an Anglo. On the scale of things, killing your mother didn't weigh that heavily, but if they saw someone on TV who'd killed a kid, they hated her. Or him. They were mostly in their twenties and thirties, I think; a few were older. Most of them came from Albuquerque and the towns farther south, down to the Mexican border. I didn't meet anyone from Santa Fe, though the Santa Fe holding pen had been jammed with locals. The biggest group, the American Spanish, were just as snotty about the Indians and the Mexicans as they were on the outside. The Mexicans were the first to talk to me, after they heard me speak Spanish. The few American Indians were extremely insular, spoke only to one another, acted as though they were back on the pueblo. (There's a pueblo not far from the prison.) The ones I knew of the American Americans, one black, three white, including Lucille, who was Irish, were the quantity dealers. The recent arrivals were mostly in for using or selling small amounts of drugs. Word had already gotten around that Grants wasn't a bad place to be when you got tired of cooking and doing your own laundry. Or your TV broke. Some of the women were more afraid of any black than of the most dangerous white, maybe because they'd seen so few of them when they were outside. I'd never seen more than six or eight black people at a time within Santa Fe, though some people there talked as though there'd been a population explosion in the sixties and seventies—blacks and hippies.

The wake-up call was at five-fifteen, which drove some of the women crazy; every morning was the first they'd ever had to wake up in darkness, the first when they wanted to finish a dream, the first . . . It was true of some of them. A few had also never set foot in a school. One of the Texas Mexican women was nineteen and had three children and when the guard asked whether she'd never had to get out of bed before, she shook her head and said, in Spanish, that her babies all slept in the bed with her and when they wanted to feed, she just rolled over onto her side. The oldest had just turned seven, so everyone laughed. There was no way to tell if it was true. Most of them said very little that was true and assumed everybody else was lying all the time, too. A lot of them had stories about being raped by their fathers; some of the stories were probably true, but the numbers went way up any time there was a story like that on TV.

Anyway, I didn't mind getting out of bed at five-thirty. I was awake. I don't think I slept for more than

twenty minutes at a stretch. I continued to live all the
time in that sense of unreality most people get once in
a while, briefly. I cannot imagine a situation in which
I would have been any more comfortable, or felt any
more real, than I did at Grants.

〇

*I*'d entered the prison in 1990. For the first six
months or so, Ellery was my only visitor, though Laya
and a couple of my girlfriends would have taken the
bus the hundred miles or so from Albuquerque if I'd
told Ellery I wanted them to. Ellery came every other
Saturday. It was a few hours from Santa Fe because
there's no direct route; you have to go south to Albuquerque, and then west. Nobody happens to have
thought of building a good highway between New
Mexico's tourist jewel and its jailtown.

When I questioned Ellery about my brother, he
kept saying he thought Billy's anger would pass. He
wanted me to know, because he understood how
much I cared about Billy, that Cona was enormously
helpful to my brother. They'd gotten really close . . .
Pause . . . Smile . . . Billy called her Momtoo. Or
Momtwo. Ellery wasn't sure how it was spelled, but
however I felt about Cona, I should know that Billy
would have been in real trouble without her.

Thinking of Cona in full possession of my brother
made me sick to my stomach, but I just nodded. I

kept waiting to hear that Billy understood what had happened and wanted to see me. In the meantime, I started teaching a couple of the women how to read. Ellery liked that and suggested that when I got out I might be able to get a degree in education and teach. I just pretended to listen.

In August, Ellery took Cona and Billy to visit his parents and his sister in New York. There were no prison visiting hours on Monday or Tuesday, but that Wednesday afternoon was when Keith came for the first time. It took me a moment, when the guard told me my visitor's name, to remember who he was, and I almost sent him a message to go away. I didn't do it because Ellery had mentioned his son's leaving Taos and coming to live with him and Cona while he decided what to do next. Ellery blamed himself, his dissatisfaction with his marriage and his going back and forth (he'd left his wife twice before meeting my mother and really leaving) for everything he thought had gone wrong with Keith, just as he apparently blamed himself for leaving me alone with my mother. Ellery thought if he did it right, he could fix anything. Or keep it from happening in the first place. So he'd taken Keith in despite, he'd reminded me, their "very real" space limitations. It was because Keith was living with my brother that I let him visit me; I thought he might have something to tell me about Billy.

The visitors' room is a nice, light place with several kindergarten-height tables, and a play space in one corner for little kids. They had small children, a lot of these women who kept doing things to land back in the joint. Some who did it to get away from the kids for a while cried about missing them the whole time.

A guard ushered me in and I sat down to wait. A couple of women were there with visitors. A male visiting a female was allowed to kiss her when he came in, but then they had to sit and just hold hands, at most. Nobody was allowed to bring in food but there were candy and coffee vending machines. The kids wanted candy every five minutes.

Keith didn't even seem familiar when they led him into the room, this very skinny, bearded kid who was twenty-seven, though he looked college age. He was wearing jeans and a blue denim shirt. I'd promised myself that if I couldn't stand talking to him, I'd end the visit fast, but the sight of him didn't bother me and his manner was cool enough. It felt entirely different than it would have if my old girlfriends had come, trying to connect with me. Keith had nothing to do with my real life, even if it turned out that he thought he did.

I said it was nice of Ellery to arrange for a substitute while he was away.

Keith shook his head. "It wasn't him. Santa Fe is pretty boring, and I've been thinking of taking a construction job in Albuquerque for a while. I thought maybe you'd like a visit, with my father away."

I said, "Thank you."

I watched Keith as he looked at everybody else. He had a great curiosity about the prison and the way it ran and everybody in it. I liked that. Ellery never saw anyone but me. Aside from his age and being skinny, and having a beard, Keith looked quite a bit like Ellery. (I don't think I'd ever marked resemblances before prison. Since then, I've been very much aware of them.) Ellery always sat very still, focused on what I was saying, but I could see already that Keith was restless in a way that went with being so skinny. He never settled in. He looked around and snapped his fingers and slapped his thighs. He smiled when he saw that I was observing him.

He said, "I'm always like this. Can't sit still."

I said, "My mother was like that."

He said, "I know. She was really something, your mother."

I didn't like the sound of that.

I said, "Maybe we'd better stay away from her."

After a while, he said, "My father talks about you a lot. He cares more about you than about my sister. At least, he talks about you more. I guess you know, she doesn't want to have anything to do with him."

I said Ellery hadn't actually talked about her much, and asked what he'd told Keith about me. Keith said his father liked me, of course, but maybe we'd better leave that alone, if he couldn't mention my mother.

This might sound crazy to some people, but it was because we understood each other just enough to go along in such things, whether or not they made sense, that Keith and I connected right away. He didn't prod if something bothered me. We talked about that. He had a very strong feeling of what was private that had to do with both his parents being shrinks.

I asked Keith how my brother was doing. Keith said he supposed okay, but it was hard for him to tell because Billy couldn't stand him, wouldn't stay in a room, if he was there.

On his next visit, Keith told me he'd taken the job in Albuquerque. Construction of an office building. He'd found a decent room in a boarding house, not far from the highway to Grants. He sounded as though he thought I was expecting him to visit, and I told him that he had no obligation to do so just because his father was away. He said he didn't think of it as an obligation; he'd been curious about me for a long time. He'd liked the way I looked when he saw me outside of the restaurant that time, and now he felt like seeing me again.

In the early visits, he didn't ask as many questions about me as about the prison. He wanted to know where we slept, who else was there, how much exercise we got, what we'd had for lunch that day. The first time I told him (a huge baked potato with sour cream; a mass of melted Cheez Whiz; a little salad; apple cake with whipped cream), he said, "No wonder a lot of them are fat." I smiled, and he smiled back and said,

"Don't you get fat like that." (When I got out of jail, he claimed I hadn't gained any weight, though I'd gone from a size eight loose to a size ten tight.)

I shrugged. I could feel the flirtatiousness in it, but I didn't care, yet. He was reminding me of the kids at Yale, with all their questions about food. It was the first time I'd thought about something that had nothing to do with my life. That is, with my mother or my brother.

Keith asked me what I wanted to do when I left Grants, then quickly saw that I had no interest in the subject and switched to something else. But I felt as though I'd been punished for letting my mind roam. It was frightening to be reminded that I was not safe and secure in jail for the rest of my life.

He didn't tell me until he'd visited a few times that he was moving to Albuquerque because of me. At some point, Ellery had decided he was too interested in me and had become reluctant to talk about me . . . as though I were a patient or something. Keith had to admit, that had only made him more curious. He had what they called an inquiring mind. He said it as though it were an embarrassing thing to have, but I told him I was the opposite, hardly curious about anything, and I thought it was probably better to be the way he was.

*L*ucille and I became pals. When you speak of a pen pal, you're mostly talking about something very different from a friend on the outside. If I didn't talk to my girlfriends in high school about my mother or Geraldo, it was because of a strong sense of privacy, of what belonged to me, not to them. In prison, the flow is very controlled. And you don't tell the other women much because you can't trust them not to use any or all of it against you if the occasion arises. If they can get good time for giving you up, or earn some favor from a guard, many of whom are curious—unhealthily so—about the cons, even the ones who don't want sex. Information might buy cigarettes, or get a message sent outside. A lot of the guards come from the same towns and neighborhoods in New Mexico as the inmates. Some are related. A couple of the guards are hopped-up all the time, as though the basic situation were sexy. The competition for the attention of the male guards was fierce among the women who wanted to have anything to do with them, whether or not they claimed they didn't. There were women who wore earrings every day, and tons of makeup, and claimed it was just habit. One of them cried rape when the night guard who'd been fucking her decided he liked somebody in the next bunk better.

Lucille and I became pals because we were smarter than most of them and came to trust each other after we'd lived together for months. Each saw the other wasn't a talker. More than on the outside, you

couldn't tell who might turn out to be crazy or violent
or just a rat. There was another dealer who acted cool
except she bitched constantly about the drinking water, which she was certain was poisoned. She wanted
bottled water, which hardly anybody there had heard
of, yet. Someone finally asked if she wanted a nipple
on her bottle. She lost it. Attacked. There was a
screaming, socking, hair-pulling fight in which she did
that neat little trick I call the prison twist, though it
must be used on the street. The prison twist was the
reason some women had begun to keep their hair real
short. You grab the woman by her hair, if it's long
enough, wrap it around your hand, then twist her
away from you so she can't lay a hand on you while
you're beating on her. If one of the few black women
hung out with a white, one of the other black women
was likely to fight with her. There was one who'd been
a housekeeper until she was caught stealing. She cried
for the little white boy she'd been taking care of, she
missed him so much. But she had to pretend she was
crying for somebody in her own family or one of the
other black women would've beaten her.

Lucille was thirty-three years old and had two kids
who were in school in Alamogordo, where they lived.
She'd been a major dealer for a Mexican known as
Roberto, whom she'd refused to give up to the police
when they caught her. A CCA guard dealt for Roberto. One of the worst sons of bitches there. Lucille
was completely cynical about the whole system, in and

out. Her parents were poor whites who'd moved with the kids from Mississippi to Texas and then to New Mexico so her father could find work. Most of the women didn't talk about the families they came from, only about their kids, but once we were pals, Lucille talked about hers a lot, especially about her mother's parents, who were still in Mississippi. She'd started dealing to earn money for plane fare to visit them. She was sixteen. She wasn't caught (first time) until she was twenty.

She had been transferred to Grants after doing time someplace much worse. She had a boyfriend who was visiting her the first day Keith came to see me. Until she saw him, she didn't know anything about me except what she heard in the dining room. She assumed Keith and I were already together. She didn't like the lesbians. She hardly liked anyone. If we hadn't been bunkmates, and if it hadn't been so easy, we probably wouldn't have become lovers. We did, but that word still doesn't sound right to me.

Lucille was beautiful in a strong way that made the word *handsome* a better fit. Tall. Big. She said she gained twenty pounds every time she came to prison, lost them when she got out. Her boyfriend and Keith waited for us together, but they never spoke. Her boyfriend was living with her kids. She didn't know where their father was.

●

*E*llery didn't come to see me for a long time after he returned from vacation. I assumed he was just too busy. In the meantime, it was Keith who told me that Billy had gone back to school.

"Back?"

It didn't worry Keith that he'd given something away.

"Maybe my dad didn't tell you. He wouldn't go after . . . you know. He just started again. They let him into the right grade. With his friends." Keith grinned. "It wasn't as though they learned anything while he was away."

I said, "School was my favorite place."

"You figure you'll go back when you get out?"

I said, "I never think about what I'll do when I get out."

"I got that idea. Is it really true?"

"Yes."

Keith mulled that over for a long time. It was his most endearing quality, while I was in jail, really to listen to what I said and think about it.

"So," he finally asked, "what *do* you think about?"

I shrugged. The real answer, of course, was that I thought about my mother. And Billy.

"I think about what I'm doing, what I did, and what I have to do next. I don't read. I used to be a big reader. The only stuff I read is in the law library. Some of the women ask me to read stuff for them, or figure out what it means. Those're the ones who want to get out. Some of them like it here. It's better than home. The TV works. Somebody else cooks. The word's gotten around already. If you're tired of housework, you can arrange to get busted."

Keith got a big charge out of that. "What about you?"

"A lot of the time I read crappy magazines. My bunkmate's boyfriend is a trash collector in Alamogordo. He brings fashion magazines, garden, house ones, all that stuff." Except for the romance magazines, which I couldn't stomach, they were more fun in the joint than outside because they were even more like science fiction. Lucille and I had begun reading each other some of the advice columns. Everything from how not to get AIDS (after each paragraph, one of us would make a comment, like, "And keep men away from your asshole") or how to get bloodstains out of your clothes ("Stay away from anyone with a knife") or how to enjoy sex ("Get out of jail").

"How many hours are you awake?"

I shrugged. "Twenty. Sometimes maybe more."

He whistled. "Don't you work? Get tired?"

"We dig ditches. Chop brush. Cafeteria duty. I don't get tired. Not sleepy, anyway."

He reached for my hands, put his on top of them. I was more affected by that gesture than I'd been by anything since my mother died. Tears welled inside me, though they didn't come farther north than my throat. I took my hands out from under his.

I said, "It's not all that bad. They get us up at five-fifteen, when I'm up, anyway. We have a meeting, they assign jobs. Then we have breakfast, then we work unless we had an early job. In the afternoon there's aerobics some days, if you want them, or different activities, usually bullshit kind of stuff. Mostly what everybody does is watch the soaps. And then there's dinner, evening meeting, more group activities, voluntary, and the place gets locked up at midnight."

After a long time Keith said, "Being shut up would drive me nuts."

I said, "I wish something could drive *me* nuts."

I meant it, but it wasn't something I'd thought about, certainly not in those terms. What I'd thought about was being able to leave my brain someplace, so that my mind could wander far enough not to land on my mother. Not to wake up hearing "Perfidia." In English *or* Spanish. Usually someone else was singing it *to* her, though I couldn't see either of them. My dreams still had no pictures.

After a while, Keith said, "I think I know what you mean. I guess that's what dope is about. Getting out of your skull." He smiled. "I don't suppose you can get dope here."

I shrugged. "Some people do. I find it too tricky. Sometimes it just sends you into a worse part of your head. When my mother did acid, she could be an angel, or she could get . . . horribly upset."

He was surprised, I guess, that I'd said something

about my mother. I held my breath, hoping he'd understand it wasn't all right for him to do it.

He said, "I pretty much stuck to weed, even in the old days." He grinned. "I was glad I got my dad hooked into it, but then I lost interest."

I nodded.

"That makes sense to you?" he asked.

"It doesn't have to make sense," I told him.

He said, "That was the biggest fight I had with my parents, both of them, from the time I could talk, practically. They always tried to force me to make sense of what I did, or what they did. The same sense as they made. As though the whole world would change if you understood it their way. One of us was responsible for every goddamned thing that happened."

I started to say I wondered which was better, explaining everything you did, or not having them care enough to explain anything, but then I was afraid Keith would think that was an invitation to talk about my mother, so I stopped.

He said, "My girlfriend was pretty nutty. Sometimes I caught myself trying to do the same thing with her. Show her what she was doing. Then I freaked."

I smiled as well as I could but my face felt funny doing it, as though it had forgotten the correct way.

He said, "And it doesn't work, anyway."

I said, "Nothing works," but when he asked what I meant, I couldn't answer.

After a while, he said, "I know it's a touchy subject, where you'll go when you get out of here, but—"

I said, "It's not touchy. It just doesn't interest me."

He said, "I think about it a lot. About where I want to go when we"—he laughed—"I leave Albuquerque."

I heard his slip, *we* for *I,* but I didn't mind if he was thinking that way. He was talking about all the different ideas he had, and since he clearly liked me, it seemed reasonable for him to hope they'd include me. I liked him, too. By that time it would have felt strange not to see him again. But the subject of what I was going to do a year later just couldn't grab hold of me. I shifted around in my seat and then, when he didn't take the hint, I stood up.

He stood, too, and said, "I think my father might visit next Saturday."

I shrugged.

Keith asked if he could come on Sunday. I said sure, why not.

He said he'd thought maybe I wouldn't like it if he sounded as though he took me for granted just because he was visiting me in prison.

I smiled. "I like having somebody to take for granted. I don't even take Ellery for granted. If my brother wanted him to stop visiting, he'd probably do it."

◗

*W*hen Ellery finally came, I attributed an awkwardness between us to his having been away for so long. I asked how his vacation was, and he said it had been all right. His father was feeble and his mother complained about having to wait on the old man hand and foot, but they were doing better than a lot of very old people.

When he didn't go on, I said, "I guess you know, Keith visited me while you were away."

He still didn't speak.

I said, "He told me about Billy. About school."

A nod. He looked a little grim.

I said, "Billy's not coming to see me. Right?"

Ellery nodded. Still grim.

I asked if something else was wrong. It took him a while to answer.

"I'm concerned about Keith's visiting you. He'd barely met you. In fact, he checked it out with me after he moved in with us, and I told him I thought it was inappropriate."

"Inappropriate?" I was upset. "I don't know what that means. Do you think you should be my only visitor in the whole world?"

"No, Madeleine. That's not what I think. And you had girlfriends who wanted to visit you."

I was stung by his use of Madeleine. He'd never called me anything but Maddy. Was it because Keith was a boy that his visiting me was a crime? I was at a loss for something to say, so I told Ellery I was thinking I was going to have to change my name, when I got out of the clink. (I'd never thought before then about changing my name.)

He just looked at me.

I got very nervous in the silence and I began singing "Perfidia" because I couldn't think of anything to say. Apparently, he couldn't either. I told him somebody was always singing that song to someone else in my dreams but I couldn't tell who was singing and who was listening. That was the sort of thing that would have interested Ellery once upon a time, when he was my friend, but now he just stared at me. I felt giddy, but also nervous. The way I was when I was a little kid and something I thought was funny looked as though it was about to infuriate my mother and I couldn't understand why.

Ellery asked, rather grimly, if there was some reason I was feeling so good.

I shook my head. "I'm not feeling good, though I felt a little better when Keith was coming than if I had nobody. Are you really angry with me about Keith? Is that why you didn't come after your vacation?"

He looked at me for a long time before he said that he wasn't exactly angry, but he was concerned, and, yes, it was about Keith. I told him that I still didn't understand, and he said he thought it was "not a great" idea for the two of us to get together.

"We're not together," I said. "He's outside, and I'm

here. He visits me once or twice a week. Will you please tell me what's wrong with that?"

I admit to being a little ingenuous at that point. But I felt I was being put on the defensive for no reason—except maybe that I was a jailbird, so Ellery didn't want his son to be involved with me. For the first time I was feeling, instead of just knowing, that I would probably be outside in a year. And that my life was going to be a continual attempt to overcome having been inside.

Ellery appeared to be struggling with himself. When he finally spoke, he sounded like the judge, pronouncing sentence and wanting me to be sympathetic because it was hurting him more than me.

"Well, first of all, you were already involved. Okay. Scratch involved. You were part of the same, let's say, extended family, in a sense. Before you ever met. I'm a father to him and I've been a sort of father to you."

"Some father," I said, upset. "A father who left when I needed him most."

"That's something I still feel bad about," Ellery said after a long time. "I can't undo what happened, but I'm trying to make up for it, to the extent that I can."

"You mean, you're making up to my brother for what you didn't do for me."

"All right, Madeleine," he said, loudly enough so heads turned toward us. "There's no point in going through . . . Let's talk about real possibilities."

There it was again. Madeleine.

"Keith is bored with his life. With this business of pretending to be an artist. Not exactly pretending, but he doesn't have enough talent to carry him through the difficulties. And besides, he's a real academic. He loved school before he decided to drop out. There's a real chance he'll go back, now, and the last thing he needs is to get involved with someone before he . . ."

I smiled bitterly. "Especially with an ex-con."

"With *anyone*. It's the last thing either of you needs, Maddy."

It was as though he thought of me as Madeleine, now, but he went back to Maddy when he wanted to make a point. Or make me believe that he was concerned about me, not just about Keith.

"You need to figure out what to do with your life, too. You're very young. *You* loved school, too. Perhaps you should . . . think about . . . finding a school."

Which school did he have in mind? UNM, where everyone knew me? Dartmouth, where there was only my stupid father? Or someplace where I was a total stranger to everyone? It was hard to tell which was the scariest. Anyway, in school I would just sit and think about my mother for another four years.

"Oh, yes? What did you have in mind? The same school as Keith?"

He started to get angry, but stopped himself.

"Look, Madeleine, you don't know how you'll feel

about anything, once you're out of here. You're going to need some time to adjust. You might want to find a good therapist. And you'll be able to afford it because—"

I couldn't listen any longer. I stood up. I wasn't even out of jail and he was preparing to turn me over to some shrink.

I said, "I don't believe you give a shit about me. If you're worried about Keith, talk to Keith. Tell him not to visit me anymore. The only thing I can do is, not come out to the room once he's here. And then I'll have no visitors. Because you're not coming, anymore. I don't want to see you. I won't come out."

After a while, Ellery stood and told the guard, who was hovering near us, that he was ready to leave.

◐

*T*hat night, my dream had a picture. I dreamed I was getting married to someone I couldn't identify, and when I held up my hand for him to put the wedding ring on it, my ring finger was gone. It was just a bloody stump.

◐

*I* didn't talk to anyone, even Lucille. I did everything I had to do. In my free time, I looked at one magazine after another, not reading, barely registering the pic-

tures. Lucille knew something had gone wrong but she
never pushed me to talk. When a couple of the hard-
boiled eggs made nasty remarks about how a kid with
all the "uhdvantages" managed to land in the joint so
young, she got them to lay off me. But she never
treated me like a kid.

◗

When Keith came, we were awkward in a different
way than before. As soon as we were seated, he said he
knew his father had been there. He asked if I was
upset.

I asked, "About what?"

He smiled as though in complicity, but I wasn't
being a wiseass, it was an inquiry. He nodded. He said
he hadn't wanted to mention it before, but the shit
had hit the fan as soon as they'd all returned and he'd
mentioned having visited me.

"What do you think it's about?" I asked.

"You really don't know?"

I shook my head.

Keith looked at me for a long time, then said, "He's
afraid I'm getting involved with you. You're here for
six months to a year, if you keep the good behavior.
Right?"

I just waited.

"He can see that I like you. I mean, it's true that I
was curious about you even before all this."

"Why?"

He shrugged. "Dunno. He talked about you a lot. You and . . . You know . . . There's nobody very interesting out here and he talked about this terrific girl who just needed to put some distance . . . you know . . . who needed to get away from Santa Fe. When you blew . . . He wasn't totally shocked. He kept saying he should have known. He should've tried to get you away from her. It nearly wrecked him, last time he visited, when you said he hadn't been much of a father. He came home in a state. Went through this routine about how he should've tried to explain that he didn't have to be a good father for the symbols to be there."

"Symbols," I said. "I don't know about symbols. When my mother was about to blow, I went there and I practically begged him to let me stay at his house until I could go away to school. Did he tell you that?"

"Shit, no. Why didn't he do it? Cona?"

I didn't answer.

"I have to say, living there I get a slightly different feeling for what she's about."

I still didn't speak.

He grinned. "She's as bossy as my mother, but not half as smart."

That got a small smile out of me.

"He thought you were amazing," Keith said. "The way you mostly stayed cool through all the . . . Am I allowed to say, through all the shit?"

I nodded. "There was a lot of shit."

"Do you know about my sister?" he asked after a while.

"I just know you have one."

"She's close to my mother. She and my dad don't get along so well. He compared your tolerance, the two of you. She'd get hysterical when anything didn't go her way. I'm the one who got along with him. Until now, anyway. It's all the opposite of the way things're supposed to be."

I said, "I don't see where the *supposed to be* is. I thought parents were supposed to love all their kids. I'd never have them if I couldn't love a boy and a girl." Suddenly I felt very self-conscious. I'd never meant for one minute to have any children, and I didn't know where that had come from. Keith seemed to be listening seriously, but he was thinking about something else.

He said, "We lived in this big, dark apartment in New York. When I went to camp every year, it was like getting out of, mmm, a jail. I felt that way when I first came out here, but now . . . There's hardly anyone to have a real conversation with. Until you meet another New Yorker."

I smiled. "I'm not a New Yorker."

"I know." A funny little grimace. "But I feel as though you are. You're smart enough. Oh, shit. That's the kind of thing they say New Yorkers say."

"Anyway," I said, "what's all this got to do with your sister?"

He laughed, but he turned bright red. "I guess I was thinking that I miss her. We were good pals. She's only three years older than me. The women I've been with, none of the women, we don't communicate all that well. We don't like the same things."

"What kind of things?"

"Anything except sex," he said—and blushed again, or stronger, or still. "The girls I've met out here, a couple of them have a little talent, but nobody has much in the way of brain."

"Your father said you didn't have enough talent to make it as an artist."

Keith looked upset but he didn't speak.

"Anyway," I said, "you might find more interesting girls in Albuquerque. My smartest high-school friends are at UNM."

He was even more wounded, asked if I was trying to pass him along. I said, Not at all, that he was very important to me, especially now that Ellery wasn't visiting me anymore.

Keith said, "I liked a lot of school, actually. I was just too restless . . . and horny . . . to sit still for all of it. And my parents wouldn't pay unless I matriculated. That was why I quit and came out here. My girlfriend had friends we stayed with while we looked around. My then-girlfriend. I was mad. It wore off, but I was really mad. Now, neither of my folks has the kind of money they had when they were together. They couldn't pay for school even if I wanted to go."

I said, "I guess that's why I was thinking of UNM."

He said, "I'll tell you what. I'll go there if you will."

Of course, that was the end of that.

I said, "You haven't mentioned my brother since they came back."

Keith shrugged. "He disappears when I go up there. And I'm hardly going up, anymore."

○

*M*y hearing was about three months away when Ellery came to see me again. He told me he'd asked Keith not to be there for the first hour. I asked if it shouldn't be fifty minutes.

Ellery said, "It's nice to see you in a good mood, Maddy."

Which, of course, sent mischief flying—squeezing —through the bars of the visiting-room window. I think he'd done it on purpose.

He said he wanted to talk to me about planning for the time when I was released.

I said, "It's not that close."

He forced a tight little smile. "It's soon enough to start thinking about."

"How's my brother?" I asked.

"He's doing much better."

I was about to ask if maybe Billy would finally let

me get a copy of the photo of him with my mother and Lion, when Ellery added, "Actually . . . he's here."

I stopped breathing.

"He wants to see you, although he's not sure he'll be able to talk. He thinks he might not have anything to say. I told him you'd understand if he just said hello."

I began to cry and couldn't stop. At first, I didn't want to stop, it was such a relief after two years of feeling the tears in there, refusing to come out. When I stopped and wiped my eyes on the tissue he gave me, it was because I was afraid I'd do it through the end of visiting hours and I wouldn't see my brother. Finally, I nodded and Ellery told the guard to bring my brother into the room. The guard led Billy in, walking ahead of him so at first all I could see was that he was much taller. But then, when the guard left us, Billy just stood there, looking at the floor, so I had plenty of opportunity to stare at him.

He was so different, I could hardly tell he was the same boy. He wasn't just much taller, he'd gotten very skinny-gangly, and his bones had developed in a way that made you know what a handsome man he'd be. It was true what my mother had said: He was terribly handsome. His hair was darker and wavier than it had been. I couldn't see his eyes, of course, because he wouldn't look up. Ellery suggested he take the seat between us, to my left. Billy obeyed.

I said hello. He pushed his head up and down a little.

I wanted to thank him for coming to see me but I couldn't get out the words. It seemed laughable, when he wasn't seeing me, at all, but only sitting near me. All he was *seeing* was the table.

Ellery started to talk. To do his psychologist thing. He said he knew I understood that it had been difficult for Billy (he called him Bill, which made me feel even stranger) to visit me, and that it might take longer before we could really speak together like friends. Meanwhile . . .

I began to do a slow burn. I wanted to tell Ellery that Billy and I weren't friends, we were sister and brother, and that was more than friends, whether he liked it or not. But I kept quiet, at first. Finally, when he'd been going on for a while, I asked Ellery if I could talk with Billy alone.

Billy bolted to his feet and around to the back of Ellery's chair as though I'd asked for permission to murder him.

I stood up almost as suddenly, so that my chair toppled backward and into the empty chair at the table in back of me. I could feel Lucille looking at me from the other side of the room, but it didn't matter, then.

Ellery stood, too, put his arm around my terrified brother as though he were the only person in the world who could protect the poor baby from the Madeleine monster. Then he did some Ellery routine about how I had to remember that Bill had been through a very bad experience and didn't know what to expect.

By this time, the guard was at our table to see what was going on.

I ignored him.

"Oh, well, I haven't been through anything of course. I don't know what it's like to be scared." I could hear my voice sounding as though hands were around my throat, trying to strangle me. "Maybe my little brother had better just stay away from me because I'm such a dangerous character, nobody knows who I'll kill next."

The guard asked Ellery if it was time for this visit to be over. Ellery told the guard he was just going to take the young man outside to wait. He wanted to come back to talk to me. But I told the guard I'd had enough company for the day. Ellery said it would be a really good idea for us to talk, and the guard reminded me that my "other visitor" was waiting outside. But I was too upset to talk to Ellery or Keith or anyone. I sent a message out to Keith that I was sorry, I'd see him next time.

❍

*I* didn't tell Lucille. Whenever there was nothing compulsory, I lay on my back, feeling like an animal that's been trapped and left alive with steel teeth in its flesh. I'd finally been able to cry and it had been for my brother, who was scared of me. Who thought . . . God only knew what he thought. I tried to push him out of my mind, but he was there even more than he had been, if only because I knew what he looked like, now.

❍

*E*llery came back on a midweek afternoon to inform me that it was reasonable for Bill to have been scared. He said I might know how I'd felt when my mother came at me with the bottle, but Bill hadn't been there, hadn't seen my terror, and even if he had, he might not have believed, as I had, that my mother was capable of smashing me in the face with a broken bottle.

Of course, there hadn't been anyone named Bill around when it happened; she wouldn't have lunged at my face with a broken bottle if a Bill or a Billy had been around. Anyway, what I saw was that Ellery was now "understanding" how my brother felt to the exclusion of understanding how I felt. I was happy for Billy that he had found a new family to take care of him. I wasn't angry with him any longer; that had been just at the moment. On the other hand, I had nothing to say to him and it didn't make sense to see him again if he was so scared of me. The desire I'd had, from the time my mother was gone, to make contact with the human in the world whom I'd thought of as closest to me, was gone.

I told Ellery that I perfectly comprehended what he was saying, and I was really happy that my brother had found a good home. In fact, I thought he, Ellery, should stay at home with Billy and Cona and leave me alone because I had nothing to say to any of them. Then I told the guard I wanted to go to my cell.

Ellery was still sitting there when I was escorted from the room.

Back in my bunk, I felt reasonably calm, but my face was wet and it stayed wet for a long time, though I wasn't really crying. I've looked up the definition of *crying*. I wasn't sobbing or shedding tears; they were just dripping, like coffee through a filter. The steel teeth had made little holes in my eyes so water could seep out. I stayed in bed and kept magazines in front of my face when I wasn't working.

❍

*I*t was a few nights later, after lights-out. I was still leafing through one magazine after another, staying in the same position at night, with a magazine propped on my legs in the near darkness. My face was still wet a lot of the time; I only noticed when my pajamas or my T-shirt got damp. I'd been feeling that Lucille wanted me to talk to her but was waiting for a sign from me. Finally, she came and sat down on the edge of my bed.

She leaned over, put her hand on my shoulder, and whispered that, whatever it was, she was sorry.

I covered her hand with mine. The feeling of her warm flesh against my palm and my fingers was so exquisite, so intense, that I began to really weep; my fingers hadn't felt another person since I'd held my mother after I killed her. I'd had my pulse taken, my fingers held down one at a time while prints were made, and Keith had briefly set his hands on top of mine, but I hadn't touched a warm hand. I couldn't let go of it. I put my other hand under hers and kept crying.

That was when we began.

A night keeper came over but it was someone with a few human genes, maybe an experimental case, and whoever it was, he left us alone, though the room was never totally dark and anyone who tried could get a pretty good idea of what was going on.

The warden was said to be a man who got nervous if he saw your elbow bump into another woman's when you walked down the hall. There were running jokes about the various ways he thought you could get pregnant: grabbing a volleyball at the same time as a teammate; bumping against somebody in the shower room; putting someone else's Cheez Whiz on your apple pie. They said he understood why a man had to fuck a woman—the church and the farmers needed babies—but he couldn't figure out why one woman would ever come near another. The rules about touching were absurdly strict, mild infringements punished with major subtractions of good days. On the other hand, word that something bad had happened to me in the visitors' room had gotten around, and I'd been observed by one genius or another to be depressed. I was scheduled to see the doctor for meds the next time he came in, and in the meantime, they didn't want to lose another paying guest to suicide, so the dyke watch was more benign than usual.

I moved back without letting go of Lucille's hand. She stretched out next to me on her side. She brushed my hair away from my forehead with her free hand. I curled up against her, my head close to her bosom, except that there were the sheet and her night T-shirt between us. I didn't think about what I was doing when I pulled away the sheet to get closer to her skin. I think we both pulled up her shirt so I could rest my face against the skin of her breasts, but then, before I knew it, I was holding a breast in my hand, sucking her nipple like a baby. And like a baby's, my tears dried. Finally, we began squirming against each other, all excited in a way that had never happened to either of us outside of jail or in it.

Once it was there, though, it was there, and we didn't fight it. We found the best ways we could to pleasure each other, and during the day, we talked. She talked about her family—mostly about her grandparents, and her kids. I told her about my mother and the Sky and she just listened, so I told her about Lion,

and about his death, which I'd never said a word
about until then, and about coming cross-country
with my mother and three suitcases and the record
player and a carton of records.

For the first week or so, until the doctor came and I
convinced him I didn't need medication, they left us
alone. The trouble happened after the doctor left
without orders for me to be medicated, and I appeared
to be okay, anyway.

One night, when Lucille had gone back to her own
bed and I'd been sleeping soundly, I awakened excited. I was lying on my side, facing the bunk wall,
wearing my pajamas, of course. I thought Lucille had
gotten into bed with me, but as I awakened further, I
realized there was a penis between my legs and a
guard, otherwise fully clothed, holding me from behind. I began to squirm to get away from him (you
become trained not to make noises so that you have to
think before you cry out) but he got one arm around
me, underneath, to hold me. Finally, I cried out for
Lucille. As I did, the filthy pig shot his load between
my legs, all over my pajamas and the sheets. Meanwhile, Lucille had scrambled out of bed. She grabbed
him from behind, by his collar, and pulled him out of
the bed.

He fell to the floor. It didn't make a lot of noise
because he just grunted, though the floor was cement,
but the women nearest to us were already awake and
Lucille's voice, calling him a rotten motherfucker,

awakened others, even though it was low. There was some giggling.

By now, I was sitting up, wide awake, of course, and as disgusted as if I'd been raped, feeling his sticky jism between my pajama legs but not able to take them off because he was still there, struggling up from the floor.

Frank Delez. Not the sharpest knife in the drawer, but also not somebody you'd have thought of as a rapist. Or whatever they call it when they don't force their way into you. Whatever they call it, it's nearly as revolting. He stood up, pushed his cock back into his pants and zipped up. What hit me even before he opened his filthy mouth, with Lucille standing there and a couple of women from nearby bunks trying to see past the dividers without being observed by Delez, was that he didn't look remotely ashamed. Not even sheepish. In fact, he was casually defiant.

"I thought she liked it any way she could get it," he said, loudly enough for the listeners to hear him.

I almost jumped for his neck, but Lucille held me back, staying calm, as she always did at bad times.

She said, "That's because you're an asshole."

He shrugged. "I don't like assholes. Maybe *you* do."

There was nothing we could do, of course. We could give him up to the warden, and Delez would deny it, and maybe we could convince the warden, which wouldn't be the same as his admitting he was convinced, or doing anything about Delez. Anyway, the only chance we had of Delez's not telling on us would be to keep quiet. We'd end up losing good time if the warden was told. I didn't really care, for myself. My brain had begun to register that I'd be leaving, though most of the time I felt I'd be just as glad to stay as long as Lucille was there. But she had more than a year left to her sentence, and she wanted to go home to her kids.

So I just sat there, and Lucille stood there, while Delez waited to see if we were going to do something. And finally, with a grin intended to show everybody watching that he couldn't care less, he adjusted his shirt and pants and strolled away. I took off my pajamas to wash. Lucille told me to save them so I'd have proof, if Delez made trouble. Not that they'd accept the proof, but it made us feel as though we were doing something. I slept without sheets until we all got clean ones.

○

*I* hadn't intended to tell Keith what happened with Billy or with Delez, but Delez told Admin that he thought Lucille and I were getting too close, and they moved her to another unit, where I couldn't talk to her. This was the first time I'd felt pain since my mother's death, and I ended up telling Keith about it. Not about the sex with Lucille, of course. Just what Delez had done to me. Not only was Keith furious with Delez and enormously sympathetic (he wanted to go to Admin; I had to convince him that would only make things worse) but he'd already heard Ellery's version of what had happened with my brother, and he was entirely on my side. He'd told his father he suspected Billy could have been prepared better for the visit. Ellery had been very sardonic, said, just like Keith could have been better prepared for college. But Keith and I agreed it was very different, between Billy's age and the circumstances of his living with Cona and Ellery. Keith thought they'd gone beyond sympathy and were spoiling Billy. He'd suggested that some of his father's concern for my brother was at my expense and that if Ellery couldn't care about me, he should just leave me alone.

Ellery had said that he would leave me alone if Keith promised to do the same.

There was no way that was going to happen. In fact, it was becoming more and more certain that when I got out of jail, we were going to be together.

◗

*I* began to feel more human. I was never happy, that would have been inappropriate. But the great mother stone inside me lightened somewhat. Grants was barren and I began to miss trees and flowers and bushes. Keith brought me gardening books and magazines and botanical encyclopedias. For the first time I was able to give names to flowers and trees I'd been seeing in Santa Fe for most of my life. When I asked the assistant warden about starting a gardening program, I was told that the management was working on something; it wouldn't be "appropriate" for me to start anything on my own. When I said I could get hold of the small amount of money that would be needed to begin, I was told that there wasn't a good area designated, yet, for such a project. When I pointed to the big dirt yard, I was told it wasn't like me to be pushing so hard. I said, "Oh, fuck!" and I was threatened with detention. I stopped. For the first time, I had a reason not to want to lose my good days.

Lucille was happy for me when I managed to tell her one day in the lunchroom.

Aside from my mother, she's the only person from my old life I ever miss.

◑

When his construction job was finished, Keith applied for work to the Corrections Corporation of America, but they wouldn't have him. Not because he was my friend. Half the employees are related to half the inmates in one or another of the prisons, but they come from Grants or nearby towns, where their families live. Keith was an outsider with no record of the kind of low-life job most of the prison employees have. They probably knew he'd leave when I got out, which wasn't going to be that long. Or maybe he just seemed too intelligent. He got a job with a painting contractor and stayed in the boarding house where he'd been renting a room.

By this time I had less than two months to serve. Though it had become bearable to think of leaving prison, I couldn't imagine how it would be. Going back to Santa Fe was out of the question but I couldn't picture myself anywhere else.

Keith talked about various places. He felt very independent, because he was good at everything connected to construction work and could always get jobs in restaurants, as well. He knew someone who was in an artists' colony in Mexico and he'd thought about going down there but he wasn't sure I'd like it (I wouldn't have gone) and besides, his father's saying he had only a small talent had unnerved him. He had friends in various parts of California, Northern California, especially. There were other possibilities, but he kept coming back to California.

I listened, nodded, never argued. I wasn't holding back, as he later thought. I didn't know, really, until I was scheduled for release, how scared I was of going *anyplace* unknown to me. I understand this wasn't logical; I should have been more scared of places where I was known. But I wasn't.

I had to take it slow. All I wanted to do was to go to Keith's room in Albuquerque that he'd described to me and stay there for a while. I couldn't imagine myself anywhere else.

And all he wanted was to be with me. Anyplace and everyplace. He wanted to take care of me. Make up to me for what I'd been through.

He said, "I guess . . . you've been in a very small space for a couple of years. And it's a very big country."

I was so grateful for his understanding. We were holding hands across the table, as we always did by then, and he squeezed mine, and I felt a sexual longing for him for the first time. I squeezed back.

The boarding house in Albuquerque was run by Mrs. Ruiz. He'd told me about the room. It had plain white walls, except for a Jesus Christ over the headboard, and a soft, lumpy mattress on the big bed. My mother and I had stayed in rooms like that when we came across the country, and she'd made fun of the people who ran them and the Jesus Christs on the walls whenever she recollected the trip, but they'd always been comfortable, those big, soft beds we shared. She never left the room while I was awake. I could picture Keith making love to me at Mrs. Ruiz's.

I asked, very timorously because I was feeling like a little kid, not sure of what was acceptable, "You're sure Mrs. Ruiz will let me stay there with you?"

"Sure she will. She doesn't want me to leave." He grinned at me. "I'm a perfect boarder. A perfect human being. Besides, she thinks you're my wife."

It sounded peculiar, not the wife part, the perfect-human-being part, though it was just the way New Yorkers talked, he assured me later on, when I knew him well enough to question some of his remarks. Right then, he was my lifeline. My sole tie to the outside world. When something he said sounded odd to me, I thought it was *me*. I felt as though I'd been away from the world for a hundred years. I didn't even know what to *ask* about it. I tried watching the television news, but aside from the world stuff, which wasn't interesting, it was all about mothers leaving their babies in garbage cans or drowning them in bathtubs, which totally turned me off. All I wanted to do was sit with him for the rest of visiting time. I felt so grateful to him for his understanding. I didn't think of understanding, then, as being something you granted or withheld according to your mood. I thought it was a gift you possessed or didn't.

I didn't mention the money left from my automobile accident after the lawyer costs, not because I was concealing it from him, but because it had no importance in my mind. I knew, without thinking about it, that it would be there if we needed it. Ellery had possession of my bankbook and everything else but he was so closemouthed, he'd never have mentioned it to Keith. Nor did we need it. Keith was making good money. More than enough to support us in Mrs. Ruiz's little house in Albuquerque.

# Chapter 7

I was released from Grants on a Saturday morning, two years and a week or two from the time I'd entered. Keith was waiting for me in the reception room when I walked into it, wearing the sweater and jeans he'd brought me the previous time, holding the black plastic bag with my belongings. He kissed my cheek, took the bag from me, warned me the reporters were outside, waiting for me. I'd barely noticed them during the trial time, and I didn't think I'd care now, but I was wrong. The moment when I walked out the front door was worse than the one when I'd entered through the rear, maybe just because I was a human with feelings, by this time. The sun was blinding-bright, though it was nine o'clock in the morning. The air smelled like dust; if you breathed deeply, you choked.

I wanted to turn around and run inside, but Keith put an arm around me and led me to his pickup truck, which was dark blue, though I could hardly tell that between the harsh sun and the dust that covered it. The press had been kept out of the parking lot, but nobody had stopped them from blocking the exit. The warden could have made them move back, if he'd wanted to, but not protecting us was one of the favors he could do to make the ones who were interested in prison conditions lay off him for a while. There wasn't a guard anywhere. I didn't see the TV truck with the camera mounted on top or the three cars until the first reporter called my name. I looked up, and they photographed me from a distance.

I ran to the truck and scrambled in when Keith got my door open. He slammed it. It sounded worse than any of the jail's clanging, sliding, locking gates ever had. He turned the key in the ignition and drove up to the entrance, which the truck and cars were still blocking. Then he got out of the pickup and talked to them. When he returned, he said they promised to leave us alone if we gave them one shot, me with my head out of the truck window, preferably waving at them.

I told him, barely able to get out the words, that it wasn't that I minded doing it, I just couldn't.

He leaned out of the window and called that I was too upset, and then someone shouted, "Are you sorry you killed your mother, now, Madeleine?" At which point Keith yelled that if they didn't move it, he'd ram the fucking truck. They cleared the exit and we shot onto the road and toward the highway to Albuquerque faster than I would have believed the pickup could travel.

Everything felt dangerous. The narrow road felt wide and horrendously curvy. The mountains looked much higher than they had from the E unit. It was hard to keep my eyes open to the brightness, but when I closed them, I felt sick. Dizzy. Keith offered me his sunglasses but I didn't want them; I just kept one hand over my eyes.

The press followed, but at a distance. They knew they'd be able to find us when they wanted to.

◑

"So, Chiquita, here we are."

I stared sideways, wondering where he'd gotten Chiquita. Geraldo would never have called me that. I felt a momentary longing for Geraldo, whom I'd not thought of in jail.

I said, "I don't like that name." But my voice was shaky, which made me sound timid. While I sounded that way, I could say whatever I felt like saying.

He apologized, asked if I wanted to get a bite to eat.

I said that all I wanted was to get to Mrs. Ruiz's and settle in.

He said, Okay, maybe it was just as well, with the creeps following us, but once we were on the highway, he couldn't stand the quiet. That would have been the hardest thing for Keith about prison. The quiet a lot of the time. After a while, he started explaining about having the truck. He'd bought it in preference to a car because it was better for transporting his paintings.

I asked, "Are they big?"

He smiled, "That's the only question you ever asked about them."

There was nothing I could say to that. For the first time, I had qualms about going to live with somebody I didn't know except for a few hours a week in the visitors' room. For the first time, it occurred to me that you don't get close to someone when you're in prison and they're not. You might think they're there with you, but they're really someplace else.

I said, "I didn't think about anything on the outside. It's still hard for me to do it. We could be in China, or in a dream, for all the . . . It's completely strange."

He said, "I'm sorry. I understand. I didn't mean to rush you."

I couldn't tell if he meant it, and I didn't exactly care. But I had to keep things as calm as possible, and in order to do that, I had to communicate with him.

I said, "Thank you."

He kept quiet for the rest of the ride, which was a relief. It was just before we got off the highway that he said, "Remember, I told you, Carmen thinks you're my wife? You're just moving down from Taos. So we wouldn't have to deal with, you know, names." He reached into his pocket and pulled out a gold-looking band. He held it out to me without turning his head. "Here, Kiddo. With this ring I thee bed." Then he got embarrassed. "Or whatever."

I put it on, but it made me edgier than I'd been before. All I could think about was wanting to pull it off.

I hate rings.

❂

We got off at the exit where the huge Sheraton Old Town is. Carmen Ruiz was employed there as a housekeeping supervisor, and some of Geraldo's Albuquerque friends had worked there or in the fake Old Town that borders it—a bunch of Navajo rugs and silver jewelry in tiny stores that were once Indian homes. Old Town is much worse than anything in Santa Fe, not only because of the hideous Sheraton that dominates it, but because it's surrounded by the elevated highway and commercial slums.

Keith drove in the opposite direction from the hotel, along Rio Grande Boulevard, past innumerable low buildings with auto-supply stores and tire shops,

until we turned down Carmen Ruiz's narrow little
street. My body coiled more and more tightly as we
traveled, so that by the time he stopped the pickup
and came around to get me, I couldn't move. He
thought I was upset by the place, or, rather, by the
neighborhood, but it wasn't that bad. There were no
garages, just small houses, some pretty run-down.
Mrs. Ruiz's needed a paint job. I couldn't have cared
less. I just couldn't move. All I wanted was to be back
in Grants. I regretted letting myself go so far with
Keith, but I had no idea of how I might have left jail
without him.

He took my plastic bags, somehow got me down
from the truck, led me, still a zombie, into the house. I
knew there were more reporters down the block but I
didn't care. I had no intention of leaving the house
again.

❍

*I* felt a little better after I met Carmen Ruiz, a chubby,
anxious little woman who was thrilled to have a reli-
able boarder in the house while her husband was
"away." (In the men's prison in Grants.) She said
hello, she was so happy to meet me. Very nervous. She
started to tell Keith something about the pipe under
the kitchen sink, then stopped, confused, as though I
were going to put an end to his helping her out. Keith
was just so good at things, she apologized, she always

. . . When I didn't answer, she said I must be tired. Did I want to see the room? I said yes, that was what I wanted and I appreciated her understanding. She relaxed a little. Keith led me upstairs.

It was a decent enough room. Keith had warned me it was very small, but it was about nine by twelve. It was darker than the room at Grants because it faced the back of the alley between Carmen's house and another one, but that was also okay. I wasn't accustomed to total darkness; there was always some light on in Grants. The walls were pinkish, almost the color of my prison pajamas. The bed was a decrepit double that looked huge to me. The wood headboard was ancient. The blue cotton blanket was clean but frayed. There were two lumpy-looking pillows. A small fan hung in the corner over the dresser where the walls met the ceiling. The Jesus over the bed made me feel as though I were back on the road.

Keith said, "I brought down your clothes from Santa Fe. Two suitcases and cartons. The cartons are in the closet, but there was no room for the suitcases, so I left them downstairs, for now."

I thanked him although I didn't know, yet, what suitcases he was talking about.

He was watching me, trying to gauge my reactions. Later, that watching of his would make me feel like a patient under observation. Or a prisoner. I *was* his prisoner, in a sense, but at first it didn't get to me. There was nothing I wanted to do, so I didn't feel as though I were being prevented from doing it. The only part of my old life that still felt like mine was the part when I'd killed my mother.

I sat down at the edge of the bed. Keith was looking at my breasts, under the sweater. He saw that I was watching him look at me, but he wasn't embarrassed. He was waiting to see how I would be. I was aware of myself, of how I looked, in a way I'd never been in jail, even when he was visiting. That was a little bit of a turn-on. He looked sweet. Very nervous. My hostility toward him was evaporating. I smiled, and he came to me eagerly, sat next to me on the bed, twisted to wrap himself around me and kiss me. Then I got turned-on, too, and was happy to let him kiss me, cup my breasts with his hand, push-fall with me to the bed.

Madeleine watched in astonishment. She kept watching as we kissed in that good-frantic way that has you all over each other, clutching, kissing wetly, trying to gobble up each other's insides, having trouble with every button and zipper you try to undo. I barely had my clothes off when he came into me. One leg of my pants was still around my ankle. He felt incredibly good. To my body. My mind, the Madeleine part of me, a tiny Madeleine, perched on the headboard, observing us. She was scornful, kept saying Keith was nowhere the lover Geraldo was. I don't know why she said it. It wasn't true. He was fine. Later, he would ask too many questions about what I liked, but he really knew as well as Geraldo, he was just more inclined to ask questions about everything.

We spent the rest of that day and night in bed. He slept for a little while after each time we made love, but when he was awake, he wanted to talk. I didn't mind as much as I had before, because the sex was so good that I felt friendly.

Before the second or maybe it was the third time that night, he said he had condoms but he couldn't have borne to put them on right away.

I said, "Yech."

He said, "I know. But. I don't guess you have a diaphragm, yet."

I said, "No. I don't get pregnant."

He asked, "Why not?"

I said, "I just don't. I never used anything."

He said, "You sound as if you've done it with everybody in Santa Fe."

I said, "No. Just Geraldo."

He liked that, though he didn't like hearing Geraldo's name. He knew about Geraldo as well as everyone who watched the evening news, but he didn't want to have to remember.

At some point, it got dark outside. Keith dressed and went out for beer and pizza. I asked him to pick up some magazines, but when he came back he said there was no place nearby to get magazines; he'd pick them up the next day. So we ate pizza and drank beer and I showered and washed my underwear. And then we made love some more.

I figure it's okay to call it making love because making it isn't the same as being in it, which is about your brain, as far as I can understand. If you're not in love, your body might feel the same as if you were, but your brain's out there in the cold, a little orphan, watching the warm room with the books and the fireplace through a window.

◐

*I*n the morning, when my eyes opened, Keith was sound asleep. The shades were down. The room was still cool. I took a bath, just because there were no tubs in Grants, only showers. I stayed in the bath forever, didn't want to come out, but when I did, Keith was still sleeping. I got dressed and went downstairs. I was very hungry.

Carmen was in the kitchen and she greeted me very warmly, offered me breakfast. I thanked her. She nodded. Very serious, but I could tell she'd heard us. I didn't really care; I wasn't accustomed to privacy. I sat down at her old white-painted metal kitchen table, and she gave me coffee and breakfast burritos, and when I was halfway through the second burrito, she asked if I'd like some more. I admitted that I would and she prepared two more, poured coffee for both of us and started a fresh pot, then sat down across from me.

She said, "Your husband missed you."

I said, "He's not my husband."

She nodded. She knew it.

I finished my last burrito. I could easily have eaten another two but she didn't offer them. I felt like a vast crater that had to be filled.

I thanked her, smiled. "I don't know what's wrong with me. I'm starving."

"They didn't feed you good?" And then she blushed. *They.*

"I was in prison."

She nodded, looked down at the table.

"You knew?"

"From the television."

"My face was on television?"

"Keith's truck. The two of you walking. They didn't have the faces good, but then . . . They told the story. About your mother drinking and beating you. They showed the newspaper pictures." She waited. When I didn't get hysterical, she said, "I think they're out there. Down the block. You better just stay inside awhile."

I thanked her, told her I meant to stay in. My voice was trembling, so she thought I was going to cry.

She said, "My husband's in Grants. He had some drugs planted on him."

Practically everybody who was caught with drugs had had them planted. I just nodded.

"He has another three months. My daughter lives a few blocks away. She has a baby."

I smiled. "You look too young."

She smiled back. "I have a good job at the hotel. I supervise the floor. I don't clean."

I said, "Cleaning doesn't bother me. I can do it here."

She liked that, of course.

Keith came down the stairs and appeared in the kitchen, well-rested and smiley. Carmen moved aside and he came over and kissed the top of my head.

He said, "So, you two are getting acquainted."

I said, "Carmen knew. We were on the news. Me. The truck."

He looked at me to see how I was taking it, but I told him it was fine. I'd just stay inside until they went away. I didn't bother to tell him that was where I wanted to be, anyway.

Carmen gave him coffee and made him burritos.

I asked her if there was somebody who could shop for us if we gave him or her money. She said she would do it.

Keith said, "We have to go out sooner or later."

I asked why, which we brought up later as a sign of my having been unreasonable from the beginning. But it was also a sign that he was eager to move out from the minute I got there. He wasn't looking for an argument then, so he just smiled as though I'd said something adorable, and told me there was no rush.

"Just don't get her so comfortable she never wants to leave," he told Carmen.

I asked why not.

He said, still smiling, "There isn't even going to be room, when her husband comes home from Mexico."

I asked Carmen, for Keith's benefit, when her husband was coming home from Mexico. She said she thought in three months, when his job was done. Keith didn't ask about the job; he didn't think it was going to matter to us. We were silent for a while, drinking our coffee.

Then Carmen said, "It's true, I cannot have the suitcases in the living room when Felix comes home."

Keith was pleased to hear it, but I didn't know what she was talking about.

"Remember?" he asked. "I told you yesterday. I brought down your clothes from Santa Fe."

I shook my head.

"The living room is not large," Carmen apologized. "I'll show you."

I nodded and she led me down the short, narrow hallway into the living room, which was a little larger than the bedroom, and full of cheap, ugly furniture: a black sofa, a green chair, a big TV console, a Mexican-Oriental rug. Jammed into one corner was a large suitcase with a satchel on top of it. Nothing about them was familiar to me but Carmen was waiting for me to say something, so I told her I could see that they really did take up a lot of space.

Later, Keith and I went back upstairs. He asked if I wanted him to carry up the luggage so I could take out some clothes; there were two empty drawers in the dresser. I wanted to open the cartons, not the suitcases. The suitcases made me uneasy because I was supposed to remember them. It turned into a problem because there was no clothing in the cartons, just other stuff like my old toothbrush and dried-up toothpaste, and some earrings, and papers from school. My high school diploma and yearbook. And, in a taped shoe box, more earrings, my wallet, my bankbook, showing eight thousand dollars in savings, and the CD papers and other stuff that Ellery had been taking care of for me. He had paid my lawyers out of the money from the sale of my mother's half of the Sky to the Hanas. The rest of the money would be Billy's. I didn't want it. I had four ten-thousand-dollar CDs. When I finally unpacked the big suitcase, it was because I needed clothing to put on top of that stuff in the drawer. A lot of the clothes still had the store's price tags on them, and the tags made me remember the night I went shopping with Geraldo.

❍

*I* didn't leave the house until days after the last reporter had given up. Carmen didn't mind. She loved having me there, began to say she wished Felix would never come home. I helped her clean, did all of it, really, after the first time, and she taught me how to cook the dishes she made. At first, Keith seemed pleased with the arrangement. And I was content there on my own, during the day. I slept a good part of it, usually awakening when Carmen came home at around four. Keith arrived between four-thirty and five. At the beginning, he and I were making love or sleeping (or eating) most of the time, and he was tired during the week, and he didn't care so much about going out. Later, he got restless and sometimes insisted on going to a restaurant, or for a beer, or to a movie. The last was difficult because I wouldn't go to the blood-and-gore stuff and that was what most of the ones that came to Albuquerque were about. Our first bad moment was when we accidentally watched one of those on TV with Carmen. Somebody's eye got gouged out with a screwdriver or something like that. I ran out of the house. Keith came after me, though I'm not sure why he bothered, since it was just to tell me he'd forgotten about the eye scene but it was the only bad one in the movie, so we could go back.

I said, "I don't want to go back."

He grinned at me in what he doubtless thought was an engaging way.

"Great. Let's talk about where to go next."

I said, "I meant *now.*"

He said, "I know what you meant, but maybe

you're in the mood to think about living someplace where we can go to a decent movie when we feel like it, or walk around streets where there are things to look at, or see people."

I began to cry because, aside from the good movie, he was describing Santa Fe.

"All right," he said. "You're not ready. I'm sorry. I'm not forcing you. Let's just go back to the house."

❍

*I* think he would have been willing to go on like that for longer, but then he got a letter from Ellery, whom he'd not spoken to since picking up the luggage. He told me, for the first time, about the fight he'd had with his father that day.

Ellery had said he didn't believe Keith was in love with me; I was just one more delay in making himself a "real life."

Keith had shouted, "You don't know who I'm in love with or what my real life's supposed to be."

Keith had been pleased with his own response, at the time. But now he was terribly upset. He showed me the letter.

Ellery had written, in his professional Ellerese, nothing you could recognize as too human, that he was moving back to New York with Cona and Billy— or, he should say, moving to Manhattan, since Cona had once lived on Long Island, but not in the city.

Both the house on Acequia Madre and Cona's little house had been sold. They had purchased an apartment on the East Side of Manhattan, just eight blocks from where Keith's mother lived. They would move in June, when Billy's school term was finished. Did Keith want them to ship his paintings or would he like something else done with them? He gave Keith the address of the apartment they'd bought, in case he didn't have a chance to contact them before they left. He wished us both the best.

Keith was coiled up in himself so tight that he practically sprung out of his chair when he tried to sit. I took a really long walk with him for the first time, along Rio Grande Boulevard.

Trying to make him feel better, I asked how big a difference this was going to make in his life when he never saw his father, anyway. He said it was a ridiculous question. I asked why.

He said, "Please don't play dumb. You sound like my sister, when she used to drive my father crazy. Pretending she didn't understand something so obvious a five-year-old could get it."

I said, "And you sound just like your father, pretending to understand everything in the world and see through everybody."

He stopped walking. We were in the middle of this neighborhood that managed to stay gray, even when the midday sun was shining down on it. Ahead of us, the elevated highway cut off all but the top floors of

the Sheraton Old Town. On either side of Rio Grande
were dingy strips of stores and buildings nobody was
going in or out of. Everything was dry and hot. I felt
as though the sun were melting my skin into my flesh.

He asked, "Don't you care if you never see my
father again?"

I didn't understand exactly what he wanted to
know, but I could tell I had to be careful with what I
said about Ellery.

I said, "Ellery was like a father to me. But, after all,
I've managed without a father."

*"Managed?"*

He had stopped walking again and I turned back to
him, not knowing what he was getting at. The sun
made it impossible to look at him in an ordinary way.

"You call what you did *managing?*"

A calm came over me. The sun stopped burning
me. The place I was in could have been anyplace.
Keith could have been the warden. Or anybody. My
body was too hot and tired to run away from him
right then, but my mind did.

"What do you call it?" I was very calm.

He said, "Okay, okay. You managed. But it was a
desperate kind of managing, don't you think?"

I shrugged. "Sure. Sure I was desperate."

"That's all I meant."

I forced myself to believe him.

We had lunch at Walgreen's. Keith said he understood I wasn't ready to travel, but I had to let him

ramble on about places where we might want to move *someday*. There were parts of California he thought we'd both love. And there was New York. When I pointed out, very calmly because nothing he said could really get to me anymore, that he'd never said anything good about New York before, he shrugged and said he meant the East. Boston was actually a great city to live in, and cheaper than New York. Plus, there were a lot of schools, some not all that difficult to get into.

"Schools?"

He smiled. Keith had an engaging smile.

"I figure, one of us ought to be in school, and you don't want to go."

I made a face, which was all that line deserved; so he tried another one.

"I can't do construction and housepainting forever. I'm getting bored. I have a couple of friends who went to Rizdee. Rhode Island School of Design. I don't know if I could get in there, but it's another possibility. What my father said about making it as an artist . . . It's true, it's nearly impossible, unless you're great, or you're going to turn out the kind of predictable crap most of the guys in Taos and Santa Fe are doing. And if I'm going to do that, I might as well think about commercial-art work."

I didn't say anything. I got dizzy when I thought of the places it was possible to go. I understood a little even then, and I understand better now, that it was difficult for Keith to remain in that small room in a dull town like Albuquerque. He didn't have the friendship with Carmen, the woman's kind of friendship, that sustained me. He needed more of an outlet for his brain, and for his talent, than he had there. But I just couldn't imagine, yet, traveling far from the places that were familiar to me. However it sounds, I was still very tied in to Santa Fe. I guess I mean to my mother. Maybe when I was in jail, however tortured I was by what had happened, I felt (not thought, *felt*) I'd be able to set things right when I returned to the real world. It sounds crazy to say I thought I could bring my mother back to life, or that it would turn out she'd never died, but something *like* that is the truth. And when Keith talked about moving far away, it meant giving up hope that I could straighten out matters. I can't defend it; I'm just stating the truth. At the very least, I needed more time to get used to the idea. I don't mean to Keith. Deep down, I was finished with Keith. I mean, to get used to the idea that my mother was gone. Forever.

Keith said, "You don't seem surprised that I'm ready to give up the painting. You never even asked to see any of it."

I shrugged. "From what your father said, it just seems as though you're being sensible."

Keith stared at me for a moment, then he stood up, asked the counterman for a check, and before I'd even joined him at the cashier, he had bought a monstrous map of the United States, with little bits of northern Mexico and southern Canada, as well as a box of thumbtacks. When we got back to Carmen's, he tacked the map to the wall over the bed. He had to take down the Jesus to do it, and I was upset. He pointed out that since I cleaned the room, Carmen never came into it, but that wasn't what really upset me. Every time I came upstairs, Keith would be kneeling on the bed, holding onto the headboard, marking up the map, or just looking at it. I couldn't get interested in any of the places he spoke of going, but I still wasn't imagining being anyplace without him.

I'd gotten a bright red burn on my face and arms from our midday walk; my skin wasn't used to the sun after more than two years in the detention center and Grants.

❍

Carmen didn't want me to leave Albuquerque any more than I wanted to go. We began to talk around the ways I could stay even if Keith insisted on leaving. It was she who suggested that I get a job that would cover my rent if he left. She told me I could use her as a reference to apply for waitress or cleaning work at the Sheraton. I said waitress hours might make traveling with her more difficult, but cleaning rooms would be easy—except I was an ex-convict.

She said a friend of Felix's arranged IDs for a hundred dollars. All I needed was a new name, etc. She was very casual about it, which startled me, because I hadn't thought of her, as opposed to Felix, as doing anything remotely illegal. On the other hand, I wanted to get a job and not use up my money or be dependent on Keith. I told her I had more than a hundred dollars from the money I'd earned in prison.

I had to find a new name because the Sheraton would check out Madeleine Stern for a prison record. I wanted to use Ruiz but she said I shouldn't have the same name as hers in case something went wrong. So I took Perez. Finding a first name turned out to be a much bigger deal. I suggested Anita, but she said that with a Spanish last name, I should have a more Anglo first name, because of the way I looked. So I ended up with Ruth Perez, at least for the time being. She arranged good references. Once the ID had come through, she took me to the employment office at the Sheraton, where they hired me to clean rooms. I didn't tell Keith until a few nights later, when I'd also seen a real apartment.

Carmen had a friend who had a friend with a two-family house near the hospital. The people in the rented half were leaving. She drove me there when her shift was finished. It was big and very light. Keith liked light and I'd become accustomed to it, by this time. We would be on the second floor. The only problem was, Keith was paying $125 a month for our room, plus most of the food bills since we'd been eating there, but this apartment was near the hospital and it was going for $300 a month, and of course we'd still be buying food. He was getting paid well, and he was saving some money, but I knew it was his Getting-Away Cash, and he'd be loath to spend it on an Albuquerque rental. That was why I'd had to get the job before I told him about it. It seemed to me that if he was interested in a compromise—that is, in staying with me—he might find an apartment a compromise between remaining at Carmen's and leaving Albuquerque altogether.

Carmen's house was miserably hot. I was lying on the bed, naked with the fan trained on me, when he came home at around four-thirty. He was tired and sweaty. He took off his clothes and was about to stretch out beside me, but changed his mind and took a fast shower. When he came out, I was still awake, lying on my side.

He lay down facing me and said, in a friendly voice, "You're really not sleeping as much. Are you."

I smiled. "I think I'm feeling better."

"Good, good." He kissed me, reached for one breast. He was turned-on, which hadn't happened in a while. I would have waited until after we made love and he'd had a nap to tell him, except that he kept talking. Whenever my nipples weren't in his mouth, he talked. He was excited about some crazy new plan to drive up to Seattle and get a job as a salmon fisherman and earn enough to pay his RISD tuition the following year. Seattle was one of the coolest towns of all.

He was in me, by this time.

I said, "I got a job."

He came.

I had to giggle, but he didn't think it was funny. He withdrew from me quickly and sat up, Indian style, ignoring the wetness, which reminded me of Frank Delez and made me feel hostile to him.

"What are you talking about?"

I stayed very calm. "Well, we have to leave here because it's too small for us. You keep saying that. Right? And I found a beautiful apartment over near the hospital, a friend of Carmen's, but it was too much money, and I went to the Sheraton with her and I got a job cleaning rooms."

He stared at me. "Just like that."

"Well, not just like that. I had to get an ID. Carmen's husband has a friend who does good IDs and she—"

"Carmen," he said. "I knew you two were getting to be a conspiracy." He got out of bed, wiped himself with the edge of the sheet, without ever ceasing to stare at me. "How long has this been going on? And what's it got to do with the fact that we're not staying in Albuquerque? At least, *I'm* not staying in Albuquerque."

I got a little bit upset because he sounded as though

he was about to take off and I wasn't actually prepared for that.

"I thought that was partly about finding a bigger place."

"Only partly. That's the immediate part."

"I guess I thought this was a compromise."

"We both know we need a bigger place. What's the compromise?"

He had adopted the super-reasonable tone people get when they think they're the sole possessors of the truth.

I said, "We can go someplace else later, if we want to. Rizdee. Whatever. Meanwhile, we can save some money and I can . . . you know."

He gave me what my mother had once called El-lery's Shrinkeye.

"No. I don't know. Tell me."

"I don't know, either, Keith. That's the truth. I only know I'm feeling better a little at a time. I'm afraid to move because I'm afraid something will happen if I move."

He nodded. He could tell it was the truth. Then he put on his pants.

"Keith, these last couple of weeks, I've just begun to feel as though it's possible, I don't know, to live until the next day."

He looked at me to see if I meant it the way it sounded, and saw that I did.

"I'm afraid to go too far. I'm afraid the feeling

won't move with me. It hardly seems any time since we've been here."

"More than six weeks."

"I know, but—" I didn't finish because I registered the expression on his face at the same moment that I heard what I'd said: It was almost two months since we'd moved to Carmen's and I hadn't had a period. I'd never gone that long without my period except right after I killed my mother, when it hadn't come for months. I hadn't realized it until they asked me in Grants. I'd been surprised when it finally started again. I guess I'd thought it was finished.

Keith said, in a voice that suggested a bank had been robbed and he'd stumbled upon me holding a bag full of cash, "When did you have your last period in jail?"

"I don't remember exactly."

I thought it wasn't long before I'd been released, but his expression was making me feel guilty, and then I got confused. He was staring at me. I was no longer just someone with a bag full of cash; I'd left a dead man at the bank.

He sat down at the edge of the bed. He never took his eyes off me. I was getting a little upset, but what was peculiar was, I'd always been convinced I couldn't get pregnant and now, in thirty seconds, I'd come to believe not only that I could, but that I had. Maybe even stranger when you look at it from a distance, I was not at all unhappy about it.

"Approximately?"

"Just before I got out."

He said, "You didn't tell me you were late."

"I didn't think about it." I smiled. I was trying to be pacific, because he was so upset.

"Is that true?"

"Yes. I swear it's true, Keith."

"Get dressed. We're going out to dinner."

I laughed because of the incongruity of words and manner, but he didn't think that or anything else was the least bit funny.

I said, "I guess we can, but Carmen prepared something last night for—"

"I don't give a small, rotten fuck what Carmen prepared," he interrupted.

I was startled, of course. I'd never seen Keith's temper. Even on the rare occasions when he was especially tired, or irritated about something that had happened at work, he'd never been seriously angry, certainly he'd never cursed at me. I stared at him, waiting for the old Keith to return, but the new one just stared back. Very hard. Very angry.

I said, "It's not even five o'clock. Do you want me to get dressed now?"

He said, "Yes."

So I washed and combed my hair and put on my chinos, which had gotten just a little tighter than they'd once been, and a T-shirt. He never moved from his position at the edge of the bed until I said I was ready, and then he got up and practically pushed me aside to go downstairs first.

Carmen wasn't there so I followed Keith out to the pickup, where he climbed in and slammed his door. He'd started the engine and I'd settled on my side when Carmen's beat-up old Chevy came down the street. Keith stepped on the gas pedal so hard that the truck jerked forward as though something large had slammed into its rear. My door wasn't closed, yet, and I was holding on to the handle, but I was thrown forward and I had to push my left hand against the dashboard to keep from being thrown into it. I began to cry because that hurt my left wrist badly. Keith didn't look at me. He just kept driving. At the first red light, I slammed my door, and made myself stop crying.

He drove as though he were late for something important. He got onto the northbound highway and it occurred to me that he meant to drive to Santa Fe, but then he left it at the next exit. We rode around the streets there for a while, and then, before I realized what he was doing, we were heading back toward Albuquerque.

I began to feel ill. At first I was afraid to say anything, but then I asked him to stop for a minute, I didn't feel good. He ignored me.

I said, "I think I'm going to throw up."

He said, "So, throw up."

I said, "Do you mean that?"

He glanced at me—stared, really, for much longer than was safe on a highway where almost everyone's doing seventy-five or more—but when our truck veered so sharply to the left that the car on that side honked him a long, angry honk, he pulled over to the side and screeched to a too-rapid stop.

I put my head out of the window but nothing happened. After a while, I drew it back in. The nausea hadn't gone away but I had nothing to throw up because I hadn't eaten in a few hours. Finally I asked him, in a choked voice, to tell me what was going on.

He said, "You really don't know?"

I said, "No." My voice, my whole body, was shaking. When he didn't speak again, I opened the door and stepped down from the truck. All I wanted was to vomit.

Keith came out of the truck. He'd put a cage around his fury but I could see it wanting to climb out.

After a long time, he said, *sneering* at me, "What do you look so scared about, for Christ's sake? *I* never killed anyone."

I forgot about being nauseated and just stared at him. I knew now, positively and for the first time, that we would not remain acquainted for much longer. I suppose we'd never exactly been acquainted. Certainly I'd had no idea of the way he thought about me. How could he have made love to me with such abandon if he thought of me as a killer? During sex, or after, he'd often said he loved me. How could he have said that? I thought of the classification form at Grants, where they decide how dangerous you are. Here was this person who'd made love to me and wanted to be my best friend in the world, who would have classified me as a killer!

A police car stopped to ask if there was a problem. I thought they sensed that I was being abused, and so I told them we'd stopped because I was carsick, but we were now having an argument about whether I was still sick. I smiled at the officer, who made Keith show him his license. He returned the license to Keith and asked me if I was certain I was okay. I assured him that I was. They left after suggesting to Keith that he stay in the right lane so he could stop for me if I felt sick again. Keith was boiling.

We got into the truck, not speaking or looking at each other. I assumed we were driving back to Carmen's or some nearby restaurant, and that was fine. It must have been close to six, by that time, and I was hungry instead of being nauseated. Back in Albuquerque, though, Keith didn't leave the highway for local streets, but instead got onto Route 40, heading east. I wasn't about to ask where we were going. I was pretty sure, by now, that he didn't know.

For more than an hour, maybe two, he drove without speaking to me. He left the highway for a gas station someplace before Tucumcari. When I asked him for a little money, he threw a five-dollar bill at me. I went to the bathroom, bought a Coke and a bag of Fritos from the vending machines. He just got a Coke. When we were back in the truck, I thought he'd head toward Albuquerque, but instead he returned to 40 east.

There began to be signs for the Texas border. At that point, I got a little nervous. Not for myself, but for the baby inside me.

I asked where we were going. My voice was hoarse from not having been used.

Keith said, "Texas, looks like."

I asked why.

He said, "Because I *feel* like it."

*Savage.*

I wished I'd bought a purse to hold money and stuff. Then I could have gotten out of the truck whenever he stopped and made my way back to Albuquerque. I was pretty sure from the police I'd seen already that if I needed help, I could ask them. But in fact, whatever Keith was trying to do, I still felt human. I kept the seat belt on and when I looked down, one hand or another or both were always there, on my stomach. There might not be a way to be pregnant without feeling human.

It was more than an hour after we'd crossed the Texas line before Master Keith decided to stop. We were in Amarillo, at the edge of a section with office buildings. A clock on one of them said it was ten after nine. He pulled into the lot of a big bar called Mexas

Vic and got out of the truck. He didn't tell me to follow him. I just did.

The place was deep but narrow, longer than it looked from the outside. The bar was lively and very crowded, but there were free tables. Keith took his time to choose one against the wall in the front, where it was much noisier; then he was extremely impatient for the waitress, in her cowboy hat and fringed skirt and boots, to get to us. When she did, he ordered a whiskey and a bottle of beer.

I kept a straight face. If I didn't think it was safe to drive home with him, I'd refuse to get into the truck. I ordered a beer, put my arms on the table, rested my head on them and fell asleep. When I awakened, Keith had a fresh beer, a couple of empty whiskey glasses and a huge combination plate in front of him. When the waitress saw that I was sitting up, she asked if I wanted some food and I said I'd have the same plate as Keith. He asked for another whiskey and beer. The waitress glanced at me but kept silent. He didn't speak until the waitress had brought my plate, and I'd said, "Thank you," and she'd left.

Then he said, "Such a sweet, polite little girl."

His words were slurred, which sent a chill through me. But I had no idea what was coming.

"That's what I heard when my father talked about you. He compared you to my sister, who had this easy life and complained about everything. Married to a nice guy. Two kids. Good job. Nice house. And she was never happy. And here was this wonderful little girl who'd been given such a rough deal with this lunatic bitch of a mother and she just went along and hardly ever—"

"Aren't you afraid," I asked—I know I sounded very calm, "that if you make me angry I'll break a bottle and kill you, too?"

His face emptied out in a way that was very satisfying to me.

"I was just asking," I said when I'd been eating for a while and his face hadn't filled up again. "And I was telling you to stay away from my mother."

He finished that whiskey, drank some beer. Then, after a long time, he said, "Fine. I'll stay away from your mother. Now, let's talk about this . . . this fetus."

I wasn't being cute when I asked what he meant.

He took a long gulp of his beer to finish it, signaled the waitress to bring another. I didn't bother to say anything about driving. He was already too drunk to drive anyplace, and much too drunk to listen to me say so. There was no way I was getting in the truck with him.

"Do you expect me to pay for this abortion with the money I've been saving to move? Go to college?"

Then I got it. We were operating under two different assumptions.

I said, "First of all, I don't expect you to pay for

anything you don't want to. I have some money, and I can use it."

"Good, good. Glad to hear it. Sounds fine."

"Second of all, I'm not having an abortion."

His eyes opened on me as though I'd jabbed him with something so sharp he hadn't known it existed.

"I'm very happy that I'm pregnant. I can't wait to tell Carmen. There's no way in the world I'm having an abortion. If I had to commit a crime and go back to jail so I could have it there, I would. They have all the facilities, and the first few months, you get to see the baby a lot. After that, they take it away. So, I guess I'd have to commit a small crime and get out fast. Motor vehicle theft." I smiled. "I could steal your truck, say, or receive stolen property, or drive while intoxicated. Except, I wouldn't do any of that because I don't want to go back to jail because I'm pregnant. And I don't *have* to do any of it because I have some money my mother got for me when I was hit by a car. I don't know if your father ever told you, but my mother got me a very good settlement and she put away the money for me. Never touched any of it. And I haven't either, except for the lawyer's fee."

I felt free in some way I hadn't before. It occurred to me that driving to a new place might have been good for me.

Keith's eyes were wide open, but he looked as though he'd been hypnotized.

*"You* never told me."

"I didn't think much about it. Your father had all the records. They're in the shoe box. I thought of it as emergency money."

He said, "You're having an emergency."

I said, "No, I'm not. I'm having a baby."

He said, "Don't say that again."

I shrugged.

His eyes closed. He wasn't even talking to me anymore. He was talking to himself.

"We could've gotten out of Albuquerque the right way." He was having difficulty holding up his head.

"But I didn't want to get out of Albuquerque."

I noticed that I had used the past tense, and I thought that Keith might find this a hopeful sign, but he didn't hear it. He stood up so suddenly his chair rattled around in its crowded little space. The man in back of him turned, irritated, but Keith didn't even notice him.

"Fuck you," he said to me. "Fuck Albuquerque." And then he crumpled into himself and crashed past the chair across the aisle and down to the wooden floor.

Falling didn't wake him up. Nothing did. The crash was so loud, I thought something terrible might have happened to him, but the men drinking at the bar checked him out and assured me there was nothing wrong with him that twenty-four hours of sleep and a lot of juice wouldn't cure. They were very solicitous. One said he reckoned I'd need some help getting my boyfriend to the car.

I said, in my quivery voice, that we were from Albuquerque, and it was a truck, and I didn't know how to drive it.

He scratched his head and said they were going to have to figure out what to do for me. The waitress said she hoped I knew how to find his wallet and pay the bill, which I did. She hadn't been nice, and I wanted to stiff her, but the men were watching, and I thought I'd better tip her right. It was a Friday. Keith had gotten two hundred dollars in cash when he deposited his paycheck, and he hadn't paid Carmen the rent, so he had plenty of money even after I paid the forty-two-dollar bill.

Keith didn't move, but he snored louder.

The men were wonderful. They figured out the closest, cheapest motel, right on 40, heading back west. Three of them carried Keith to the truck and stretched him out in the back. Then one of them drove us to the motel in Keith's pickup, while the other two followed in another car. At the motel, they told me to register, they'd get my husband into the room. I couldn't thank them enough when it was done and Keith lay, snoring, on the bed, but they assured me it had been a pleasure to do a favor for a sweet little lady like me.

I think these guys had learned their manners from Gary Cooper. I saw some Westerns while I was in

Grants; they were the nighttime soaps. These men had accents that were more Western, very cowboyish, and they all wore denim jackets, as though they couldn't feel the cold. They didn't seem to think it was a big deal for us to have driven three hundred miles for dinner at Mexas Vic.

○

*I* took a warm bath but it was still a long time before I fell asleep. It was one of those small, noisily air-conditioned motel rooms that look dirty even when they're clean, with an awful smell I couldn't identify, then. Now I know it's old cigarette smoke they try to cover up with some air spray because the windows don't open. I didn't mind any of it that much. I was feeling pleased with myself. I'd come to another state, not the opposite end of the earth, true, but still different, full of strangers, and they'd been lovely, and everything had been fine. Better than Albuquerque, in some ways. The world had opened up. It was less frightening to think of going East with Keith, or even north, for a while. (No, in spite of everything, I still couldn't imagine taking off on my own.) I remembered how I'd loved the cold weather and the snow when I was little. I was excited. I was rubbing my belly in circles. Maybe it sounds foolish, to have been less afraid of traveling with a baby than without, but travel is uncertain, and a baby, born or unborn, felt like some sort of anchor. A way of not being lost while I was floating.

Keith awakened before five, when I'd finally fallen into a light sleep. He turned on the night-light, saw me next to him, my eyes just opening, looked around and more or less figured out what had happened. He felt stupid, which was appropriate and also convenient because it made him act nice for a while. I didn't move. He went into the bathroom and took a shower. When he came out, he said he was starved.

I said, "Me, too."

We drove to the first place on the road going west, a real greasy spoon where we both had orange juice and bacon and eggs and toast with something awful that wasn't butter. He had a couple of cups of coffee. I didn't want any. Then, saying he had to get the taste out of his mouth, he drove to a doughnut place and bought a bag of doughnuts and two coffees to have in the car. We started with the cinnamon doughnuts, but I didn't want coffee.

Keith laughed. "I've never seen you eat like that."

I said, "Lucille told me she was hungry all the time when she was pregnant. In jail, or pregnant. Those are the two times . . ." I stopped talking because his expression, his whole self, had changed.

I asked, "What happened?"

He shrugged. "I wasn't thinking about that."

"About what?"

"That you think you're pregnant."

We were back on Route 40, by this time. He was driving too fast for the pickup, if not for the speed limit, and I put on the seat belt a little high around my belly.

He said, "I'm taking you to a doctor."

I asked, "What for?"

He said, "To find out if you're pregnant."

I pointed out that they had tests in the drugstore, but he said he wanted me to go to a real doctor. At a hospital. He didn't continue because he knew what it would sound like if he told the truth, that he wanted a Great White Chief Doctor, or maybe a shrink who would tell him the baby was in my mind, not in my belly.

I said, "Okay." I decided not to mention the apartment, even though it was right near the hospital. I would show him that I'd become open to the idea of leaving Albuquerque.

"You know," I said, "it doesn't have to be that big a deal, traveling with a baby."

"I wouldn't know," he said. "And I'm not planning to find out. I don't want anything to do with a baby."

It had a much more definite and unpleasant sound than before. I didn't bother to try to describe how I would feel about killing the helpless creature who was closer to me than anyone in the world. We just had another silent ride back to Carmen's. When he parked, she came running out, saying she'd been worried about us. I told her we were fine. Keith charged inside and then I gave her a brief summary, beginning, of course, with my being pregnant and Keith's not wanting it.

She nodded. "They never want it."

I smiled. I felt very good to be home with her. She knew about life. About babies. Men. At that moment, I felt that I might not want to go even so far as the other apartment when I had my baby; I'd want to be right there with Carmen. I put it out of my mind because there might conceivably be enough space for a baby and me, at least until Felix came home, but certainly not for Keith, as well, so it meant thinking about not having Keith. Having wiped him out of my mind didn't mean I was ready to not have his body around.

◑

We mostly stayed clear of each other for the rest of the weekend. At night, when I reached in his direction, he said, "Not without birth control." Which seemed pretty funny, under the circumstances. He avoided Carmen and me when we were in the same room, always suspicious (correctly) of what we were talking about. On Sunday night, he said he would pick me up after work on Monday and drive me to the hospital. I said that would be fine, then realized he meant *his* work. I had to remind him that he would be picking me up at the Sheraton. When I did, he walked out of the house.

He was in worse shape than I'd realized.

❁

Cleaning in the hotel was very different from doing it at home, or at Carmen's, where I knew whose refuse I was dealing with and what I might find. Changing the bed linens and vacuuming weren't bad, although the bulky spread was difficult to get back on the bed. The worst part of it was doing strangers' bathrooms, often left as though no other human would be entering them: gathering their towels, dropped on the floor, occasionally half-fallen into an unflushed toilet; finding used, unwrapped tampons stuck to the bottom of the wastebasket that the plastic liner had been borrowed from to be used for something else. That sort of thing. Disgusting, though not painful. You wondered whether they were poor people who'd never learned how to behave or rich people who just didn't give a shit for the slobs who cleaned up after them. The neater guests, often in the less expensive rooms, tended to be the ones who left tips, and I did get a great kick out of having some cash in my pocket that I hadn't had to ask Keith for. I'd used up my prison money. I think I picked up nine dollars that first day.

When I got into the car, I was in a good mood and I told Keith I'd treat him to ice cream or something.

He looked at me in a way that reminded me of how Ellery looked at my mother when he was getting set to leave. So I stopped talking to him.

We drove to the Presbyterian Hospital at Central and Chestnut, and I—we—were sent to the clinic, where I went through the examination while Keith waited outside. He had told the doctor he wanted to talk to him afterward, so the doctor asked him to come in, and said I appeared to be having a very healthy pregnancy. He congratulated Keith.

Keith said, "What if she wants an abortion?"

The doctor, who was quite young and Spanish, glanced at me and said that it hadn't appeared to be an issue.

I said, "It isn't, for me."

The doctor got a little uncomfortable, naturally. He said that was between us. He himself didn't terminate pregnancies, but there were competent clinics, and he wished us the best of luck, whichever path we chose. Keith asked whether he had a supervisor. He said, with a little smile, that *he* was the supervisor. Keith asked, hostile, straight-faced, where we would go for abortion counseling. The doctor told him.

When we left the office, Keith was so tight beside me that it felt as though he'd topple like a bowling pin if I bumped into his side. At the front desk, when the receptionist asked how we intended to pay the bill, he said to me, clearly not caring whether she heard him, that since I was so rich, I might as well pay it.

I said, "I'm sorry, Keith, I don't have a checking account, yet. It's mostly in certificates your father got for me, and a little in a savings account. I'll be happy to pay you back as soon as I can get cash."

The woman at the desk was looking at him disapprovingly.

Finally, he took out his AmEx card and slapped it on the desk. But then, as we were walking out, we passed a phone booth and he said he wanted to see if we could get an appointment at the other clinic.

I told him I was too tired.

He said, "Are you really tired, or you don't want to talk about it?"

I said, "Both."

His face, always red from working outdoors, seemed to swell up and get redder.

I said, "I worked all day."

He said, "So did I."

I said, "But you *want* to do it, and I don't."

He turned and walked away, out through the doors to the parking lot, staying ahead of me the whole time until we were back in the pickup.

I would have preferred him to be nice. My brain said it would be better for both of us if he were nice. But I didn't care deeply because I was too happy that the doctor had confirmed that I was pregnant.

Keith dropped me off at the house, but he didn't get out of the truck. Before I'd reached the front door, the pickup was down the street, and I didn't see him again until the alarm awakened me in the morning. He was awake already, and dressed, but lying beside me. I leaned over to kiss him, but he turned away from me and got out of bed.

We went through the rest of the workweek that way, barely speaking.

At some point he said, in a voice suggesting he was being so reasonable it hurt, "I can imagine being settled with you, married, or whatever, and then wanting a baby later, but this way . . ."

I thought he was making it up. Trying to trick me into having an abortion. He'd talked about going back to school, about salmon fishing, plenty of other things, but never about being married.

I smiled sweetly.

"I understand. You're willing to marry someone you think murdered her mother as long as she's willing to murder her baby, too."

He stared at me for a long time, as though we were playing freeze-tag and I'd told him to freeze. Then he left the room. And the house. Again. I wasn't sure it was a bigger deal than the other times until his foreman called later that morning, wanting to know where Keith was.

I said, "Oh, dear, he was feeling awful this morning when he left. I hope nothing's happened to him."

The foreman asked me to phone him if I heard from Keith.

Carmen and I talked about what we would do if

Keith really cleared out. I thought I might be ready for
him to do that, but there were a lot of things I'd have
to figure out. I asked if she would take me to the
motor-vehicles bureau to get a learner's permit.

She said, "You're going to do just fine, *Muchacha*.
Learner's permit!" But she was uneasy.

I said, defensive, "Well, I'm going to have to learn
how to drive if he's gone!"

She nodded, but she wasn't reassured.

I asked if it was about money. "Because I have
enough to pay the rent, for a while, and my share of
the food. I'm not going to be a drag on you." I didn't
tell her I could get my own apartment and car if I
wanted to. I didn't have to. She relaxed. That night
she spoke of a house on her sister's block that she
thought was going to be sold. Maybe, if we didn't
have enough space when Felix came home . . .

I smiled. "I don't have that much, Carmen. Less
than a thousand dollars."

Meanwhile, she'd take me to get my learner's permit.

◑

*K*eith came back on Wednesday night when Carmen
and I were sitting in front of the TV with our dinners.
In the dim light, it was as though somebody different,
someone skinny and hunched over, had walked into
the room.

He ignored Carmen, said to me, "Can you come upstairs? I want to talk to you."

I followed him up to the room. He closed the door and used the hook to lock it. Neither of us had ever locked it before. I sat on the edge of the bed. He pulled up the window shade and sat on the sill, but he didn't stay there. He was up and down as he spoke, walking the four steps to where I sat, looking as though he were dragging chains instead of just pacing in a small area, going back to the sill, sitting, standing up again. When he finally spoke, he sounded as though he were going to cry. I suppose that's why I wasn't angry with him.

"I've thought and I've thought and I've thought. I don't see any way this is going to work. I don't want to be a father. I'm just beginning—I don't know what I'm just beginning to be. I only know I don't want to be it around this lousy town. Any town out here. Doing ball-busting work forever. Or sitting around waiting to sell pictures nobody wants. Or maybe somebody'll want. Eventually. Anyway, that's not the issue. I want to go back East. New York or Boston. School. I don't know for what, yet. I just know I'm going back.

"I've been talking to my father. I'm going to drive his station wagon back to New York for him. Full of their stuff. They were going to hire someone. They'll go in the Toyota. The three of them. Once I'm there, I can live with my mother for a while. Until I know where I'm going to school. Maybe for longer, if I go to school in New York." He stood, walked the four steps, turned and went back to the sill, sat down. He took a deep breath. "If you want to go with me, that's okay. My room at my mother's is bigger than this. But no baby. I don't want to be married, and I don't want to have a baby. My father told me how much money you have, so I know you won't be in trouble if you don't go. If I go—I mean, *when* I go. I *am* going. You understand that, don't you?"

I nodded. I was about to ask if he wanted some of my money to repay him for what he'd spent, but then he said, "I think . . . my father thinks . . . you should have an abortion for your *own* sake. Not just mine. Before this—this fetus—becomes more like a baby. He'd be happy to discuss it with you if you want, before we leave. I leave."

I smiled and decided not to say anything about money, after all. I was going to need it to take care of my baby.

"I mean it, Madeleine."

"I don't think my name's going to be Madeleine anymore."

"Call yourself whatever you want. Your school records are Madeleine. You are who you are. My father says you were a terrific student and you should probably go back to school and find yourself a reasonable career."

This person who was preparing to walk out on me

had also decided what I should do with the rest of my life. I just kept smiling.

Keith shrugged. "I can see I'm not getting to you."

I stood up and stretched. He was only a couple of feet away from me, and before I knew it, he was holding me, kissing me in a frenzied way, and then we were making love, and he was just the way he'd been at the beginning, frantically excited but careful and loving. I don't know how long it was before he came, but then we both fell asleep.

When I awakened, Keith and all his possessions, except the map on the wall over the bed, were gone.

# Chapter 8

I learned how to drive very quickly and passed the test for my license in Carmen's car. I kept my Ruth Perez birth certificate and other ID. While Carmen was at work, I investigated buying my own car.

I stayed with Carmen until a few weeks after Felix came home, when I was in my fourth month. From the beginning, I could see that he was trouble. A macho Latino who was going to charm me and fuck me, or get more money out of me, or get rid of me. I began carrying my bankbook and CDs with me to work but I wasn't concealing my handbag well enough when I was home, and he went through it and began

to complain that I wasn't paying enough of the household expenses. I started locking my door. That, I
think, was what convinced Carmen that he was doing
the number with me that he'd done with plenty of
other women. She grew alternately remote from me
and critical. One day she announced that a woman
should not leave a man while she was pregnant with
his child. When I laughed, she stopped speaking to me
for two days. Then I knew it was time to go.

I was in my fifth month. One of the Sheraton managers had asked if I was pregnant (Carmen might have
told him) and I'd given notice but I didn't particularly
intend to wait for the date I'd told them I was leaving.

Using my real ID, I cashed in one of my certificates
and bought a Honda Civic, which I arranged to leave
at the lot. I kept the keys and papers in my bag, the
bag with me all the time when I was home, under the
mattress when I slept.

Awake in my room, I spent a lot of time kneeling
on the bed, reading Keith's map. Finally, I bought a
duplicate map as well as a bunch of guidebooks, which
I also kept under the mattress. I took them out at
night after I'd locked my door. It's hard to get a good
sense of a city from most guidebooks; I know now that
some of the best ones sound dull, and the worst, de-
lightful. But I made a plan for my first couple of weeks
on the road.

Felix was pumping gas at a station that was far
enough west of Albuquerque so they didn't know his

ID was false. He drove Carmen to the Sheraton in the morning, then went on to the station.

On a Monday morning, I played sick until Carmen and Felix had left for work. Then I packed my bags, walked to the car lot for my Honda, drove back to the house for my belongings, and took off for Amarillo. I chose Amarillo first simply because I'd been there. I had to get accustomed to driving.

After Amarillo, I did things somewhat differently than I'd intended. I had planned to get off Route 40 in Oklahoma and go up into Kansas, but I found myself reluctant to leave this road that had come to seem friendly, so I followed it all the way through Arkansas, and then into Tennessee. In Nashville, I retrieved a second CD and got papers made out in another name, which I kept until my child was old enough so that we needed permanent ones. (When you have a feeling for how false papers are obtained, it's not very difficult to find the people who do them in any city of a reasonable size. Insurance is more difficult, and sometimes I don't have it.) It was in Nashville that I took the price tags off my college clothes and cut the store labels out of them, even though it would be a while before I could wear them. Finally I found the courage to leave Route 40 and head north on Route 65, through Kentucky. By this time I was near the end of my sixth month. It was my intention, and I fulfilled it, to be settled somewhere in the East before my baby was born.

I'm obviously not going to tell you our new names, or where we are or what I have been doing during these years. It is important to me not only that I be able to start a new life but that my child not be burdened by my old one. I've destroyed my original ID. I have yet to find a city Madeleine and her mother don't persist in coming to with me, but at least they don't have to shadow the child. I own a small radio I get the news and weather on. I don't listen to music.

The city we've settled in is of reasonable size and has good public schools. I hope it will be comfortable for longer than any of the places we've been until now. There is that in me that needs to be settled, even to have another child. If I don't find a person, or people, I'm comfortable with in this city, there are numerous others in the Eastern and Northeastern United States.

And, of course, if none of those works out, we can always go farther north. To Canada.